Deadly Stuff Players

Dear Reader:

Many times, people find themselves caught up in tragedy when they are sitting at home minding their own business. Such is the case in Flo Anthony's *Deadly Stuff Players*. Money can buy a lot of things in life, but it can also buy trouble; hence the saying "more money, more trouble." In this witty, engaging novel, Anthony spins a tale of billionaires, high-stake equestrian races, drug dealers, deception and ultimately, revenge.

When a billionaire's estranged wife is murdered in what appears to be a drug deal gone bad in Las Vegas, two celebrities that moonlight as crime solvers are quickly on the case. No one is whom they appear to be, old friendships are either strengthened or annihilated, affairs are revealed or newly cultivated, and no one is sheltered as bodies upon bodies begin to stack up, both in Las Vegas and in Los Angeles. Readers will surely enjoy the characters and the fast-paced action.

As always, thanks for supporting the authors of Strebor Books. We always try to bring you groundbreaking, innovative stories that will entertain and enlighten. For a list of complete titles, please visit www.zanestore.com and I can be located at www.facebook.com/AuthorZane or reached via email at Zane@eroticanoir.com.

Blessings,

Zane

Publisher
Strebor Books
www.simonandschuster.com

ZANE PRESENTS

Deadly
Stuff
Players

FLO ANTHONY

SBI

STREBOR BOOKS

NEW YORK LONDON TORONTO SYDNEY

Strebor Books
P.O. Box 6505
Largo, MD 20792
http://www.streborbooks.com

ISBN 978-1-59309-507-9
ISBN 978-1-4767-3068-4 (ebook)
LCCN 2013933669

First Strebor Books trade paperback edition November 2013

Cover design: www.mariondesigns.com
Cover photograph: © Keith Saunders/Marion Designs

10 9 8 7 6 5 4 3 2 1

Manufactured in the United States of America

For information regarding special discounts for bulk purchases, please contact Simon & Schuster Special Sales at 1-866-506-1949 or business@simonandschuster.com

The Simon & Schuster Speakers Bureau can bring authors to your live event. For more information or to book an event, contact the Simon & Schuster Speakers Bureau at 1-866-248-3049 or visit our website at www.simonspeakers.com.

Acknowledgments

This book is dedicated to everyone of us who is sometimes inflicted with pain. It doesn't matter whether your pain is physical and the result of illness or disease, if you are undergoing financial difficulties, challenges with loved ones, or, perhaps emotionally you are struggling with the challenges that life presents on a daily basis. Fear not. I can assure you that God's favor is headed toward you. Please believe that prosperity and joy are on the way.

I also want to dedicate this book to the memory of my mother and father, Joe Savoldi Anthony and Doris Johnson Anthony, who are no longer upon this earth. Thank you for giving me life and for always encouraging me to go the extra mile to achieve my dreams, in spite of any obstacles that might come before me.

I have also written this book in memory of my two cousins, Selena Anne Thorne and Delores Thorpe. They died five months apart in 2010 and 2011. I love and miss you ladies very much. Sometimes, I forget that you are gone and pick up the phone to call you. But, you're no longer there. So, I always say a prayer and know that as angels up in heaven, you can hear me talking to you.

Thank you, God, for breathing talent into my body and for always directing my path.

To Suzanne de Passe, thank you for inviting me to the premiere of *Zane's Sex Chronicles* at the Urban Film Festival several years ago, and, for introducing me to Zane. You have always been a wonderful role model and so kind to me every time that I see you. You are living proof that blondes have more fun. That's why this blonde followed in your path.

Zane, I will never be able to thank you enough for publishing my book. I know that my writing style is a challenge. Thank you for helping me out. Thank God that I met you again at the Book Fair and you were kind enough to give me your card. You have truly made a difference in my life.

Thank you, Charmaine Parker for helping this poor computer illiterate person along and giving me examples of your work to show me the way.

To the love of my life and my soulmate, Claude Stanton. Thank you for listening so patiently as I read passages from the book to you. Thank you for running all the errands and helping me around the house so that I could concentrate on writing this book while continuing my daily work on the radio, as well as writing columns and doing interviews. I love you more than life itself.

To my Untouchable 31 line sisters of Delta Sigma Theta Alpha Chapter, Howard University. I made you all a part of this novel. I love you all. An extra shout-out to Dr. Patricia Baranco, Dr. Suzanne Randolph and Attorney Sharon Stickland. You ladies are too wonderful for words!

To my specials of Delta Sigma Theta, Sandra Hall-Mays and Jaizelle Dennis Rome. The word "Special" doesn't begin to describe you two.

To my Nu Lambda Bama soror and dear friend, Ethel Dawson Stewart. Thank you for always having my back.

To the Ann Arbor, Michigan crew, Barbara Jean Patton and Theresa Dixon Campbell. My life would be nothing without you two. You are the best!

To Johnny Newman, Charles Oakley, Trent Tucker, Wynton

Marsalis, Roger Goodell, Steven Marcano, Ted Watley, James Hester, Kenneth McCoy, Nathan Hale Williams, Angelo Ellerbee, Michael Spinks, Tony Turner, George Pryce, Robert Sauthoff, Steve Manning, Ary Tolerico, Ephraim Walker, Karl Griggs and Peter Wise. Thank you for being my favorite guys.

To my posse, Renell Perry, Irene Gandy, Shelley Brooks, Adrienne Lopez, Jocelyn K. Allen, Marva Lee, Lu Willard, Helen Shelton, Lisa Arcella, Sylvia Winrich, La Toya Jackson, Ayanna Bynum, Janis DaSilva and Sue Ann Henderson. You are my girls!

Thanks to Dhonna Goodale for giving me the laptop which I used to write this novel.

Lastly, thank you to the three authors whose work inspired me to become a gossip columnist. Thanks to the late Jacqueline Susann for writing your fabulous celebrity novels beginning with *Valley of the Dolls*, that made me fall in love with New York City, fashion and celebrities, when I was a kid that shouldn't even have been reading them. Thank you to the late Helen Gurley Brown for writing *Sex and the Single Woman*, which made New York City the only place I ever wanted to live when I grew up. And, thank you, Jackie Collins, for all of your wonderful characters, especially Lucky Santangelo, who my cat Lucky is named after. These three ladies gave me the burning desire to write Hollywood murder mysteries.

To my Sheroes, Oprah Winfrey, Cathy Hughes, Hillary Rodham Clinton, Suzanne de Passe, Shonda Rhimes, Tracey Edmonds, Mara Brock Akil, Diahann Carroll, Camille Cosby, Kathryn Bigelow, Cindy Adams and Janet Langhart Cohen. Thank you for your never-ending inspiration.

To every young African-American woman out there, always follow your dreams. I know first-hand that they can come true.

Love,

Flo Anthony

Prologue

As the yacht exploded into flames, the man fumbled with the keys as he attempted to unlock the orange Bugatti Bordeaux. He hit a button and the luxurious vehicle opened.

"All right now!" the man exclaimed. "I have the right key ring." Moving swiftly before any fall-out from the fast-moving flames or smoke from the explosion could engulf him, the man threw his bag in, eased behind the steering wheel, thrust the key into the ignition and quickly drove away. He sped right past five fire trucks, three EMS units and at least ten Broward County Sheriff's Office cars that were racing toward the blazing yacht. The man was headed toward Interstate 95.

As he exited onto the freeway, he snuck a glance into the Louis Vuitton duffel that he had taken from the yacht. As expected, it was stuffed with one-hundred-dollar bills that were supposed to equal $500,000. He sighed with relief again and tossed the bag into the backseat. He would count his new found fortune later.

Reaching for the glove compartment, he slowly opened it. True to the word of the man now lying somewhere at the bottom of the ocean, there was a wallet that matched the satchel inside. Pulling it out, yet keeping his eyes on the road, the man sifted through it. There was at least $10,000 in the wallet, along with a Black American Express card, a driver's license, and nearly a dozen other credit cards inside.

It was too bad his cousin, Rolando, had to die. But, hey, that's what happened to no-good drifters. After all, the man was Royale Jones, a famous retired baseball player for the Los Angeles Wildcats. He had conquered baseball. Now, he was about to take the entertainment world by storm. There was no reason to look back on the events of the last few hours now. It might take him a week to drive across country, but he had a car full of money and a head full of dreams of conquering the world. Driving this Bugatti was almost a religious experience. There was no turning back now.

Smiling, Royale shouted to himself, "Hollywood, here I come!"

Chapter One

December 2013
Valerie

As much as she loved a good party, at the final thrust toward turning into a seasoned citizen of age, Valerie Rollins also loved the comfort of her beautiful wrought-iron bed. A glass of Kendall Jackson chardonnay, a good Zane or Danielle Steel novel, a rerun of *Law & Order: Special Victims Unit* or a good Lifetime movie, and Val was good to go for the night.

Valerie Rollins was the gossip queen of Black Hollywood. She had a daily syndicated radio show, "Gossip On the Go With Your Gal Valerie Ro," wrote a weekly syndicated column, and published her own magazine, *Black Noir*. Val was also a regular talking head on TV One's *Life After*, and she still popped up on entertainment news shows here and there.

Her tiny two-bedroom home, or "cottage" as she liked to call it, was nestled on Fountain Avenue beneath the Sunset Strip. After a busy happy hour at Tisha Campbell Martin and Duane Martin's hot spot in North Hollywood, Xen, Val had fallen fast asleep around nine. So, here she was half asleep/half awake at four a.m. on Saturday morning, catching an old episode of *Entourage*.

That Adrian Grenier was one gorgeous specimen of a man. However, her DVR was set to it and she couldn't bring herself to open her eyes. She lay back, enjoying the dull roar of the television. All of a sudden, her beautiful solace was shattered by the ringing of the phone. Val glanced at her cat, Lucky, who had pounced on the phone as if she could answer it.

"Is that the TV?" It kept ringing. No, it was her phone. She managed a groggy, "Hello."

"Val, it's Rome."

"Rome, what do you want? Do you realize what time it is? What's going on?"

"Oh, can it, Val. Anybody who knows you, knows you're watching *Entourage*. Listen, I'm on my way to your house. I have to talk to you and I can't do it on the phone."

"Rome, it's four a.m. Are you crazy?"

"I'll be there in less than twenty minutes."

With that, he hung up. Rome Nyland was one of the finest black men on the face of the Earth. Six-foot-two with a body that looked like a Greek statue, Rome's skin was as smooth as mahogany velvet. At one time a star wide receiver for the Los Angeles Rams, Rome was now a private detective. Val had met him around five years ago after his cousin, Charmaine Sutton, was murdered. As a journalist, who some people referred to as a "celebrity snitch," Rome sought Val's help in uncovering Charmaine's, who people called "Charlie's" murderer.

As a result, he and Val had discovered there was a serial killer running around Hollywood. Together, they had solved the huge case, which resulted in them uncovering the death of actress Jennifer Sands. Now they were best friends.

Val first met Jennifer when she was on Broadway, starring in the play *Sally Hemings*. From the start, the two girls had been BFFs. Although they had been tight, Val was shocked when Jennifer's will was read and she had inherited $100,000, a Rolex watch, several diamond rings and a Bentley Coupe. Although she still drove her fabulous Cadillac XTS on a daily basis, Val loved to move around Hollywood in the beautiful white Bentley.

An only child, even though she was fifty-one, Valerie considered herself to be an orphan. Valerie's parents had conceived her later in life, when they were in their late-forties. Her father, Clifton Rollins, died during Val's senior year of college, when she was nineteen. Her mom, Stella, lived to be ninety. In the latter part of her life, she had relocated from Ann Arbor, Michigan to Los Angeles to live with Val.

Valerie had only been married once, in her early twenties, to a former heavyweight boxing champion. She never had any children. Her only living relatives consisted of a few cousins who resided in Michigan. Despite the lack of a biological family, Val was the opposite of lonely. She had sorors as well as wonderful friends. Her philosophy had always been the family that you selected was often much better than the one that selected you. She believed in living life to the fullest and had made Rome the brother she never had and his son. His son, Romey, made a devoted nephew. It would still be nice to find that special someone to enjoy her sunset years with. She was not ready to give up on that dream yet.

Royale

Rome and Val weren't the only two people in Los Angeles with four a.m. plans on a Saturday morning. Royale Jones was holding court at Peppy's Playhouse, an exclusive after-hours spot ensconced in the basement beneath a sports bar he owned in Compton.

Royale was in the middle of a hot dice game. He had been rolling sevens and elevens all night and planned to leave Peppy's with a fist full of money. After that he was going to take care of the unfinished business he had back at the Horizons Hotel....the sexy and nubile reality star Roshonda Rhodes, who was a bronze beauty. She had worked for Royale back in Las Vegas, and he had promised her a clothing line endorsement. He was positive that she'd be waiting when he returned.

Even though his ambitious plans to conquer Hollywood as a

film producer had not panned out for Royale in the manner that he had envisioned when he left Florida three years ago, he hadn't done badly. After making a brief stop in Las Vegas and establishing connections there, he had finally gotten to Hollywood where he had opened a boutique entertainment company that encompassed record deals, party promotions and talent management. He also secretly had a lucrative side hustle that included prostitution and operating an international drug ring. However, Royale was ready to go legit. He was almost financially to the point where he could kiss the street life goodbye. The final deal he was currently working on would definitely bring those plans to fruition. Aside from aiming to represent Roshonda, Royale had recently signed actress Jermonna Bradley to his stable. Her addiction to drugs and fast living enabled him to get her to join the escort business. In fact, she was in Las Vegas right now servicing a client. Little did Royale know that arrangement would never take place.

Valerie

As Val was heading into the bathroom to jump into a quick bubble bath before Rome arrived, the phone rang again.

She picked it up. "Rome, I know you didn't get me out of my bed to say you don't need to talk now."

"Val, it's Jermonna. Please help me…Ro…Ro…" With that, the phone went dead.

Val yelled, "Jermonna? Jermonna? Where are you?"

Val quickly dialed Jermonna's cell number, but it went straight to voicemail. Then she tried to *69 the call back, but it was restricted.

What had Jermonna gotten herself into this time? And who is Ro? Did she mean Rome? Maybe that's why he was rushing over to her house before dawn, to tell her something about Jermonna.

One of the most well-liked characters on television, Jermonna Bradley portrayed Tiffany on the now cancelled Black Hollywood dramatic series, *Baldwin Hills*. But the girl was living her life as some sort of Hollywood hellion copycat, in and out of drug rehab, constant conflicts in clubs from Hollywood to New York to Miami and Europe. A magnet for lunatics, Jermonna had dated every crazy loser in the entertainment and sports world, not to mention a few street pharmacists, and was now a hot mess. For some reason, Val felt she had to take care of her. Hopefully, Ro was Rome, and, maybe he could tell her the latest calamity in Jermonna's life.

Just maybe he might know where Val could find her little friend. It was the first Saturday in December. Val had planned to get started with Christmas preparations today. It looked like those plans were a thing of the past.

The weekend was off to a banging start! Unfortunately for Val, she had no idea how literally "banging" the next few days were about to become!

Chapter Two

Jermonna

S tanding five-foot-three and weighing one hundred ten pounds wet, Jermonna Bradley had a body all women envied and every man she came in contact with lusted over. Once known as the raptress "J Body," Jermonna had broken into acting after a cameo on *A Match Made In Heaven*, a pilot that was never picked up.

Ironically, Peter Unger, the producer of *Baldwin Hills*, had somehow seen the show, fallen in love with Jermonna, and tracked her down. At the time she didn't even have an agent, but Valerie Rollins had taken an interest in her and was always talking about her, taking her to parties with her, as well as introducing her to people.

Somehow, Peter recognized all of this, and contacted Val to get in touch with her. He felt that Jermonna would be perfect for the part of Tiffany, the zany bookkeeper on *Baldwin Hills*. That seemed like so long ago. After Jennifer Sands was killed by her crazy, lookalike, long-lost sister, Mavis Butler, *Baldwin Hills* was cancelled. Jermonna had found a little guest-starring work, but not another series.

To make matters worse, she had been busted twice for DUIs, ended up the star of an internet sex tape and, even though she was never indicted, it was suspected that she had killed Black Mike, a rapper that had been gunned down the previous year. Jermonna had been the last person to publically see him alive. So, now she was even having trouble getting on a reality show. As great of a dancer as she was, *Dancing with the Stars* didn't even want her. And, now she was locked in a basement in Las Vegas waiting for some guy she didn't even know to let her out. She was so desperate that she had started to date high-rollers that wanted to be seen with a celebrity for money. Why now?

Yesterday, she had received a call that Vance Dumas wanted her to appear in a commercial he was doing for a new boxer ad. He was not only one of the few black jockeys in horse racing, but he actually owned the race horse Wildin' Out. Vance was the son of Victor Dumas, a black dot.com billionaire. Vance may have been tiny, but he was handsome as all get out! She had envisioned it was a stroke of good luck when she had run into his mom, Andrea, at Tao earlier in the evening. Knowing Andrea had a penchant for cocaine and young men, Jermonna had eagerly followed her off the Las Vegas strip to what the older woman described as a hot spot where they could really get their party on. However, the sports bar that Andrea had taken her to was bizarre. It was virtually empty, with no real wait staff, and the few men present had ogled her like she was a piece of meat.

Taking Andrea's lead, she had followed the one named Sincere into a private room where they did a few lines of coke together, but he also must have spiked her drink. She had awakened with bruises on her arms. Her cash was also missing from her Hermes clutch bag. The door was locked and she had no idea what had happened to Andrea.

All of a sudden, she had heard Andrea yelling from the other side of the door. "Please, don't kill me! I'll give you as much money as you want! Please, let me live!" Andrea had pleaded.

There were two shots, then silence. Jermonna had called Val to find someone to get her out of the place, but her phone had died as soon as Val picked up.

Why did her cell phone go dead? If she could only get a hold of Val, she was convinced that Val would come and rescue her.

Chapter Three

Valerie

Val was pouring herself a cup of Constant Comment tea when the bell rang. In a matter of seconds, Rome was at her door. Letting him in, she said, "This had better be good. You know I only get to sleep in on Saturdays and Sundays."

Giving her a light peck on the cheek, Rome asked, "Do I get a cup of tea, some juice, a how are you? Something?"

Val had the herbal tea and honey ready for him, just like he took it. Rome eased back on her red, leopard-trimmed couch. "I got a call from Victor Dumas. He believes his estranged wife, Andrea, may be in danger. He's afraid whatever trouble she's in could put his son and his horse in jeopardy. It has to do with some baseball player and a gang threatening to kidnap her. Do you know anything?"

"Yeah. I have this fabulous new St. John suit trimmed in crystal fox with a hat to match to see their son Vance ride Wildin' Out on the fifteenth. Kentucky Derby contenders start on their Road to the Roses in the $750,000 Cash Call Futurity at Hollywood Park. Then, I'm on the committee for the Santa Sleigh Ball that follows the race that night at the Beverly Hills Hotel, and I, had planned to head out today to get a dress for those festivities. In addition, I'm planning to bet on and win big with Wildin' Out. And, now you're telling me the extra Christmas shopping money that I was looking forward to winning, not to mention a fun night that in-

cludes raising money for Sickle Cell Disease, is in danger. Thanks
for ruining my day before it's even light outside. And, you can kiss
your Christmas gift 'goodbye,' Scrooge."

Shaking his head, Rome asked, "Seriously, Val. What's going on
with these people?"

"To be honest, Rome, I don't know what happened to Andrea.
She's a woman I've admired for a long time. She revolutionized
the fashion industry by refusing to lose weight and becoming the
first plus-size woman to stroll runways all over the world. Now,
all you hear about her is that she vips and vops with street pharma-
ceuticals. In other words, she's known to be a veteran cocaine
user, who also smokes tar heroin to smooth out the high. Even
though Vance doesn't use drugs, he runs with a very fast crowd
that not only rides horses, they've been known to shoot and snort
a colt here and there, too. I got a weird call from Jermonna right
after you called. I know she's been chasing Vance around.

"Maybe she was trying to tell me something about the Dumas
family. I need to get on the horn and see if I can find her. I also
got her a gig hosting a Bronner Brothers Hair Show next Friday
night in Atlanta, so I have to make sure she's there."

"When did you start hanging with the high-rolling, horse-racing
crowd?"

"A friend of mine founded an event called the Grand Gala to
get African-Americans involved in the Kentucky Derby. She invited
me there and I loved it. So, I started following Vance's career.
Now, when or wherever he races, I'm there. "

Seemingly, out of nowhere, Val's phone rang, causing the normally cool and calm Rome to jump! Picking it up on the second
ring, Val answered, "Hello. I see. Are you sure? Has anyone notified
her husband? Okay, I'm heading there."

Hanging up the phone, Val told Rome, "Well, Andrea Dumas is
no longer in trouble. She's dead."

Rome was shocked. "Where did they find her?"

He couldn't believe he was too late to save his client's wife's life. Although the media wasn't aware of the situation, Victor no longer lived with Andrea. However, he was still very concerned for her welfare and continued to allow her to live in the style she had become accustomed to as his wife.

Rome had given his word to Victor he would find her and make sure she was safe.

Val responded, "Las Vegas, at some sports bar off the strip. We also solved the Jermonna mystery. She was there with Andrea. She's unconscious, but she's alive. The source also says a witness swears he saw Roshonda Rhodes leaving the scene."

"Roshonda Rhodes? That gorgeous woman on the reality show *Diamond in the Rough*?"

"That would be her." Val smirked. "If she was there, I don't know if she's a suspect or another victim. Let me get dressed and pack an overnight bag. We're heading to Vegas. If we hurry, we can catch the seven a.m. flight and be there by eight."

"Forget packing a bag. I need to get to Vegas right away and try to do damage control for Victor before the media gets a hold of this. If we have to stay overnight or longer, I'll buy you some clothes. You said you wanted to go shopping for a new ball gown. Here's your chance. We'll call it an early Christmas present."

Val was way ahead of him. She poured at least two days' worth of Meow Mix into Lucky's bowl, threw on a pair of XCVI gray-graphite leggings with a matching cotton lace and knit long-sleeved coat, and her black Chanel ballet flats.

Despite what Rome had insisted, she tossed her always ready toiletries and makeup bags and two pairs of panties (she refused to leave town without extra clean underwear) into her Hermes Birkin bag, snatched her mink poncho and headed back into the living room where Rome was finishing up a call.

"That was Victor Dumas. I didn't tell him Andrea was dead, just that she'd been involved in an incident and we are on our way to check it out. He keeps a Dumas Electronics jet at LAX. Victor is notifying the crew that we're on the way. I'm going to leave my car in your garage; let's take a cab to the airport."

"I've never met the man, but I already love Victor Dumas's style," Val replied anxiously. "Let's roll!"

Chapter Four

2012
Roshonda

Growing up in Cleveland, Mississippi, a small town in the Mississippi Delta of 13,841 people, Roshonda Rhodes had constantly dreamed of becoming a Hollywood actress. A cross between Halle Berry and Beyoncé, Roshonda had used her exotic looks and lithe body to enter beauty pageants around the state. After winning titles at Delta State University, and in Jackson and Hattiesburg, she had finally won Miss Bronze Mississippi and headed to the national Pageant held in Las Vegas.

Placing in the top ten of Miss Bronze America had gotten her noticed by a small talent agency called Topaz Entertainment, which was based in town. The owner, Rebecca Fuqua, was a former designer who liked the procuring profession better. She was recently divorced from late-night talk show host, George Fuqua. She had convinced the naive Roshonda, who had never been out of the state of Mississippi prior to the pageant, that she could make more money letting her book her jobs right in Sin City rather than competing with seasoned actresses for jobs in Hollywood as an ingénue starting out.

After fronting money to get Roshonda breast implants, veneers on her teeth, and a flashy wardrobe, most of Roshonda's "bookings" consisted of escorting high-rollers to events around Vegas that always ended up with her servicing them in bed. Whenever she complained to Rebecca, the buxom blonde would pull out her records and calculator, then punch up thousands and thousands of dollars in expenses that Roshonda still owed her.

"You see these numbers?" Rebecca would constantly ask the young beauty queen. "Once these bills are paid off, you're free to do anything or go anywhere you want to go."

So, for the past three years Roshonda had been stuck in Las Vegas. Back in Mississippi, her friends and family thought she was on the brink of landing a starring role in a casino revue. Instead, she was a glorified call girl.

It was a quiet night on the Vegas strip. Roshonda hadn't received any calls from Rebecca about a date for the evening, so she thought she would take it easy, head over to the Forum Shops at Caesar's Palace, do some shopping, then treat herself to a steak dinner at the Palm restaurant. That definitely sounded like a plan. There would be no grimy hands up and down her body tonight.

She hopped into a pair of MiH Marrakesh jeans, a simple tee shirt and a pair of Tapeet by Vicini heels. They were wedges and would be sexy, yet comfortable enough to walk around the Forum Mall in.

After dropping $1,300 on two pairs of Christian Louboutin stilettos, Roshonda headed inside of the Palm. Deciding to eat at the bar, she was surprised when a bottle of Cristal was placed in front of her as she perused the menu.

"Compliments of the gentleman at the end of the bar." The bartender placed a champagne flute in front of her and poured some bubbly into the glass.

Roshonda almost started laughing as she lifted her glass to toast a "thank you" to the tiny little boy who was smiling at her. How could a kid buy a three-hundred-dollar bottle of champagne, and why was he being allowed to sit at the bar?

Oh no, she said to herself, *the little smurf is coming down here.*

Barely as tall as she was sitting, the munchkin stretched out his hand. "Allow me to introduce myself to you, Pretty Lady. My name is Vance Dumas. I was mesmerized by your beauty. There's no way I can let you sit alone. Would you like to join me for dinner?"

Not wanting to laugh in the little guy's face or hurt his feelings, Roshonda explained that she was enjoying a quiet night by herself. At that moment, former NBA stars Charles Oakley and Johnny Newman walked into the restaurant, making a beeline to Vance.

"What's up, man? What are you doing here; shouldn't you be training? We got you and Wildin' Out in the Derby," Charles said.

"I'm in town for the fight, then I'm heading home to Kentucky. I was trying to convince this beautiful woman to let me treat her to dinner," Vance explained.

Smiling, Charles told Roshonda, "Girl, go with the man. He won't make any fast moves. His horses do all the running for him." With that, the hostess escorted the two men to their table.

"So, what do you say?" Vance asked. "Will you join me or what?"

"I would love to." Roshonda thought to herself, *He's only four feet tall. If he tries anything, I'll step on him.*

Dinner with Vance turned into dessert. Roshonda had no idea a man could be so interesting. She had totally misjudged Vance's age. He told her he was thirty, one of a few winning African American jockeys, and that he owned the horse he rode, Wildin' Out. Looking at his platinum, diamond-studded Rolex watch, Vance told her, "It's almost midnight. I've taken up all of your time. Let me have my driver take you home. Can I see you tomorrow?"

Roshonda didn't want to be seen around the strip with Vance for fear that someone would give her vocation away. He seemed so nice. She quickly decided to invite him for lunch at her apartment. That way they wouldn't run into any of her clients or fellow call girls. "You were so nice to treat me to dinner. If you're not busy, why don't you have lunch with me at my apartment tomorrow? I live in the towers at the Las Vegas Country Club. Would one o'clock be good?" Writing it all down for him on the back of the restaurant's card, Roshonda continued, "My address is 3111 Bel Air Drive and my number is 702-555-1310. I drove here. It's very sweet of you to offer, but I can see myself home."

He smiled. "I'll walk you through the mall."

Great, now everyone would see her with this shorty worty. As they strolled past Gucci, Vance suggested going in for a moment. Never one to pass up browsing at Gucci, Roshonda followed him into the store.

"Hello, Mr. Dumas."

"So nice to see you, Mr. Dumas."

"Welcome back, Mr. Dumas."

She now knew he was a jockey, but this man seemed to be as famous as Denzel Washington or Will Smith. Who was this little guy?

Speaking of Denzel, the movie star and his wife, Pauletta, were actually walking right toward them. "Vance, my man," Denzel said as Vance shook his hand and kissed Pauletta on her cheek.

Vance told them, "I see you guys are doing a little pre-fight shopping."

Denzel gave Vance a pound on the fist as they walked off.

Roshonda couldn't take it anymore and eyed Vance. "How do all these people know you?"

"Friends of the family, beautiful; just friends of the family. I need to pick up a suit I had tailor-made for me. Do you see anything you like?"

"I've already exhausted my shopping budget for today, but I love their entire shoe and purse collection for the summer. When I build my bank account back up, I'll probably come and pick up a bag with shoes to match." She paused. "I'm going to get out of here. You go ahead and do what you have to do. I'll see you to-morrow at one."

"Are you sure I can't see you home tonight?"

"I'm sure. Enjoy the rest of your evening." With that, Roshonda left the funny little guy lusting after her in Gucci.

Chapter Five

Roshonda and Vance

Roshonda rose early the next morning to prepare lunch. Vance hadn't seemed to eat or drink much at dinner, so she decided on a lobster and pasta salad that she could pick up at the gourmet deli right behind the strip. As she got ready to embrace her daily cleansing ritual, the doorman rang her.

"Yes?"

"There's a delivery down here from a Mr. Dumas. Is it all right to send everyone up?"

Everyone? Who was everyone? Pulling her pink satin robe tightly around her, Roshonda told him, "Yes.

She ran into the bathroom to quickly brush her teeth and run a brush through her hair. The doorbell was already ringing. Well, "everyone" was here. Roshonda opened the door to at least three men pushing carts filled with shopping bags from Gucci.

"What the hell is going on?" she yelled. After filling her living room with all the bags and boxes, one of the guys handed her a card that read:

Since you love the entire collection of shoes and bags, here it is, with all the dresses and clothes to match. See you at one. Love, Vance.

Okay, it was time to Google this guy. There had to be a half-million dollars' worth of clothes, shoes and purses, not to mention scarves, belts and fragrances. Roshonda didn't really know her way around the Internet, but, she had an iPad to check her emails from Rebecca and schedule her dates. She found Google and typed in "Vance Dumas."

She couldn't believe what she was reading on Wikipedia. *Vance Dumas. Born: November 5, 1982. An American Jockey. Vance Dumas is the only son of American dot com Billionaire Victor Dumas and his wife, Andrea. The elder Dumas is among the eight Black billionaires in the world who include Oprah Winfrey, Mohammed Al Amoudi, Aliko Dangote, Mike Adenuga, Patrice Motsepe, Mohamm Horahim and Foloransho Alakija. A millionaire in his own right, Vance has a personal wealth of over $60 million.*

Single, he resides in Versailles, Kentucky. Son of a billionaire, a multi-millionaire? Had God finally answered all of her prayers? Was this a dream that could turn into Roshonda's worst nightmare if this little guy really liked her and found out she was nothing but a two-bit whore? Roshonda thought about Julia Roberts' character, Vivian, in *Pretty Woman*. She had told Richard Gere's character, Edward Lewis, a rich and powerful guy, that she wanted the fairy tale, and in the end, he had given it to her.

Maybe the same miracle could happen for her. Well, even if it didn't, she had an entirely new Gucci wardrobe to try on and hang up, and she had to run out and get lunch. She decided to use her last few hundred bucks to purchase a couple of bottles of Cristal to serve Vance. Lunch had to be delectable. She would treat this little smurf so good, he would never want to get rid of her.

Roshonda

As Roshonda dashed back into her apartment, laden down with grocery bags and two bottles of champagne, her cell phone was ringing. She glanced at the number and wanted to push the "Ignore" button, but she'd have hell to pay if she didn't answer.

"Yes, Rebecca?"

"Darling," cooed Rebecca. "I have a job for you tonight. Jacques Michel from Paris is in for the fight and wants to book you for the night. He'll need you to escort him there and pick up the usual bag of happy dust for him and anything else he might need. He's paying $5,000. His car will be there to get you at seven. Dress to impress."

Without even giving her a chance to respond, Rebecca hung up. Her command had been given. Roshonda would have to get Vance out fast and explain she had already promised an old friend she would accompany him to the fight. With her bubble burst by Rebecca's call, Roshonda let out a deep sigh, and went about the task of setting her table for lunch with Vance. She placed an elegant gold lace table runner on it, then set two places with her prized Versace Medusa Dinnerware and matching champagne flutes. Designed by the late Gianni Versace himself, a golden Medusa set in the middle of the plates on a solid red/black background. A wide band in a black, red and golden scroll motif bordered the plate. The matching champagne flutes had the head of the Medusa in the stem. She placed a candelabra on the table with three white tapers in it, and a bowl of floating white roses in front of that display. The champagne chilled in a silver bucket. Finished there, she jumped into the shower.

It was time to get dressed. Roshonda hadn't had time to totally look through all of the clothing racks that now filled every inch of her bedroom. However, she chose the flower print silk georgette kaftan dress that she'd had her eye on in the store forever. With its gigantic price tag of $2,400, she had never imagined she could figure out a way to own the beautiful dress. Slipping it over her head, it fit perfectly. How had Vance known her exact size? Gucci stated that the night-blooming flowers on the garment would create your own enchanted evening. She hoped the store knew what it was talking about.

Roshonda intended to definitely have an enchanted afternoon. Looking through tens of boxes of shoes, she decided on the light-pink patent leather high-heel platform-shoe with Mary Jane-style straps and an open toe. The heel would add five-point three-inches to her already five-feet-five-inch height. Roshonda didn't want to make the little fellow feel like a dwarf, but she figured he must have desired to see her in the sexy shoes or he wouldn't have bought them for her.

The buzzer rang.

"Mr. Dumas to see you."

With an anticipation she had never felt before, Roshonda whispered into the intercom, "Send him up."

This little luncheon could be her pot of gold at the end of the rainbow. It wasn't every day a girl was about to have the heir to a billion-dollar empire eating lunch at her table. *Please, God, let him want to stay for dessert.*

"My, my, you sure make Gucci look good," Vance proclaimed as he walked through Roshonda's threshold. Kissing her lightly on the lips, he handed her a beautiful bouquet of sterling silver roses with one hand, and a bottle of Cristal with the other.

"Thank you. I already have a glass of bubbly chilled right here for you. I'll put this in the fridge. The flowers are lovely. Let me put them in some water. Have a seat," Roshonda told him as she put the champagne flute in his hand.

As she was walking into the kitchen to get a vase, Vance noticed her white baby grand piano. "Do you play?"

She told him, "Yes," and then set the roses on top of the piano.

"Play something for me. I'd love a little entertainment before lunch."

Few people that were in her present life knew that Roshonda played classical piano. She had won the talent competitions in every pageant she had ever competed in. For some reason, she felt she should play Chopin for this tiny, yet oh so elegant and wealthy man. So she sat down at the piano, her most prized possession, and began to play Chopin's "Prelude in E Minor."

As her fingers glided over the keys, Roshonda forgot about Rebecca, she forgot about all the horrible men with their hot breath, clammy hands and hairy bodies that violated her body almost daily. As she played the beautiful medley, she imagined herself to be onstage at Carnegie Hall or an opera house in Vienna. She slowly brought the song to a close, not noticing Vance was standing over her.

"Bravo," he clapped. "That was almost as beautiful as you are."

Amazingly strong to be so small, Vance lifted Roshonda up from the piano stool and leaned her back across the keys and up on the top. With the swiftness of the second hand on a watch, he took a sip of his champagne and poured the rest of the glass down the front of Roshonda's pricey dress. With one hand, he ripped the expensive threads apart, saying, "Your skin makes a much better glass."

Without speaking, he began to lick the cold liquid off the space between her breasts. Looking up, he slowly kissed her. As his tongue met hers, Roshonda didn't know what to do. Did he know she was a prostitute? If so, did he expect to collect his money for all of the clothes with sex?

Sensing her uneasiness, Vance whispered in her ear, licking it at the same time, "If you want me to stop, I will. Baby, I don't want to do anything you don't want to do. I've been fantasizing about making love to you from the minute my eyes met yours in the restaurant."

For some reason, Roshonda felt paralyzed and mute. She couldn't move a muscle or force any words out of her mouth. Vance pushed her further back on the piano, ripped off the dress, her bra and panties, and proceeded to crawl up and down her body, licking every spot until he reached her g-spot. At that point his tongue dove into her clitoris, sending chills throughout her body, causing her to quiver. He slowly eased his head up, pulling down his pants at the same time.

Roshonda was afraid to look, but it must be true that big things come in small packages. The man's penis eclipsed his entire body. It was as if it was an appendage all to its own. Like a magician, his hand produced a condom, and he was in her. The sounds of their bodies pounding up and down on the piano seemed to be a concerto unto its own. Gasping, Roshonda came and Vance, letting out a huge yell, came right behind her. He slowly pulled out of her and eased up.

Roshonda shook her back out and sat down on the piano bench. Smoothing down her hair, Vance asked, "Are you all right, baby?"

Not answering his question, Roshonda whispered, "What just happened?"

"We not only made love. I'm in love with you. I've been waiting for someone like you for a long time. Forget going to the fight. This is Las Vegas. Marry me tonight."

Roshonda felt him slip something on her finger. She held up her hand and saw the biggest diamond you could imagine staring down at her. *Where had that come from?*

Stuttering, she told him, "Vance, we only met last night. I feel something, too, but are you sure?"

"I'm sure. Which way to your bedroom?"

"Why, do you want to see the clothes?"

"No, I want to make love to you again; this time properly. Then, we'll get dressed, head to a chapel and you will become Mrs. Vance Dumas."

Dreams can come true. Still wearing the five-point-three-inch Gucci stilettos and nothing else, she led him into the bedroom.

The ringing of Roshonda's cell phone caused her to open her eyes. She could hear Vance talking to someone on his phone in the living room. She must have drifted off to sleep. It was dark outside. She glanced at her phone. Oh my God! Rebecca! Jacques Michel! She had six missed calls. Well, she certainly wasn't going to call Rebecca back now. She inched up. My God, this man had rocked her world. Had this all been a dream? No, the ring was still on her finger.

Vance entered the bedroom.

"I see you're awake. Your doorman rang up to tell you that a Monsieur Michel was downstairs. I took the liberty of saying you were unavailable. You are unavailable for him, aren't you?"

"For Monsieur Michel and everyone else in the world, yes, I'm unavailable. For you, I'm available for the rest of our lives."

"That's what I like to hear. I called the marriage license bureau. They're waiting for us. I also called the Little White Wedding Chapel. If it was good enough for Michael Jordan, Darryl Strawberry and my man Slash to get married there, it's more than good enough for us. Get dressed. We'll celebrate here tonight, then head to Monte Carlo in the morning and get on my father's yacht. Let's escape this world for awhile. I want you all to myself." He paused. "Listen, I'd like to keep our marriage between the two of us until the time is right to tell my parents. Okay?"

That was fine with her. She had quite a few secrets of her own. One more wouldn't hurt. Roshonda kissed her future husband on the lips and dashed into the shower. When she got out, she put on the burnt light georgette one-shoulder Gucci dress he had bought her, and paired it with her new Isabel contrast suede high-heel sandals with studded netting.

Not exactly a wedding ensemble, but it was gorgeous. Vance was waiting for her in the living room. Handing her a check, he said, "I believe you're going to need this. We can drop it off to Ms. Fuqua on the way to the chapel."

In Roshonda's hand was a cashier's check made out to Rebecca for $500,000. "I don't owe her this much." Roshonda gasped. "But, how did you know?"

Laughing, Vance responded, "I knew everything about you within five minutes of meeting you at the Palm. Come on, the future Mrs. Dumas, let's start our new life together."

Chapter Six

Jumping into her silver Bentley EXP 9 F SUV, Roshonda sped away from the Las Vegas club. She had driven here all the way from L.A. when she'd overheard Royale talking about making a big score off of Andrea Dumas. He had provided the exact address to whomever he was talking on the phone. She had written it down as he was reciting it. While she and Vance had been married now for a year, no one still knew about it. She often wondered why he had married her. He still showered her with clothes, jewels and furs, but who cared when she couldn't show them off being on his arm. He had also forced her to take the offer to be on *Diamond in the Rough*, a reality show about grooming young talent. She had run into one of the producers when she was having drinks alone, as usual, in the Beverly Hills Hotel's Polo Lounge.

He had judged a pageant she was in years ago and thought she would perfect as a judge on this particular show. Hey, it didn't exactly pay *American Idol* or *The X Factor* judge money, but it was pretty good and had proven to be great exposure for her. Plus, Vance said if she was working, no one would ever imagine that she was his wife.

Her old friend, Royale, had implored her to meet him at that Horizons Hotel dump back in L.A. to discuss a possible endorsement deal for her. Upon arrival, it was obvious that he had other ideas. Even though she hadn't known him personally when he had played baseball, he had the reputation of being a stand-up guy. Now, he was looking very sleazy. Well, even though Andrea didn't know she was her mother-in-law, Roshonda felt she needed to protect her. So, she'd left a note for Royale saying she had an appointment that couldn't wait and hightailed it through the desert to Vegas.

As soon as she pulled up in front of the address that was a sports club, she heard shots. Hopefully, her mother-in-law was all right. Now that she had come all this way, she was afraid to go inside. She had to find Vance fast and tell him what was going on. He hadn't answered his cell phone all day. Maybe she should catch the next flight out of Las Vegas to Kentucky. But, what would she do with her car? She needed to get out of there before the shooter or shooters came outside. The best she could do for Andrea now was to call nine-one-one.

"Nine-one-one, what is your emergency?"

"Shots have been fired at the Three Points Sports Bar; 4892 Dean Martin Drive. Please come quickly."

With a sigh, she hung up the phone and backed out of the parking lot. She was going to head back to L.A., as fast as she could. She would take the Lancaster route down I-15 to the 58 and ease into the 405 and take it all the way back to Los Angeles. She would deal with Vance when she got home. She prayed that his mother hadn't been in that dreadful place when those shots rang out.

Chapter Seven

Valerie

Val felt an elbow nudging her. *What was happening now?*

"Hey, sleepyhead, we're getting ready to land."

Val looked around. She was stretched out on a bed on Victor Dumas's jet. Boy, that was the fastest hour she had ever experienced.

Laughing at her, Rome asked, "How do you fall asleep so fast? You were out before we took off."

"Well, funny you should ask," Val replied. "When some fool wakes you up at four o'clock in the morning, you tend to be a little tired by eight." She sat up further and stretched, then headed into the bathroom. "Let me freshen up real fast, then let's face whatever tragedy lies in front of us. Did you call ahead to rent a car?"

"I didn't need to. Victor has a limo waiting for us. He also took the liberty of hiring a security guard to go to the crime scene with us."

Heading out of the bathroom with a warm towel in her hand and wiping her face, Val shook her head in dismay. Wherever they were about to go this morning, it wasn't going to be pretty.

Moments later, she inhaled and then exhaled a deep breath as they landed. The wind hit Val as soon as she got out into the Las Vegas air. It was a cold December morning in the desert.

Pointing to a Rolls-Royce limousine that had pulled right up to the private runway, Rome said, "That must be our ride."

"Don't you think that's a little too ostentatious, Rome? We need a truck to get around in, something that doesn't scream, 'Here they come!'"

"You're right. I'll tell Victor."

A tall, brown-skinned man with dreadlocks emerged from the car. "Master Rome," he said, as he opened the car door for them. "My name is Amir. I'm here to assist in whatever you need. Welcome to Las Vegas."

Shaking his hand, Rome let Val get in the car first. Snuggling down into the seat, Val asked Amir, "What is the temperature here? It's freezing."

"Fifty-two degrees, Madame Valerie, but I'm afraid it's going down to thirty-seven tonight."

Val sighed. "Well, by tonight, I intend to be headed back to L.A., or *Master Rome* here is going to have to buy me a new fur jacket."

Rome glanced at her and smirked.

"Where to?" Amir inquired.

Scrolling through her BlackBerry, Val replied, "The Three Points Sports Bar & Grill, 4892 Dean Martin Drive, near the In-N-Out Burger."

It never ceased to amaze Rome how Val had sources from every realm of life.

Rome said, "You never told me who gave you this tip."

"No, I didn't," Val responded. "I never reveal my sources. But, you're going to see her when we get there. My line sister, Dedra Thorne, is the Deputy Chief of Police here. My phone number was the last number dialed on Jermonna's phone. That's why she called me. She threw in that she thought the dead woman might be Andrea Dumas. So, I told her that Victor Dumas had hired you to find Andrea, and to keep the crime scene sealed off and we'd be there in two hours. And, guess what? We're here in an hour and a half.

"I hope Jermonna's not too bad off and we can take her back to L.A. with us."

"I don't get it," Rome stated.

"Get what?"

"Why you keep fucking around with Jermonna. The girl is a lost cause, Val. Why do you keep wasting your time saving her over and over and over again? You and her lawyer, Shawn Holley, need to call it quits. You see she finally threw in the towel with Lindsay Lohan. She needs to kick Jermonna to the curb also."

"I can't do that. She's been my little buddy since she was rapping. She's a product of New York State's foster care system. She became an emancipated minor at fifteen. She doesn't have anybody but me, Rome. I can't turn my back on her."

At that point, Amir broke into their conversation.

"There's an envelope in the pocket in front of you from Master Victor," he directed toward Rome.

"Thank you."

Rome took out the envelope. There was a smaller cardboard wallet inside of it. He opened it and saw it was stuffed with hundred-dollar bills. There were also papers giving him Power of Attorney to act on Victor's behalf.

"Wow!" Val exclaimed. "That has to be at least fifty grand. I can see myself strutting around Vegas in my new lynx jacket tonight."

Laughing, Rome counted out $10,000 and then handed it to her.

She pushed it back toward him. "I can't take this."

"Yes, you can. This is part of my retainer and, if it weren't for you, I wouldn't have a clue what had happened to Andrea. Thank you, Val."

She knew when to follow orders. Smiling, she stuffed the money into her Birkin.

They were now entering West Las Vegas, also known as the "Historic Westside," a predominantly black community with some of the oldest streets, homes, and businesses in Southern Nevada. It wasn't a long distance from the strip, but it was a whole other world. They pulled up to the address on Dean Martin Drive to what looked like a war zone. There were at least a dozen LVPD cars, four EMS trucks, and what looked like all of the news crews in the city all jockeying for prime property right in front.

"I thought you told me that they were keeping this quiet?" Rome said to Val.

"How long did you think that was going to last? Jermonna is a major star and if they have a hint it may be Andrea Dumas's body in there, there's going to be a media feeding frenzy. Her husband is one of the most respected, as well as one of the wealthiest men in the world, and her son is a living legend."

Rome and Val were out of the car before Amir could open the door for them. Standing in front of the club, Dedra ran straight to Val. She was followed by every camera crew that was out there.

Reporters yelled out questions to Val from every direction.

"Val, what are you doing here?"

"Is it true Jermonna Bradley is inside dead?"

"Are there any other casualties?"

"Was this a gang-related shooting?"

Stopping for the cameras, Val calmly stated, "I just landed in Vegas. Give me a moment to speak with Assistant Deputy Chief Thorne and go inside, so I can check things out for myself. When I come out, I'll attempt to address some of your concerns."

Another reporter shouted, "Mr. Nyland, what are you doing here? Do you have a client in there?"

Rome pushed Val through the throng of people and inside as he replied, "No comment."

Turning to Dedra, Val hugged her, "It's been a long time. You still look great." The two of them had pledged Delta Sigma Theta together at Howard University. The name of their line was the "Untouchable 31."

"This is Rome Nyland," Val said, doing a formal introduction.

Dedra smiled at her line sister. "You look good, too." Dedra then turned to Rome, proffering her hand. "It's nice to meet you, Rome. Come on, guys. Let me show you what's going on inside. I wish this morning's outcome had been different."

The inside of the sports bar had seen better days. But where most sports bars had paraphernalia from every team, every wall in this place was covered with Los Angeles Wildcats posters, jerseys, photos, banners. It was like Wildcats heaven.

"This way."

Val wanted to hang behind and let Rome enter the room Dedra was leading them to. She hated seeing dead bodies so much that she rarely attended funerals.

Dedra pulled the sheet back. Val let out a gasp. The woman lying in front of them was a far cry from the Andrea Dumas Val had seen in photographs and from a distance at events over the years.

Andrea Dumas had been a full-figured beauty. The first super plus-size model, she was the role model for every woman over size fourteen in the country. She had a flair for fashion that no one could touch and her hair and makeup were always camera ready. This woman was all skin and bones, with gray hair that hadn't seen color in months. She was wearing a red St. John pants suit, trimmed with a mink collar and cuffs that had stains on it.

With all that money, time had not been kind to Andrea Dumas.

Val noticed she wasn't wearing any jewelry. Had it been stolen? The Andrea Dumas she had been observing for years was always dripping in diamonds. She still clutched a crocodile Hermès Birkin bag in her hand.

"It's her," Rome announced, verifying the obvious.

Dedra nodded.

"Okay. Notify her husband, then let me know how he wants us to handle this."

"Did Jermonna tell you anything that happened?" Val asked Dedra.

"No, she's really out of it. She kept screaming your name and Ro. Do you know who that is? Could she mean Roshonda Rhodes? A guy out front believes he saw her pull up and leave."

"Well, they do know each other, but I don't think they hang out. I'll see what I can get out of Jermonna at the hospital. Where are the people who work here, or own this place?" Val asked.

"That's the problem," Dedra replied. "This place has been abandoned for the past few months. I don't know how they got in here or what they were doing here."

Rome was on a serious phone call with Victor. It wasn't easy telling a man that his wife had been shot twice in the head in what seemed to be an after-hours club. "I'm sorry, Victor. Okay. I'll see you tonight." He turned back to Dedra and Val. "Listen, Dedra, Victor is placing a call to Palm Mortuaries, Cemeteries and Crematories to send a casket over here. He would rather you let their people carry his wife's body out of here in a casket, rather than a body bag. He wants to give her some dignity. Is that all right?"

"No problem. I'll instruct the medical examiner to wait until they get here."

"How soon before the body can be released?" Rome asked.

"Hopefully the autopsy can be completed by tomorrow. I'll call you as soon as they're done," Dedra assured Rome.

"Okay. Val and I will address the press real fast. Then, Victor will hold a full press conference when he's up to it. Val, you ready?"

Val said, "Yes, I'm as ready as I'll ever be. Let's do this. I need to go to the hospital and check on Jermonna."

With solemn faces, the three of them headed outside to a barrage of flashing lights and cameras.

Val held up her hand to get everyone's attention. She suddenly had a flashback to years ago when she had been a reporter for the *New York Post*, but had fronted a press conference for Ike Turner and his then wife, Jeannette, about a book on domestic violence they were promoting. Just like what was about to happen right now, she'd had to explain her involvement with the controversial music icon.

"Good morning. I realize I'm usually the one breaking stories, but today I'm here as a friend of Jermonna Bradley. The actress was shot in this establishment sometime early this morning. I don't know how long she's been in Las Vegas. Her injuries are not life-threatening. I accompanied Rome Nyland here, who is employed by Dumas Electronics mogul Victor Dumas. You'll hear from him now."

"Good morning, ladies and gentlemen of the media," Rome said, jumping in on cue. "With a heavy heart, I can reveal to you that Andrea Dumas, Victor Dumas's wife and mother of Vance Dumas, was found dead this morning. There will be no further statements at this time. Mr. Dumas will hold a press conference in the very near future. He is headed to Las Vegas from New York City to handle these affairs as we speak. Thank you."

Val whispered to Dedra, "Look, Dee Dee. We need to talk. Call me when you're finished here."

Dedra gave Val a reassuring glance as she and Rome climbed back into the car. "No problem."

"Please take us to Sunrise Medical Center," Val instructed Amir, and then turned to Rome. "Rome, did you see all of that Los Angeles Wildcats paraphernalia?"

"Yes, why? There's nothing unusual about that. It's a sports bar."

"Dedra said it's an *abandoned* sports bar. Are you familiar with the Bugatti Blades? They present themselves as concert promoters, managers and independent record label owners in the music business, but I hear they're really a pretty deadly gang out of Compton that wear Wildcats gear instead of colors. Their hangout back home is a sports bar over in Inglewood. I have a feeling this same sort of place isn't a coincidence. Maybe Andrea knew some of those guys. As I said, they don't appear to be gang members. Rumor has it that they ship drugs around the country. They're nobody to mess with. My sources say they're extremely dangerous. Forget being your average players in the game. These guys are deadly stuff players."

"Okay, I'll look into it. In the meantime, Victor is arranging for us to have two suites for the night at the Palms Casino Resort. He wants us to meet him for dinner and go over everything at the Alizé restaurant around eight o'clock. I realize you prefer to go home tonight, but we have to tie up loose ends."

"That's all right. Besides, the hospital might not release Jermonna today anyway. There are worse things to do on a Saturday night than having dinner at a five-star restaurant in Las Vegas with a recently widowed billionaire."

Rome glared at her with amusement and shook his head.

"Excuse me, Master Rome," Amir interrupted. "There's a car practically on my bumper, aggressively following us."

"Amir, do you have a gun?" Rome reached in to his leg holster and retrieved his Glock. "Get down on the floor, Val."

"I already have it out, sir."

Dialing nine-one-one as she dove on the floor of the limousine, Val yelled, "I told you this car was too damn ostentatious! You should have had another one delivered while we were in the club! Oh, Jesus Lord, save us!"

A shot rang out.

"Nine-one-one. What's your emergency?"

"This is Valerie Rollins. I'm in a gold Rolls-Royce limousine with the license plates *Dumas II* heading down North Flamingo Road in Las Vegas. Shots have been fired. You need to get here as fast as you can!"

Rome shouted, "Amir, make a fast U-turn here! There are no cars coming on the other side of the road!"

As Amir followed his instructions, Rome slowly lowered his window, aimed his gun out of it, and fired a shot at the front tire of the navy blue Cadillac Escalade that was following them. He heard the tire blowout. Then, he inched up a little further and fired two more shots at the guy with the gun on the vehicle's passenger side. The tire flew off and the guy slumped down in the seat. The driver tried to steer the car, riding on the rims, but couldn't and veered off the road, crashing into a street lamp.

At that point, the trio in the car could hear sirens approaching. But there was another *Ppop! Ppop!* and the limo started swaying back and forth.

Amir had been hit. Rome quickly jumped into the front seat. With his right hand pushing Amir out of the way, and with his left hand grabbing the steering wheel, he eased his foot onto the brakes, bringing the humongous vehicle to an abrupt stop. By then, there were cop cars on either side of him, and surrounding the Escalade.

Val started to scream. "What just happened? Why were they shooting at us?"

The police were pulling the driver out of the SUV. He was a young black guy, whose jeans were hanging off his butt. The police officer slammed him against the car, put handcuffs on him, then read him his rights.

Rome ran over to them. "Who are you, man? Who sent you?"

The guy spat in Rome's face. At that point, Dedra pulled up, then jumped out of her unmarked car, yelling, "Val? Val?"

Val slowly eased up, whispering, "I'm okay."

Dedra walked up to her arresting officers, looked at the guy in cuffs, then told them, "Take him to the station."

Wiping the spit off his face, Rome wanted to question the guy, but it wasn't his call. He walked back over to the car and glanced over at Amir. He had been shot twice in the temple. It was obvious that Amir was dead. Looking at Dedra, he said, "Get Val out of here and take her to the hospital. I'll stay and answer questions."

"No," Dedra replied. I'm taking you *both* to the hospital right now. I can question you there."

Although she also could see that Amir was clearly deceased, she added, "Here come the paramedics for your driver right now."

For once, Val was at a loss for words and did exactly what Dedra had said. It wasn't quite noon yet, and already she had seen two dead bodies. This was not the morning she had signed up for when she left Los Angeles.

Holding Dee Dee's hand, she got into her car with Rome, who was in deep thought. Those shots had been fired by someone who wanted to kill Amir. Although Rome had been in plain view when he fired his gun out of the limo's window, the shooter hadn't even aimed at him. Yet, Amir had been shot dead in the corner of his forehead. That was no accident.

But, why? And, why had the driver been whisked out of there so fast before Rome could get his name? He also needed the identity of the guy he had shot. Dedra hadn't even asked him for his gun. Unbeknownst to her, he had picked up Amir's wallet as he got out of the car. He needed to look into this man's background, and then he would deal with the other two in the car that shot at them. First, he needed to call Victor and let him know the driver he had sent for him and Val was dead.

Val seemed to read his thoughts. "Rome, you need to call Victor and fill him in. We also need to get our own car and driver to pick us up from the hospital and take us wherever we have to go tonight. I don't know who's after the Dumas family, but we don't need them tracking our every move." She focused her attention on Dedra, who was grasping the wheel with both hands. "Dee Dee, what's a good and confidential car service around here?"

"Call Omni. They have a nice fleet of SUVs."

"Will do. As soon as we leave the hospital, I need a glass of chardonnay. No, forget a glass. Someone needs to come up off an entire bottle. All of this is spooking me and my nerves are shot!"

Rome said, "Dedra, I know you have to notify the next of kin before you release his name, but, it would be doing me a real solid if I could get the names of the guy I shot and the driver of the car. You sure you don't need me to come down to the station? I just killed a man."

"No, Rome. I'll handle all of this. If I need you, I'll call you."

Rome nodded his head and quickly dialed Victor, completely understanding Val's emotions. Being so close to death was never an easy pill to swallow.

Chapter Eight

Royale

Back in L.A., Royale was just getting back to his hide-out at the Horizons Hotel near LAX. Discovering an empty room with no Roshonda patiently waiting for him, Royale was mad as hell. He read her note.

Had a last-minute audition I had to get to. I'll give you a call on Monday.

I'm sorry.

Best, Roshonda

Smirking, he thought, *Well, I'll just have to tear that pussy up some other time.* Then his cell phone rang and the man on the other end was shouting.

"How can your people fuck up two jobs? Tell me, Royale, how? There are three people still breathing who shouldn't be. On top of that, one of our guys is dead and another one has been arrested. You've almost totally fucked everything up for me. Do you know the fate of my financial future is in your hands? Well, if you want to keep the fingers on your hands, you'd better get the next jobs done correctly, *if* I decide to trust you again. For now, let those ducks keep swimming." He paused and drew in a deep, angry breath. "Don't bother them anymore. I'll take care of them personally."

"Yes, boss," Royale said, trying to maintain his composure. He was never one to appreciate being talked down to in such a manner, but he had to suck it up this time. "I'm sorry. I thought the workers were better equipped."

"Well, you thought wrong. By the way, your boy, Amir, is no longer with us. He didn't follow instructions either." With that, the man clicked off the phone.

Casting an ashtray across the room and against a wall, Royale unleashed his anger and yelled, "Gotdamn those assholes!"

He needed to try to get some sleep. Saturday night was still in front of him and he had a lot of business to attend to that evening. He wanted to check out a new female rapper named Platinum Pizzazz that was performing at Greystone Manor in Hollywood. She was supposed to be hotter than Nicki Minaj. She was rolling with another rapper D.O.D., who also worked for him, and was his boy, Sweet Lyrics', nephew. Sweet had signed her to his new record label.

Instead of heading to his apartment in North Hollywood, Royale decided to crash at the hotel. Yeah, that wasn't a bad idea; he didn't know how angry the man was over everything that transpired earlier in the day. He definitely didn't want to end up as a statistic like Amir and those dudes did this morning, or merely another Negro in a body bag. He headed into the shower to get cleaned up. From there, he would get some much needed sleep to prepare for the upcoming night's action.

Chapter 9

Valerie

Sitting in the emergency room at Las Vegas's Sunrise Medical Center, Val was growing increasingly impatient with the staff by the second. She snapped at an attending nurse. "I told you I'm all right. I need a glass of chardonnay, some lunch and a quick nap, and I'll be back to normal. Now will someone please tell me where Ms. Bradley's room is?"

Val didn't mean to yell at the nurses, but, she really wasn't "all right." Inside, she was shaking like a leaf. First, the sight of Andrea Dumas's body was very upsetting to her. Right after that awful experience, a man that she had just been talking to got shot dead in the car seat in front of her. Moments later, another man was dead in the car that was shooting at her and Rome. She didn't know when things would be the same again. She wanted to get this dinner over with Victor Dumas and get back to the safety and comfort of her own little home. This was not what she had bargained for.

While Valerie was stressing out in the examining room, Rome was putting in a reluctant call to Victor, who was on his plane headed to Las Vegas from New York to claim his wife's body. Now, his chauffeur, one of the members of his security team, was also dead.

"Hello, Victor, it's Rome. Listen, on our way out of that sports bar, someone trailed us and shot at us. I don't quite know how to tell you this, so I'm going to give it to you straight. Your driver, Amir, is dead."

"Amir?" Victor repeated. "I don't know any Amir. My associate, Claude Hoskins, was supposed to pick you up."

"That's crazy!" Rome was shocked. "A tall guy with locks named Amir picked us up. He was driving a Rolls-Royce limousine with vanity plates that say 'Dumas II' on them. He even gave me the envelope that had the deposit for my retainer in it and all of your papers giving me Power of Attorney to conduct business for you."

"Maybe Claude had some sort of emergency and had to send this Amir. I'll get in touch with him now. I'm landing in an hour. I'll see you and Miss Rollins at dinner. Also, you told me you and Miss Rollins left Los Angeles in a hurry and didn't have time to pack. So, I took the liberty of having a suit, shoes, shirt and tie delivered to your suite for dinner. Size forty XL, right, and size eleven shoes?"

"I'm not going to even ask how you knew all that, but thanks, man. I need to make a lot of phone calls and don't have time to shop."

"Tell Miss Rollins not to worry either. Several articles of clothing are already hanging in the suite's closet for her."

"That's very nice of you. I gave her some money to get a few things, but she's had a rough morning. Since it's going down to the thirties tonight, I may call around and try to surprise her with a fur jacket for Christmas just to see her smile." He paused. "She's pretty shaken up. I didn't realize your wife was the first famous plus model or something like that. Val was a big fan of hers."

"Just leave it all to me," Victor assured him. "I'll see you at eight. And, Rome, thanks for everything."

"You're welcome, Victor. See you tonight."

Rome pushed the "end" button on his phone and headed back toward the examining room where Valerie was located. For all they had been through this morning, she didn't look any worse for the wear. Her blonde hair was still brushed flat on her head, nestling on her shoulders. Val very rarely wore makeup and her skin was radiant. And, as usual, she was smiling.

"How did Victor take it about Amir?" she asked in a soft voice.

"Things just got a lot stranger. He says he doesn't know Amir." Val gazed at him in confusion. "I'll get to the bottom of that problem as soon as we see what's happening with Jermonna and head to the hotel."

"Okay, she's in room nine twelve. Her doctor's name is Lawrence Packer. Let's go check both of them out."

As they passed the gift shop, Val told Rome, "Give me a moment to duck in here and purchase some flowers to brighten up Jermonna's room."

After purchasing a beautiful bouquet of red roses and a teddy bear, the now weary duo got on the elevator and headed up to find out what sort of condition Jermonna was in. Luckily for them, Dr. Packer was leaving the room as they were heading in. Val saw his nametag and immediately stuck out her hand to shake his.

"Dr. Packer, my name is Valerie Rollins and this is my associate, Rome Nyland. I'm a friend of Jermonna's. How is she doing?"

"Nice to meet you, Ms. Rollins; you too, Mr. Nyland," Dr. Packer responded. "I've been a fan of both of yours for years. I still remember that touchdown you scored against the Chicago Bears back in '90, Mr. Nyland. That was something to witness. I won a lot of money on that game. And, Ms. Rollins, I still watch you on *Life After*. You still look exactly like you looked back in the nineties with all the Michael Jackson and O.J. Simpson commentary you used to do, maybe even younger."

"Thank you. Call me Val. What's the latest with Jermonna?"

"I'm afraid she's an extremely sick woman, both physically and mentally," Dr. Packer answered. "I'm amazed she's even still with us. Her system had cocaine, marijuana, Vicodin and traces of ket-amine in it. Plus, she's quiet and non-responsive. We need to keep her here a few days to wean all those drugs out of her system. Once that happens, she needs to go straight into a rehabilitation facility."

Rome shook his head. He didn't want to upset Val, but he was really sick and tired of her playing Mother Teresa to Jermonna. The girl was nothing but trouble.

"Okay," Val stated solemnly. "I'll make arrangements for her to go to Promises in Los Angeles."

"I don't think Promises is a good idea. She needs to get as far away from Hollywood and all her friends and old habits as possible," Dr. Packer said. "I'd like to suggest Hazelden, in Center City, Minnesota. It offers real hope for lifelong recovery. It's located fifty miles north of Minneapolis and Saint Paul. The programs there allow for more in-depth time on special issues, mental health complications, and relapse prevention. The counselors and doctors there can also provide Jermonna with sober living skills. Check out the facility's website. Everything I'm telling you is right there."

"He's right, Val," Rome interjected. "If she goes back to L.A., she'll surely die. She may not be so lucky the next time."

Heading into the room, Val told him, "Goodness. All right. You start making the arrangements to get her there, Doctor. I'll talk to her now."

Jermonna seemed to have shrunk since Val and Rome had seen her last. You could barely see her buried under the covers, with all the IV machines surrounding her. Placing the roses on the table and the teddy bear in the bed with Jermonna, Val called her by her hip-hop name, which Jermonna used when they'd first met.

"Hey, J Body, it's me. Rome is here with me."

Jermonna opened her eyes, trying hard to focus on Val. She couldn't look at Rome. She understood that he didn't like her. "Can I get up and come home with you now?"

"No, sweetie," Val answered. "You still have a lot of drugs in your system, including ketamine. That's a date rape drug, isn't it? I mean, why would you take any of this stuff, but, especially a date rape drug?"

"I didn't take it," Jermonna replied. "That guy, Sincere, must've put it in my glass of champagne."

Rome made note of the name Sincere, then asked her, "Do you know who killed Andrea?"

"I already told the police all I know. We went to that club with Sincere and some other guys. The next thing I knew I couldn't get out of the back room. The door was locked. I must've passed out. I heard Andrea pleading for her life, then gunshots. The next thing I knew the police were breaking down the door."

Rome continued, "Where did you meet Sincere?"

"At another after-hours place. It didn't have a name on the door." She fought back tears. "I'm sorry, Val. I'm supposed to be doing better and staying clean."

"Well, you don't have any choice now." Val touched her hand lovingly. "When they discharge you from here, you're going straight to Minnesota to the Hazelden Center. You have a choice; get clean or keep killing yourself. That could've been you headed to the morgue instead of Andrea. I guess God wasn't ready to call you home yet. You have a lot to be thankful for."

"Jermonna," Rome said. "Can you describe any of the other guys to me?"

"They were all athletic-looking, tall and well-built, all black guys, and a couple of them had on hats with the Wildcats logo on them."

At the mention of the Wildcats gear, Val and Rome exchanged glances.

"And, oh… One of them was tall with locks. They called him Amir."

Val sat down on the edge of Jermonna's bed before her legs gave out. *Amir? Had the killer or one of the killers picked them up from the airport? If it was the same guy, why had that other guy killed him?*

"J Body?" Val asked. "When we got disconnected on the phone, you mentioned the name Ro. Did you mean Roshonda Rhodes? One of the guys that was hanging outside of the Three Points Bar told my friend Dedra that he was positive he spotted her leaving in a Bentley truck."

"No, Roshonda wasn't there. I was talking about Royale Jones. I'm here in Vegas for a booking he got me. But, when I got to the bar at the casino, the gentleman I was supposed to meet wasn't there. I couldn't get Royale on the phone. That's when I ran into Andrea and she suggested we go to the first club."

Val asked her, "You mean Royale Jones who used to play baseball?"

"Yes, that's him. He has Royale Talent and Booking agency now."

"Okay," Rome jumped in with a sigh. "I know Royale from years ago when we were both active athletes. Let me have his number and I'll see what's up." He headed toward the door. "We're going to let you get some sleep. We'll call your lawyer. If the police or anyone come back, tell them you've retained an attorney and can't answer any further questions. I'm also going to call a security firm here in town to place round-the-clock security on your door." He looked at Val. "Val, we also need to get her a private nurse service for security. I'm going to go down to the hospital's security office and get someone up here right away until I can get a guy here." He noticed Val was hesitant about leaving. "Come on, Val. Let's do this right away."

Jermonna shook her head. "I just tried Royale's number. Now it's disconnected. It's all real strange. Val." She tried to readjust herself in the bed but it was too painful. "They stole all my cash. I still have my passport and driver's license on me, though. Can you leave me some money?"

Fearing Jermonna would take the money, leave the hospital, and head to the nearest drug dealer, Val realized she couldn't do that. Taking Jermonna's hand, Val told her, "It will all be okay. Don't worry about money. When they discharge you, we'll see to it that you have whatever you need. The doctor said you can't have any phone contact with people while you're detoxing. I'll stop by here to see you before we leave in the morning. When you're ready to go, I'll take you to Minnesota myself."

"I wasn't planning on staying, so I don't have any clothes with me," Jermonna whined. "Can you pick up a few things for me and a toothbrush and some toiletries? I can write you a check for whatever you bring when I get home."

"Don't worry, J Body," Val said with a smile. "Consider whatever I pick up as an early Christmas present." Val let go of her hand and was about to leave but paused. "By the way, when you were with Andrea last night, did she have any jewelry on?"

"Of course she did. I remember two big diamond rings, one on each hand, a gold Rolex, and a huge necklace. It was a big black diamond, maybe eight carats, surrounded with yellow diamonds that had to be at least one to two carats a piece. Why?"

Val answered, "She wasn't wearing any jewelry when we identified her body."

She kissed Jermonna on the cheek and followed Rome out of the hospital room's door.

"Your hunch about the Bugatti Blades being involved seems to be on point," Rome told her. "This Amir must have been hired to kill us, too. Victor says he wasn't his regular driver. I wonder why he was killed instead."

Val told him, "I'm going to call Dee Dee and give her the description of the jewelry Jermonna says Andrea was wearing. She should put an alert out to all the pawnshops in town right away. If the murderer shows up at one of them, they can call Dee Dee right away."

Val couldn't take much more of all this violence and horror. She wanted to get down on her knees right there and pray that God would keep them safe. Stopping by the nurse's station, she arranged for private round-the-clock care for Jermonna.

"Can you tell us what floor the security office is on?" Val asked the nurse.

"It's down on three. You two can't miss it; it faces the elevator. I'll call an agency we work with and have a nurse in Miss Bradley's room momentarily."

To make sure the nurse moved fast, Val opened her purse and pulled five hundred-dollar bills from the wad Rome had given her out of her purse and discreetly handed the cash, along with her card, to the nurse.

"This is for your troubles. Call me as soon as everything is in place. Give me a price, and I'll pay you whatever else is needed before I leave Vegas tomorrow."

"Thanks." The nurse grinned; she could not believe her luck. Five minutes earlier, she had been stressing over how she would pay her electric bill that month. "I'll personally make sure everything is fine. Ms. Bradley will be well taken care of."

As they got on the elevator, all Val could think of was how close she and Rome had come to losing their own lives this morning. Rome's voice broke into her thoughts.

"I know you want to stop off at the security office here and hire guards for Jermonna. But, there is a good chance that we may have been followed here by whomever hired the gunmen who—that tried to kill us. I want to get out of here now and get us into hotel rooms where I know we have security. For safety's sake, let's take a regular cab to the hotel. There should be a taxi stand out front. I'll call the security for Jermonna once we get to the hotel. The nurses will make sure she's safe for now. Let's blow this joint."

"You ain't said but a word," Val quickly agreed.

She was happy to be leaving the dismal atmosphere of the hospital. As Rome had predicted, there was a taxi stand outside of the hospital. He opened the door for Val, then told the driver, "Take us to the Palms Casino."

Feeling as if the outfit that she was wearing had the smell of dead bodies all over it, Val told Rome, "Maybe he should take us to the Fashion Showcase Mall first. I have to get out of these clothes."

Not wanting to say much that the taxi driver could hear or recognize, Rome quietly explained to her, "Don't worry about that. My associate told me everything we need to wear to dinner tonight and any other clothes we'll need while we're here in Vegas will already be in our suites when we arrive at the hotel."

"What's that supposed to mean?"

"Just follow his lead. I guess we'll find out what it means when we get there." The ringing of a phone made them both jump. "That's me," Rome said, answering. "Hi, baby. Listen, I had to jet to Vegas on business this morning. I'm sorry. Of course I didn't forget it's your birthday. Yeah… Yeah…I'm, uh, I'm with Val. Remember, I told you about her. I know, baby.

"Whoa…Whoa… Look, why don't you catch a flight to Vegas? I'll be at the Palms Casino. After Val and I get done with our business meeting, we can catch a show for your birthday and then hit the casino. That's a much better plan than plain old dinner in L.A., right? Okay, baby, I'll leave a key for you to the suite with the concierge." He paused and then told whomever was on the other line, "Me, too."

"What was all that about?" Val grinned. "And who is 'baby'? I thought you and your cheerleader baby mama broke up last year."

"That was a young lady I've been seeing for a while now, and *yes*, Davida and I have totally broken up."

"Does this young lady have a name? She must be pretty special. I've never known you to mix business with pleasure."

Rome laughed. "She is very special. Her name is Turquoise Hobson."

"I know who she is. She owns Turquoise Hobson Realty. A few of my friends bought homes from her. She's supposed to be pretty cool. I'm happy for you, Rome. But, why did she seem to have a problem with you being here with me? Didn't you tell her we're just friends?"

He was not in the mood for all of Val's interrogation. They had just left three bodies, including the guy who shot at them. He needed answers on all of this. They also had no clue as to who had shot and drugged Jermonna, putting her the hospital. Plus, Rome had always been very guarded when it came to discussing his love life. Always a one-woman man, he had never been the stereotypical jock that had several of his women sitting in different sections of the stadium during football games. During his playing days, he had to help many a team mate out with that situation by entertaining the woman who was from out of town while his boy got rid of the one who lived in town. That type of deception had never been his thing.

To be honest, even though he was in his early fifties, Turquoise was only the third woman that Rome had been sexually involved with. Of course, there was the high school girlfriend he had lost his virginity with. Then, he had met Davida during his sophomore year of college. Although the two of them never married, they had been together off and on for the next twenty-five years.

He had never cheated on her and constantly asked her to marry him. Almost sixteen years ago, when their son, Romey, was born, he was sure that Davida would agree to be his wife. But, once again she turned his proposal down. He never asked her again.

A year ago Davida confessed to Rome that she had been dating other men throughout their entire relationship. It wasn't difficult because Rome had served in Desert Storm and he had played football for many years traveling to away games. But, now she had fallen in love with a doctor she'd been seeing for several months. She wanted out. Rome had been crushed. Like, Val, he was an only child and both his parents were dead. Soon after the break-up from Davida, he met Turquoise. She was gorgeous, sexy, exciting and aroused sexual desires within him that he never knew existed. Turquoise was definitely a keeper.

He answered Val, "Yes, I told her we're just friends. But, I did forget today was her fortieth birthday. So, why not invite her here? I might as well kill two birds with one stone."

Val smirked. "With all we've witnessed this morning, I wouldn't use the word *kill* so lightly."

The taxi pulled up to the hotel and Rome paid the man as they both gladly got out.

Stepping into the Palms Casino Resort was like entering a whole new world. Owned by the very wealthy Maloof Brothers, whose sister Adrienne was once a cast member of *The Real House-wives of Beverly Hills*, the Palms was directly off the strip. It was renowned for its ultra-hip hotel scene. Val couldn't wait to get into the room, order some room service and get off her feet. It was now one-thirty in the afternoon and she had been up since four a.m.

Stepping up to the front desk, Rome told the clerk, "We're Rome Nyland and Valerie Rollins. I believe some rooms have been reserved for us by Victor Dumas. "

"Welcome to the Palms Resort Casino. Of course, Mr. Nyland. You and Ms. Rollins are actually in the Trio Story Sky Villa."

"Wait a minute," Val interrupted. "We can't stay in the same suite. That has to be a mistake. Plus, he has a date arriving soon."

"Not to worry, Ms. Rollins," explained the clerk. "There is plenty of room. Mr. Dumas reserved the Trio Story Sky Villa for you all. It's three levels and there are three bedrooms. I'm sure you both will find the accommodations very comfortable and much to your liking."

Rome told him, "I'm expecting Miss Hobson. Will you send her up when she gets here?"

A man appeared next to them. "I'm Gerard, part of your personal butler staff. Allow me to escort you to your suite. Do you have any luggage?"

Pointing to Rome, Val answered, "Thanks to him and his rush to get here to meet our personal version of Armageddon, no, we don't."

Rome smirked.

"In that case, follow me," Gerard said with a chuckle.

He led them to a glass elevator that no one else got on. The elevator opened right into the suite. Both Val and Rome walked around in disbelief. Not only were there three bedrooms, but there was also a fitness center on one level, a huge swimming pool and a media room. There was also a dining room where the table was already set with a spread that was unimaginable. It looked like Christmas dinner. There was a turkey with all the trimmings, ham, salads, rolls, rice, macaroni and cheese; this was unbelievable. There was also an oversized champagne bucket filled with bottles of Kendall Jackson Chardonnay and Cristal.

Val was astonished. "Did we get shot this morning along with everyone else, and now we're in heaven?"

Rome laughed. "Let's eat and then I have to get on the horn

and get some questions answered. Gerard, if there's a jewelry store downstairs, can they send up a variety of diamond bracelets and necklaces for me to look through? And can a bottle of chilled Cristal be put in my room?"

"No problem, sir. I'll call down right now. Would you two like me to serve you?"

"Diamond bracelets and necklaces," repeated Val. "Ms. Hobson is truly going to have one happy birthday when she gets to town!"

Rome chuckled and shook his head.

Val told the butler, "Point me to my room and let me wash all this death off of me. When I get out of the tub, I'll come back here and eat."

When Val got to her room, she couldn't believe her eyes. You must have been able to see all of Las Vegas from up there. The suite reminded her of years ago when she had been a publicist for former Heavyweight Champion of the World Larry Holmes. They had given a press conference for him in one of the Fantasy Suites in Caesar's Palace. Though not nearly as lavish, it had also been all silver and chrome, with white furnishings, and multi-levels with several bedrooms. She remembered how she didn't want to leave when the press conference ended. Reminiscing, she thought about how she'd taken the luxury soap that was in the bathroom.

A note on the closet door caught Valerie's attention. "Welcome to Las Vegas, Valerie."

She opened the door. Hanging before her were three dresses. There was a Jones New York Collection Plus boat-neck, zip-shoulder dress, a fabulous Melissa Masse Plus caftan and a Karen Kane Plus sequin dress. There was also an Eileen Fisher sequined, crimson silk knit tunic and a pair of black pants. They were all size fourteen. On the floor were four shoe boxes. She opened them right away. One held a pair of Michael Kors platform pumps with leopard print that matched the boat-neck dress exactly. The other three held a pair of black Louboutin pumps, a pair of fabulous Louboutin pumps covered with Swarovski crystals, and in the last box was a pair of Brian Atwood silver and gold leopard-printed glitter booties. Okay, this was scary.

She had looked at these booties in Neiman Marcus last week, but decided she didn't feel like teetering around in the five-and-a-half-inch heels. Val slipped her feet into them. They fit perfectly. Teetering around this hotel or not, she was going to sport these bad boys tonight! How could this man have known her exact sizes and taste? Leaving nothing to chance, there was a Louis Vuitton rolling carry-on suitcase sitting right next to all the clothes for her to pack them in. There was a knock on her door.

Assuming it was Rome, Val yelled, "Come in!"

"This package arrived for you, Miss Rollins." Gerard handed her a large box wrapped in silver paper held together with red ribbon and a huge bow.

Val was excited to see what was inside. "Thank you."

She set it down on the bed and carefully removed the elegant wrapping. The box had "Anna Nateece Studios" written across it. Val was very familiar with the name and the store. Not only had Anna Nateece been Liberace's exclusive furrier, but all of the boxers that Val had worked for in the beginning of her career had purchased furs from the fabulous woman. She opened the card before unwrapping the tissue paper.

We wouldn't want you to get chilly tonight. Here's to an early Merry Christmas. Best, Victor Dumas.

Val tore the tissue paper off and pulled the most beautiful pink mink jacket she had ever seen out of the box. Slipping it on, all she could do was mumble, "Oh, my God."

It was a perfect fit. This scene was becoming surreal. First of all, she had just seen a photo of her friend LaToya Jackson wearing the exact same jacket and tweeted Toy to tell her how gorgeous it was. All of this excitement was getting in the way of business. She was acting like a kid on Christmas morning. Val almost forgot that she needed to let Dee Dee know about Andrea's missing jewelry. She pulled out her phone and texted her the descriptions of each piece. Now that she had accomplished that task, all she could do was wonder who is this Victor Dumas, a mind reader, a magician, or just an extremely wonderful, generous guy?

"I'll see which one he turns out to be at dinner," Val mumbled to herself before heading into the bathroom to slip into the tub.

Rome

While Valerie was admiring her new clothes, Rome was trying to make sense out of everything that was happening around them. Who killed Andrea? Why did they leave Jermonna alive? Why did that guy shoot at them, and why was Amir killed execution-style? He normally didn't work this way; he shouldn't have taken Amir's wallet from the dead man's pocket, but he needed to get ahead of the cops for Victor. He would get it back to Dedra before he left town. He'd tell her he picked it up by mistake. He sifted through it and counted a little over $2,000 in cash. There were no credit cards. His driver's license said his name was *Amir Lockett, 7038 S. Prairie Street, Chicago, Illinois 60649.*

Rome quickly dialed one of his best FBI contacts. He was elated when he picked up on the second ring.

"Hey, man. What's going on? Listen, I'm in Vegas." He chuckled at a comment his contact made on the other end of the line about hot women in Vegas. "No, that's not why I'm here. I got caught up in a fire fight this morning. A guy by the name of Amir Lockett was killed." His friend asked what he needed. "His license gives a Chicago address. Now, he was posing as a driver for Victor Dumas. Yes, the same Victor Dumas as in Dumas Electronics…Yes, I know his wife was found dead this morning. That's why I'm here. He hired me to find her…I have one more favor to ask. Can you text me the number of your friend in Vegas that has a security firm? I want to hire someone to guard Jermonna Bradley over at Sunrise. Okay, hit me back when you find something out. Thanks."

His next call was to the concierge.

"Can we help you, Mr. Nyland?"

"Yes, I need a rental car. Can you get me a Cadillac Escalade with On-Star in it?" The concierge assured him that it would not be a problem. "Great, let me know when it's downstairs. I'll give you my credit card when I get down there."

"That won't be necessary, sir. Mr. Dumas said all of your charges were to be on him."

"That's very kind of him, but I'm going to be using the car for personal reasons. I'll take care of it."

"Very well, sir," the concierge replied before Rome hung up.

After this morning's fire fight, Rome wasn't quite sure who was the enemy and who was on his side. He could always give Victor the receipt for the car after renting it and get reimbursed. Until he got to know him a little better, the less Victor Dumas knew about the exact moves he was making, the safer he felt it would be for Val and him. It was now three o'clock. They had five hours until dinner. He was going to head back out to the Three Points Sports Bar & Grill, see if anyone was around, and try to get some real information pertaining to the ownership.

His phone beeped, letting him know he had a text. He punched up the number that his boy had sent him.

"This is Rome Nyland. May I speak with Ephraim Rogers, please?"

"Speaking."

"Good afternoon, Ephraim. Conrad Spencer gave me your number. I need to hire round-the-clock protection for Jermonna Bradley. She was shot this morning and is at Sunrise Medical Center. Do you have any one available that could start right away?"

"Yes, I do. My charge is $100 an hour. I can fax you a contract and send someone right away."

"Forget faxing it," Rome instructed him. "I'm staying at the Palms. I'll leave a retainer of $5,000 with the concierge which will get you started. Pick that up and leave the contract. I have to run out. I'll sign it when I get back and leave it for you to get later. Please leave a receipt with the contract."

"No problem, Mr. Nyland. I'll take care of the first shift myself. By the way, I have always been a big fan of yours. It will be an honor to work for you. I also enjoy Ms. Bradley on television. We'll take good care of her."

"Thanks. I'll touch bases with you soon. I will text you my email address so that you can keep me up to date on Jermonna's condition. Bye now."

"Goodbye."

Rome counted out $5,000, tucked it between two sheets of stationery that was on the hotel desk, put them into an envelope, then wrote "Ephraim Rogers" on it and headed out of the door.

Chapter Ten

Victor

The luxury jet was beginning to make its descent into the Las Vegas airport. Leaning back in the white leather couch, Victor Dumas closed his eyes and shook his head. He had yet to shed a tear for his wife, Andrea, whose body was now lying cold in the morgue. Although they had been married for more than three decades, Victor couldn't recall the last time they'd held a decent conversation, shared a meal or a laugh together, gone to an event, or even had a glass of champagne with each other. Forget about sex. They hadn't slept under the same roof in at least five years. Now, the beautiful, vivacious, voluptuous girl with the infectious smile that he had met at the Kentucky Derby so many years ago wearing that big crazy hat was dead. Some low-life had gunned her down as if she were a deer in hunting season.

Victor tried to think back to when Andrea's partying and recreational drug use had escalated into a full-blown addiction. One minute they were happy. Then, he sold the software patent for $100 million. Back then Andrea was merely dabbling in smoking marijuana, but one night he returned home after a long couple of days of traveling on business, and she had a house full of people that he had never seen before snorting cocaine. She virtually ignored him when he walked into the house desiring a nice, quiet dinner. When he came back downstairs after changing his clothes, Andrea and her entourage were gone.

The next morning she acted as if nothing had happened. He tried to take her out to dinner, but she told him she had other plans. He later found out those other plans involved an orgy while Andrea and her new friends smoked tar heroin. It was downhill from there.

She mainly lived in their Bel Air estate, while he continued to travel. He took Vance with him as much as he could, but Vance had discovered a love of horses. He wanted to be a jockey. Victor sent him away to jockey school, then purchased Dumas Farms in Versailles, Kentucky. The farm had 150 stalls in six horse barns, including a yearling complex with six walking rings and an equipment building. Vance had a big race coming up in two weeks. Wildin' Out was running against horses that included Fast Bullet from Winstar Farm. Victor would convince his son to still race. They would hold a huge memorial for Andrea right after the New Year.

While Andrea was busy on the party circuit, Victor's business deals kept getting larger and larger. A graduate of MIT (Massachusetts Institute of Technology), Victor discovered a revolutionary drug for Sickle Cell Disease patients. His parents, who had died within eleven months of each other when he was in his early twenties, were pharmacists. They owned ten pharmacies throughout Kentucky that, together, also served as a pharmaceutical distribution company. Victor saw no reason to hold on to the business, so he sold it to Sovereign Health for a billion and a half dollars in cash. He made that money work for him by hooking up with some young geeks from Howard University and getting into the video game business. Dumas Electronics was born.

Considered a little guy, Victor was five-foot-four and weighed one hundred thirty pounds. Although he now wore lifts in all of his shoes that made him three inches taller, he should have known from the beginning that the five-foot-eight, voluptuous super-model Andrea Bell was way too much for him. However, with her deep chocolate skin and curly mane of hair that cascaded down her back, Victor had to have her. She was like a colt that couldn't be broken, always too fast for him. When Vance, who had inherited his height, was born, she tossed the baby at the nearest nanny and kept partying and spending money.

His flight attendant, Karen, approached him. "We're preparing to land, Mr. Dumas."

He fastened his seat belt and looked around his jet. Dubbed the "Flying Palace" by the media, the leather seating was inspired by Versace Couture for the Home. There were a dozen seats, two bedrooms downstairs and his master suite at the top of the spiral staircase. The jet also boasted three bathrooms, a full office, a cocktail bar and an executive dining room. All of the china, flatware and glassware was also by Versace. As the plane touched down on the runway, all he could think of was he had come a long way since he was little Victor Davidson from Louisville, Kentucky, the little runt who everyone laughed at and teased. Now it was time to say goodbye to his wife, the mother of his wonderful son.

Victor stood up and exited the plane. His plans were to have his wife's remains cremated here, scatter her ashes over the farm in Kentucky, and hold the memorial later. His staff had already contacted Andrea's family and informed them of her death. He had always been very generous with his wife, no matter what the circumstances were, so she should have maintained a decent amount of money in her account. Most likely, she took good care of her family. He would deal with her will when he got to Los Angeles next week. He had been planning to be in L.A. anyway to oversee Vance and the other jockeys and horses prepare for the Cash Call Futurity Race. Since the mansion was Andrea's main residence, he had planned to check into a bungalow in the Beverly Hills Hotel. Now, he would just head to his house that had never really been a home. He would be happy to see the staff there. They were all good people.

Rome

When Rome pulled up in front of the Three Points, there was still police activity, so he decided to go over to the In-N-Out Burger next door. Walking up to the counter, Rome ordered a cheeseburger and an iced tea. While he didn't normally indulge in this kind of food, the burgers here were said to be quite good.

As he got his order, he asked the counter girl, "Did you hear about that murder that happened next door late last night?"

The girl smiled up at Rome. *Who was this gorgeous man?* He looked familiar, but she couldn't quite place his face. "Yeah, it was awful. I had already left work when it happened, but you know, that's an after-hours spot. I hear that black jockey, Vance Dumas's mom got killed over big drug money she owed. Can you imagine that, with all the money her husband has? The word on the street is she was a drug courier for some guys out of Chicago, but snorted and smoked up the merchandise, instead of delivering it where it was supposed to go. A guy told me she was into these guys for over half a million. That actress Jermonna Bradley got shot, too. But, they didn't have any beef with her, so the bullet grazed her arm, just enough to throw the cops off."

Rome thought to himself, *This girl talks more and even faster than Val.*

He smiled at her when she finally decided to take a breath. "And you know all this how? By the way, what's your name?"

She looked nervously around to make sure no one could hear

her. "I'm Evelyn. My friend's man is down with some guys who knew Mrs. Dumas, The Three Points is their Vegas hangout."

This girl could come in handy. Rome discreetly paid for his food with two hundred-dollar bills. "Keep the change, Miss Evelyn. Maybe I can chat with you and your friend when you get off. Do you ladies have any plans for this evening?"

Evelyn wanted to jump for joy when she looked down at the cash in her hand.

Talk about a Christmas bonus!

"We planned on going by the Zebra Lounge at the Ballard around ten. There's a good old school R&B act playing in their lounge."

"Okay, maybe my friends and I will meet you there. Thanks."

"What's your name?" Evelyn inquired, still trying to place his face.

"Clifton," Rome quickly replied with much fabrication. He didn't want to give her too much information. He was still figuring out who the players were in this deadly game.

Rome took his food to a table that had a clear view of the Three Points. Police were still there working the crime scene. A red Ferrari pulled into the front parking lot of the establishment, stopped for a moment, then pulled out. It had California vanity license plates on it that spelled out: "Sweet 4 U."

Taking note of the plate number, Rome tried to get a good look at whomever was driving the sports car, but the windows had a slight tint on them. The cops were finally leaving. Good. It was time for him to try to slip back in the bar and see if he could find any evidence that the cops hadn't uncovered.

As he downed the last sip of his iced tea, Evelyn came over to his table and handed him a folded-up napkin. "Here's my number. Since you're handing out Benjamins, I know you're not a cop.

Why are you interested in what went down at the bar next door?"

"You're right. I'm most certainly not a cop," Rome replied, wiping the side of his mouth with a napkin. "I work for one of the tabloids. You know how we follow Jermonna Bradley around. And, Mrs. Dumas wasn't any slouch, either. The public loves to read about rich people having problems. We pay for information. Tell your friend there's more from where that chump change comes from."

He didn't like to lie, but, he didn't want her to know he was a private investigator working for Victor, either.

"Hope to see you later," Rome told Evelyn as he stood, discarded his trash, and walked out of the door. Instead of going to his car, Rome headed next door. There were a few real reporters milling around the yellow tape that now cordoned off the bar from onlookers.

"Hey, Rome," one of them yelled out. "I figured you'd be back this way after I saw you earlier. You found any motives for these shootings yet?"

"Not yet, but I'm working on it."

Nodding his head, the reporter informed Rome, "Andrea's death was definitely a drug hit. She owed some guys from out of town a lot of money, and I hear she was supposed to have taken them to the bank yesterday to get it. But when they got to the bank, the bank officers said her account was overdrawn. My sources said she pitched a bitch up in there. Somehow she and the guys she was in debt to all ended up here at the end of the night."

"Do you know what bank?" Rome asked, excited about the lead.

"The US Bank, over on East Charleston. One of my boys works there."

"Thanks, man. What's your name?"

"Wilson Rivera. It's nice to meet you. I loved everything you did on the field."

"Thanks again. I'm going to duck under this crime scene tape real fast and see what I can find inside."

In Rome's favor, the police hadn't sealed the entrance to the Three Points Bar. Cautiously looking around, Rome saw the tape on the ground depicting where Andrea's body had lain. He walked further in, hoping to find an office that could shed some light on who really owned this place. He saw a narrow door in the back. Bingo! It opened up into a tiny room that held a table and a couple of chairs. He opened the closet door. Although there was no file cabinet, there was a small locked cash box on the shelf. There was no lock in existence that Rome could not pick. He took a tiny knife-like instrument out of his pocket and had instant success. The box held cash, what looked like vials of cocaine and a gun. His gut told him to leave the box where he found it. He would inform Victor about his discovery, but, he didn't need any gang-bangers tracking him down for their cash and drugs. He now knew if this place was a Las Vegas headquarters for the Bugatti Blades, they were definitely drug dealers on a high level.

Rome glanced at his watch. It was almost five. He needed to get back to the hotel and pick out Turquoise's birthday gifts. The jewelry should be in the suite by now. Turquoise had sent him a text message saying she would be landing around eight. He texted her back, telling her to order room service when she got to the suite, then wait for him there. He would pick her up after his dinner meeting with Val and Victor. Then, the two of them could head over to the Ballard for cocktails. He would also bring Val along to speak to Evelyn and her friend. He doubted if Victor would want to join them there. No matter what the circumstances were with Andrea, she had been his wife for over thirty years. He was sure the man had to be mourning her death.

When Rome got back outside, Wilson and a few other reporters were still there.

"Did you make any new discoveries?" he inquired.

Never one to tip his hand, Rome told him, "Not really. "

"Okay, Wilson. I need to hit the road. Here's my card. Call me if you hear anything else. Oh, and take this for those little pearls of wisdom that you dropped on me."

Looking at the five hundred dollars Rome had handed him, Wilson laughed. "Don't worry. Your number is being added to my speed dial. I'll be in touch the minute I hear anything."

Rome jumped in the Escalade and pulled out of the parking lot. He had collected a lot of information. Now, he had to wait to hear from his boy at the bureau about Amir's background.

Valerie

Although she had attempted to take a nap, the vision of both Andrea's and Amir's bodies would not leave Val's head. She glanced at the clock on the nightstand next to the bed. Boy, was this room gorgeous! It was six o'clock. She had two hours left until dinner and still needed to pick up some clothes for Jermonna. She decided to bounce up, get dressed, and head downstairs to the shops prior to meeting the iconic Victor Dumas!

It would be good to get back to Los Angeles tomorrow. She and Rome had left town so abruptly that she hadn't even packed her laptop. She had to file stories on Jermonna being shot and on Andrea's death. Plus, her phone had been binging off the hook with text messages wanting to know if she was all right after being shot at. Every network from Fox to CNN wanted to do interviews with her. She would deal with them when she got home tomorrow. She was still a little bit too shaken up to make television appearances today.

After taking a quick shower, Val put on the Eileen Fisher sparkly tunic, leggings and the fly Brian Atwood booties. She wouldn't mind tipping around tonight in these bad boys. Arriving downstairs to the busy lobby, Val headed straight to the Palms Shop. She needed to get Jermonna a few things to tide her over until she could get over to her apartment to pack up some clothes and send them to her. These type of shops always had an abundance of small sizes, so she quickly selected several pairs of True Religion jeans in size four for Jermonna, along with some tops to match, a pair of Gwen Stefani's L.A.M.B. Dorrie leopard booties and a croco-embossed tote and a pair of jean multicolored shoes. She was good to go. She would stop by Victoria's Secret in the Forum Mall in the morning and get her some lingerie. She also picked up a couple of Twisted Heart House hoodies with matching fall Kenzie sweat pants for her little buddy.

Reaching into her purse for the cash that Rome had given her this morning, which seemed like a lifetime ago because of all the drama, Val turned around when she heard a thick, Jamaican accent purr, "Valerie, my darling. I was hoping I'd run into you somewhere in town tonight."

Val turned around to see her old pal, Rebecca Fuqua. The ladies hugged, then air-kissed each other on each cheek.

"I saw you on television this morning," Rebecca said anxiously. "Thank God that you, Jermonna, and, that luscious hunk of a man, Rome Nyland, are safe. But, listen, we need to talk. If I was you, I'd already be back in Cali. Those guys Andrea was messing around with ain't nobody to play with."

Listening to her as the salesgirl rang up her purchases, Val asked, "What can you tell me? You already know I never give up a source. No one will ever know you told me anything. Whatever you tell me will stay with me."

Nodding, Rebecca asked, "Where are you headed now?"

As the salesgirl told Val, "That will be one thousand five hundred forty-nine dollars and seventy cents," Val told Rebecca, "I have an eight o'clock dinner upstairs."

"Well, it's barely six-thirty. Let's have a drink in the Scarlet. It's right over here and I'll tell you who you're dealing with. You may want the police to handle this, Val, and be very careful about what you write."

Val paid the salesgirl, told her to have the clothes delivered up to her suite, then followed Rebecca into the Scarlet. As Rebecca located an available booth, Val observed the plush surroundings. The intimate space was adorned with sultry red accents.

"You haven't changed in ten years," Val told Rebecca with much admiration once they were seated. Once an assistant designer for Pierre Cardin, at one time, Rebecca had her own line of full-figure swimsuits. The two of them had met at Jezebel restaurant in New York back in the '90s. In her bubbly blonde mode, Rebecca had approached Valerie who was sitting at the bar and said, "I watch you on *Joan Rivers* all the time. I have a new swimsuit line for full-figured women. I would love to send you some."

Val had given Rebecca her card. When the suits had arrived, she called the designer to thank her and they had been friends ever since. However, Rebecca gave up designing for the Madame business, saying it was a lot more fun and much more lucrative.

A cocktail waitress came over to their table.

"What can I get you ladies?"

"I'll have a Grey Goose martini with olives," Rebecca told her.

"You can give me whatever your best chardonnay sold by the glass is. If you have Kendall Jackson, that would be fabulous," Val replied.

"You're in luck. We do. I'll be right back with your drinks."

Observing Rebecca's mini-dress, black Christian Louboutin

Pigallo spike heels and to-die-for black Celine bag, Val told her friend, "Girl, you still have mad style. So, what's going on?"

"You don't look so bad yourself. How is it that you're younger than you were fifteen years ago? Who is your surgeon?"

Val laughed. "Kendall Jackson Chardonnay."

Rebecca giggled. "I know you're here with Rome digging into Andrea's murder. This thing is down and dirty, Val. I hear Andrea and her little, twenty-two-year-old boy toy ripped off hundreds of thousands, possibly millions, of dollars' worth of cocaine from some cats in Mexico."

"Wow, that's not good!"

The waitress set both their drinks and some peanuts on the table in front of them.

Taking a sip of her martini, Rebecca shook her head, then continued. "This is big. This crew goes from Los Angeles to New York to Jamaica. Anyway, the guys in Los Angeles never got their shipment and followed Andrea here. She and her boyfriend had been acting as some sort of middlemen or couriers. This kid thinks he's pretty tough, and Andrea thought because she was Mrs. Victor Dumas that no one would touch her. However, they were dead, no pun intended, wrong. They definitely fucked with the wrong people."

Val asked, "Who is the boyfriend and why isn't he dead instead of Andrea?"

"That's the thing. No one really knows who he is. I've been told he's a rapper that comes from a family of entertainers. Andrea had to be in her mid-fifties. Running around with a young one like that is a bit much. He stayed below the radar and avoided being seen out in public with her. I'm sure that funding his lifestyle is why she was broke."

Drinking her wine, Val still couldn't comprehend what type of spell Andrea could have fallen under, causing her to choose such an unsavory path in life.

Both women sighed and thought about how foolish Andrea had been.

"These guys are rough. They move a lot of money and dope around. And, as I said, her and the driver's murders may have ties to weed and cocaine dealing out of Jamaica. If you insist on still investigating Andrea's murder, then you and Rome need to find this boyfriend and whomever he's working with fast."

"Where has the time gone?" Val glanced at her watch. "Thanks for all of this. I truly appreciate it, but I need to get upstairs and prepare for dinner. I don't want to be late."

"Who are you meeting?"

"Victor Dumas and Rome."

"Poor Victor. I wish I could have hooked up with him rather than that slut, Andrea. I shouldn't be speaking ill of the dead, though. God bless her. You know, one of my former girls, Roshonda Rhodes, is married to their son, Vance."

Val was astonished. "I've never heard that before."

"For some reason, they keep it a secret. But it's definitely a fact. He paid me five hundred grand to buy out her contract and they got married that very same night here in Vegas. I doubt if Andrea even knew, or if Victor knows, for that matter. She never paid any attention to Vance anyway."

"That's interesting. A guy outside of the Three Points Sports Bar swore he spotted Roshonda driving away from there about the same time Andrea was murdered."

Rebecca smirked. "It wouldn't surprise me; not at all. Maybe she was also trying to get money out of Andrea. You never know."

Leaving some money on the table for their drinks, Val asked, "Do I owe you anything for this info? Rome gave me a nice chunk of change this morning for helping him."

Laughing, Rebecca replied, "You've always been so generous and such a sweetie. Thanks for offering, but no, honey, keep that money. You've always had my back. Now, I have yours. Just be careful."

Air kissing her on the cheek, Val told Rebecca, "I love you," then dashed toward the bank of elevators.

Chapter Eleven

Rome

The first to arrive at the Alizè, Rome was already seated at their table. He liked to get places early so that he could get acclimated to the situation. After picking up the contract that Ephraim Rogers had left for him, Rome left an additional note at the front desk for Turquoise, telling her to dress for their night out. The baubles that the Leor jewelry store had sent up were beautiful. It had been a long time since Rome had been so enamored with a woman. Although he had truly loved Davida, the flame had diminished between them a long time ago. He should have called it quits when she still refused to marry him after Romey's birth. His sex life was certainly on fire with Turquoise. The woman had him doing things he had only heard his teammates talk about. Since the first time he made love to her, every experience in bed was better than the last. To let her know exactly how much he was into her, he wanted to make Turquoise's fortieth birthday one she would never forget. He splurged and spent $18,000 on a Breitling watch and also bought her a Chopard So Happy Hearts diamond pendant.

"Rome, I'm so glad to finally have the honor of meeting you in person."

Rome stood up to shake Victor Dumas's hand. Although he towered over him, Victor's huge persona made the man seem as if he were seven feet tall. Glancing over Victor's shoulder, he could see the surrounding tables had been filled in with members of Victor's security team. The two men sat down.

"Thanks for the suit, shirt, tie and shoes," Rome replied. "You can deduct whatever the expenses were from my fees."

"You came here as fast as you could for my benefit. The clothes are the least I can do to make up for you not having the time to pack your own bags."

At that point, Valerie arrived. She smiled and extended her hand to Victor. Val would be shocked to no end if she had known, but Victor had wanted to meet her since back in the day when she had defied fear and protocol by fiercely defending O.J. Simpson and Michael Jackson. Television certainly did her no justice. In person, this woman was beautiful with shining eyes and a gorgeous smile.

As he stood up and shook her hand, which he noticed, was small, dainty and wrinkle-free, he told her, "Valerie, you're a woman I've always admired from a distance. I wish that our first meeting could've been due to more pleasant circumstances, but the pleasure is definitely all mine." He glanced at her elegant outfit. It fit her like a glove. "I see you like the ensemble."

For once, Val was almost lost for words, but somehow managed to softly say, "I love it. Thank you so much for all of the clothes, the mink jacket, the shoes, and, the suitcase to take it all home in. No one has ever done anything like this for me."

Victor pulled out a chair for her. "Please, sit down."

As Val accepted the seat, she said, "I want to offer my sincere condolences to you, Mr. Dumas. Your wife single-handedly spear-headed the evolution that caused the fashion industry to embrace larger women and that has always meant the world to me."

Suddenly, it was all too much for Valerie. She could still envision Jermonna's bruised-up body, staring down on Andrea's emaciated dead body, and watching the blood pouring out of Amir's head. She collapsed into the chair in tears.

"I'm so sorry."

Rome immediately put his arms around Val. He was a tough guy, a football player, an Army officer in Desert Storm, and, a pretty seasoned private detective. But, he understood what she was feeling. Today's events had been rough on him as well. He should have been a little more sensitive toward Val and not have left her alone all afternoon.

Victor summoned a waiter. "Can you bring out one of the chilled bottles of Kendall Jackson Chardonnay I ordered and pour a glass for Miss Rollins. I'll have a Hennessy on the rocks."

Although Rome rarely drank, he added, "I'll have the same thing."

How did Victor know she drank Kendall Jackson Chardonnay? While she was impressed, Val was beginning to get nervous over all the personal information this man seemed to have on her.

She had to pull herself together. "I usually don't fall apart like this. Forgive me, Mr. Dumas."

"First of all, call me Victor. And, there's nothing to forgive you about. I admire your compassion. More people should care as deeply about others as you do."

The waiter returned with their drinks.

Valerie raised her glass. "To Andrea, to Amir's memory, and to Jermonna getting well. Mostly, to you two gentlemen...it's not often that a woman gets to be in the company of such handsome and aristocratic men."

As they sipped their drinks, Rome filled Victor in on what was happening. "The medical examiner told me they will be able to release your wife's remains on Monday."

"That's fine. I'm going to have her cremated here in Las Vegas and then do a memorial after the holidays. My son is riding in the

Cash Futurity race at Hollywood Park in Los Angeles in two weeks, and I want him to keep that schedule. We'll do something big in her honor at home in Kentucky in February."

Val asked Victor, "Did your son ever mention Roshonda Rhodes to you? Have you ever met her?"

"No, I haven't met her. I do know that he knows her, though. My assistant tells me they have been seen out together here in Las Vegas and in Los Angeles."

Never one to mince her words, Val blurted out, "I ran into an associate of mine downstairs and she tells me that Vance and Roshonda have been married for at least a year."

"Married?" Victor and Rome exclaimed at once.

"That's what Rebecca told me."

"I'll call him when I get back to my suite and see what he has to say about that. Rome, I'm glad I have you on my team now. It's obvious the investigators I had on my payroll aren't worth a damn. This is news to me. Vance never actually discussed his love life with me. However, I have always thought he was in love with a young lady who works with him in Kentucky. My son can't get married. My entire dynasty could be at stake if the girl was after money and really didn't love him."

"I didn't mean to upset you," Val said in earnest. "You've just learned your wife is dead."

Victor glanced at Val and sighed. "To be honest, her death comes as no surprise to me. I always knew one day I would get that dreaded call. I just didn't know when or where she would be." He turned toward Rome. "By the way, Rome, it's very unusual. My assistant can't reach my guy, Claude. I even tried him personally, but all of his phones keep going to voicemail. He runs a small outpost of my organization here in Vegas. Charmion, my assistant, sent someone over to the office, but he's not there."

Rome was pretty sure that Claude was probably another casualty, but he didn't want to let Victor know that. Besides, he figured that Victor had probably arrived at the same conclusion.

"I'm waiting for a report to come back on Amir, and the police here should have his prints back by now. We'll know where Claude is by morning. I'll tell you guys what.

"Let's not concentrate on all of this for now. Victor, my preliminary report is already in your inbox. We can go over it together before Val and I leave here tomorrow. This has been one hell of a day. It's a difficult thing to do when you're grieving, but let's order dinner, and try to relax for the rest of this evening. Tomorrow is another day."

Nodding their heads, they all looked over the sumptuous menu, lost in their own thoughts.

Val told the waiter, "I'll have the iceberg lettuce salad to start and the prime rib eye, medium well, for my main course."

Rome perused the menu.

"Let me try the classic French onion soup and bouquet of baby greens and I'll follow them up with the imported Dover sole."

Victor gave the waiter his order last.

"Bring me the escargots De Bourgogne as an appetizer. Then, I'll have the roasted Muscovy duck breast."

He turned to Val, "I'm sure you will enjoy your meal. Chef Andre Rochat is the best."

Taking another sip of her wine, Val smiled at Victor. This was the first time she had ever been in his presence. She had no idea he was so handsome. His skin was the color of café au lait and smooth as butter, without a wrinkle on it. He also had gray eyes and wavy hair that had a distinctive small patch of gray in front of his right temple. Val had also imagined him to be shorter. However, when he stood up to greet her, even though she was wearing five-and-a-half-inch heels, he was slightly taller. She was only five-feet-three. That would make him about five-feet-nine.

The comfortable silence at the table was suddenly disrupted by the ringtone on Rome's phone.

"Excuse me. This call might have something to do with the case."

However, it didn't. It was Turquoise texting him to let him know that she was upstairs in the suite.

"It's my lady. Today is her fortieth birthday, so I told her to fly in and I would take her out to celebrate after the three of us finish dinner."

"Nonsense. Tell her to join us now. It will do me good to spend an evening with happy people. I haven't experienced that in a long time."

He signaled to one of his security guards and whispered in his ear. The guard nodded his head "Yes," then headed toward the hostess at the front of the restaurant.

Rome returned Turquoise's text and told her to come to the restaurant. The jewelry he had purchased for her was in his jacket pocket, so this was going to work well.

Victor told the waiter to send over a bottle of Cristal for the birthday girl. He was actually grateful for the distraction. He hadn't experienced much joy for the majority of his life. A murdered wife and a secretly married son were an overwhelming combination in the course of one day. However, he was determined to stay strong.

"Listen, Victor, I have one more thing to tell you," Val informed him.

"Hopefully I don't have any grandchildren that I don't know about."

Val thought to herself for a man who just lost his wife he certainly does have a sense of humor. "No, nothing like that. I noticed Andrea didn't have any jewelry on. And, all the times I've ever seen her, she had on to-die-for pieces. So, I asked Jermonna about it, and she told Rome and me that Andrea had been wearing a Rolex, two diamond rings and a huge black and canary diamond necklace. I have the police checking the pawnshops in town, but you might want to let your insurance company know."

Victor was very impressed with Val's observation and insight. "Thanks. I'll do that. The *huge black necklace* set me back $5 million. It's an estate piece that belonged to Wallis Simpson, the Duchess of Windsor."

As Val almost choked on her wine at the cost of the necklace, Turquoise and their appetizers arrived at the same time. The billboards for her realty company were on bus stops all over Los Angeles, but this was the first time Val had ever seen Turquoise in person. Rome sure did have a "type." Turquoise looked like she could be the mother of his son, Davida's, twin sister. Nut brown, with a curvy figure and hair done in twists, Turquoise wore a tight gold dress, pink and gold sling-back stilettos, and, carried a copper, pewter and burnished gold Fendi Baguette bag. She was stunning.

Escorted to their table by one of Victor's security team, Turquoise kissed Rome, then looked as if she was going to faint when she saw Victor standing there. Completely ignoring Valerie, she held her hand out to him. "Victor Dumas. Shame on Rome. Not only has he never told me that he is acquainted with you, he certainly didn't let on that you were who he was meeting with tonight. This is the best birthday party I have ever had in my life."

Nodding, Victor answered, "The pleasure is all mine."

Looking a little embarrassed, Rome introduced Val. "Baby, this is my partner, Valerie Rollins."

Standing up, Val gave Turquoise a hug.

"Hi, Turquoise. Happy Birthday. It's great to meet you. A few of my friends have done business with you."

Untangling herself from Val's embrace, Turquoise gave Valerie a light nod. "Likewise."

Looking to break the ice, Rome handed Turquoise a menu.

"We ordered before you came. I'll call the waiter over now."

The waiter happened to be standing right there. "What would you like?"

Turquoise pointed to the bucket of champagne. "I'll have a glass of Cristal, and, whatever Mr. Dumas ordered will be fine for me. You can't go wrong with eating like a billionaire."

Val looked at her with amusement. *Where did Rome get his women?* She had never liked Davida, but, this one was really off the chain. To ease Rome's embarrassment, she decided to regale them with stories of all her gossip antics throughout dinner. And, now, several courses and hours later, thankfully, it was time for dessert. Instead of giving them menus, the staff rolled out a three-tier cake with live pink roses on it and tall sparklers glittering on top, as they sang "Happy Birthday" to Turquoise. As soon as Rome told Victor that it was a milestone birthday for his lady friend, the billionaire had instructed one of his men to arrange the cake. While Val wasn't aware that Victor had arranged the cake, she wasn't quite sure all this public revelry was good for his image with his wife lying on a slab in a nearby morgue. However, his actions were none of her business. Let his public relations people worry about his image.

As Turquoise blew out the sparklers, Rome pulled two jewelry boxes out and placed them in front of her. She opened them right away. The diamonds on the watch and necklace made the sparklers on the cake look dim in comparison.

Holding them both up, she plunged her tongue into Rome's mouth, yelling, "Thank you, Baby. Put them on me."

Val thought to herself, *This chick must think class is where you go in school.* Val was well aware of Rome's lack of sexual variety with women. She almost fainted when he confessed to her that he had only been with Davida and a childhood sweetheart. It was easy to see that Turquoise must really have had Rome pussy-whipped because he sat there with a goofy grin on his face. Although she was very happy that her best friend had found someone, Val had never seen this side of Rome. It was time for her to excuse herself.

"You know it's been a long day. I'm going to turn in," she told the table.

Victor stood up.

"If you don't mind, Valerie, I'd like to speak with you privately. Will you join me for an after-dinner drink? We can go to the private lounge."

She really didn't think it was a great idea, but the man had shown her more generosity than she had ever seen. Val supposed one quick drink with him couldn't hurt.

"It would be my pleasure."

Rome had wanted to head over to the Ballard to meet up with Evelyn and her friends. Even though he didn't have a clue as to Val's thoughts about Turquoise sexually turning him out, as usual she was right about his facial expressions. Just looking at Turquoise made his dick hard. He had been working since four this morning and it was now close to eleven at night. He would talk Val into staying here in Las Vegas a little longer and catch up with Evelyn and her crew tomorrow. All he wanted to do right now was get a taste of Turquoise's sweet juices. He stood up to shake Victor's hand.

"Thanks for dinner, Victor. What time do you want to meet in the morning?"

"Eight in my suite will be perfect. I'll arrange breakfast to be served. I'm on the floor above you. A member of my security team will knock on your door and escort you up. You two have a nice night. Again, Happy Birthday, Turquoise." He then held out his arm to Val. "Shall we?"

This was starting to feel like the Twilight Zone, but Val looped her arm through his. "We shall."

As Victor and Valerie were walking out, Turquoise complained to Rome.

"Why can't we have a drink with them? I'd like to ask Victor if he might be interested in buying a few properties I have listings for. One of them is a high-rise office building downtown."

Val's comment, "I've never known you to mix business with pleasure," had come back to haunt Rome.

He would never let her know it, but, as usual, Valerie was dead right-on. "I've been up since three this morning, baby. Come on, let's go upstairs so I can really see how good that necklace looks on you."

He grabbed her by the hand and led Turquoise out of the restaurant.

Chapter Twelve

Rome

Rome didn't waste any time leading Turquoise to his bedroom once they got into the suite. If the elevator hadn't been glass, he would have done her right there. He needed to release the tension of the day. While Turquoise would have loved to spend more time talking to Victor, (the opportunity to be in a billionaire's presence didn't knock on your door every day), she figured Rome and that $50 million she knew for a fact he had in the bank wasn't a bad catch, either. As a result, she was way ahead of him. As soon he sat down on the bed, Turquoise removed his shoes, undid his belt, pulled down his pants, then briefs, and took his penis into her hand, slowly massaging it, as she engulfed it in her mouth.

As her tongue moved, Rome pulled his shirt over his head, and kicked his pants totally off. Slowly, she ran her tongue in circles around his dick's thick tip, then ran her tongue up and down the huge organ, which was becoming bigger by the second. Turquoise slowly began to suck his balls...then encased her entire mouth around Rome's dick, thrusting it in and out of her mouth. He started to moan, then pulled her up, and slowly undressed her until she had nothing but her new diamond necklace and watch, and her pink and gold stilettos on. Rome slowly massaged her right breast, as he took her left breast into his mouth, fingering her pussy with his free hand. Turquoise let out a gasp, her juices began to flow. He switched hands, massaging her left breast and sucking her right nipple.

"Baby," whispered Turquoise, "let's continue dessert with a little more eating."

Rome flipped around again. Now his head was at her vagina, and her mouth was once again on his penis. Almost screaming, Turquoise yelled, "You make my pussy feel so good!"

Rome was so caught up in the moment that he forgot to slip on a condom. Turquoise sat up, turned around, then straddled Rome's dick. He cupped both of her breasts with his hands, then stuck his tongue into her ear. Rome rode Turquoise until his semen came gushing out into her vagina like an oil well shooting up into the sky.

Valerie and Victor

While Rome and Turquoise were lost in each other upstairs, Val and Victor were ushered into a private suite all to themselves in the hotel's high-rollers lounge. Another bottle of Kendall Jackson appeared in front of her.

"Thank you, Victor. I don't really need any more wine, but I'll just have another glass to help me sleep. I tried to take a nap earlier, but, kept seeing your wife's body, Jermonna all drugged up and wounded, and, hearing those shots that were fired at us. It was impossible to sleep. I have to pick a few things up for Jermonna in the morning before I see her, and I want to have lunch with Dedra, my sorority sister, before Rome and I fly back to L.A. tomorrow afternoon. Thanks again for the clothes, shoes and suitcase. Rome gave me some money this morning. If you like, I can pay you back."

"I wouldn't hear of it. Once again, thank you for bringing Rome here this morning. You saved me the horror and sadness of having to identify Andrea's body. I will forever be grateful to you for easing my pain.

"Rome explained to me that it was through your contacts that he was able to locate Andrea so fast and make this less of a public relations nightmare. Plus, now you've given me information about my son I had no idea of. I owe you much more."

Hoping she wasn't crossing any boundaries, Val decided to tell Victor what she thought about the cake and sparklers.

"I'm actually glad you brought up the subject of public relations nightmares. I don't think it's a good idea for you to be seen out again like earlier tonight with champagne on your table and sparklers going off. This is an ongoing murder investigation. Some people could get the wrong idea and think you're celebrating your wife's murder, instead of mourning. You don't want to end up a murder suspect."

Victor had always admired how Valerie spoke her mind whenever she appeared on television. He agreed with her. "Thank you for that observation. I did not mean to give off the impression that I don't care that my wife is dead. At one time I loved my wife more than life itself. But, we haven't been on the same page for many years. However, you are very correct. In fact, that's why I wanted to talk to you alone. You represent a few clients for public relations. Can you handle me while I'm dealing with the issues surrounding Andrea's murder? I'll pay you $50,000 from now until the end of January when I have her memorial."

Victor had looked into Val's background, and knew, even though she was very busy, he discovered that everyone that she worked for grossly underpaid her. He also knew that most of the money she inherited from Jennifer Sands had gone to pay her back taxes. Her reputation was stellar. She always did a good job. He wanted to be generous with her; plus, there was something about this woman that intrigued him.

Val was well aware that the large public relations firms charged these types of retainers, but she had never been offered large sums of money for her work. "Fifty thousand dollars for two months of work? I've never received an offer like that. That's incredible, Victor. I'll be glad to handle things for you, but you don't have to pay me that kind of money."

"It's not a problem, I assure you." He raised his hand and one of his bodyguards put an envelope into it. He extended it to Val. "Here you are, a check made out to Dottie Media Group LLC for $50,000. We don't need any further paperwork. You have a reputation of doing excellent work."

Val stared down at the check she was now holding. She had to ask him how he had so much personal information about her. There was no way Rome could have told him all of these things in the short time they had to get to Las Vegas this morning.

"Victor, I have to ask you this. How do you know so much about me? The Kendall Jackson Chardonnay, these boots I have on, how much I loved La Toya's jacket. You even know my company's name. Have you had me investigated?"

He took a moment to make sure his words came out right. He didn't want to frighten Val away.

"In the case of your favorite wine, I saw you on *The Today Show* with Kathie Lee and Hoda. The three of you were drinking wine. You told them that the owner of the Kendall Jackson Winery had recently passed. You then jokingly stated that you love his chardonnay so much that you probably got more condolences than his family. You also told the ladies that when you referred to Kendall Jackson in the novel that you had written, the winery sent you a case. As far as the boots and jacket are concerned, my secretary follows you on Twitter and saw you and Miss Jackson exchanging tweets about both of them. However, I will admit that I did look into your background and that's how I know your company's name. It's after your Aunt Doris."

Valerie absorbed all that he had just told her. While this day had been a nightmare in one respect, it was turning out to be a beautiful dream in another one.

"I don't know what to say, so I will start with 'yes,' I'll take the job. Thank you for the opportunity. I will make a statement on behalf of you and Vance in the morning. I also think that you should adopt five families for Christmas that are living in shelters due to circumstances relating to drug abuse. In Andrea's memory, get them into apartments, pay a year's rent, and give them groceries, toys and clothing. That will ease the talk when her autopsy report comes back if there were drugs in her system. And, I think you and Vance should lay low until the $750,000 Cash Call Futurity Race on the fifteenth. Have him make a donation at the Santa Sleigh Ball that night to KiKi Shepherd's Sickle Cell Disease Foundation. I understand you and your wife were estranged, but it's better for your image for people to at least think you're grieving."

Victor looked at her gratefully. "You see, you are worth $50,000 and much, much more." He didn't know where the urge came from, but he leaned forward and kissed Val smack dab on the lips. From seemingly out of nowhere, cameras started flashing in their faces.

Chapter Thirteen

Los Angeles

While all of that activity was going on in Las Vegas, back in Los Angeles, the femcee Platinum Pizzazz was staring down in awe at the necklace her manager had placed around her neck. It was a huge black diamond pendant that was surrounded with at least twenty canary diamonds that had to be at least two carats each. The stones glittered against her ebony-hued skin.

At eighteen years old, Platinum Pizzazz was the next big thing on the hip-hop scene. She had an underground cut called "Chanel Tricks," that wove a tale of girls selling their bodies and souls to whomever they had to in order to own a Chanel purse. An emancipated minor, Platinum Pizzazz, whose real name was Jo Ella Conrad, had been out on her own since she was fifteen years old. She had been rapping since the age of thirteen. It was a stroke of luck that she ran into her man, who was now also her manager, at KDAY radio station on its Music Day. That's a very important day of the week when artists and record label representatives drop new music off to radio stations. He saw her sitting in the lobby and asked what she was doing there. Without hesitation, Platinum Pizzazz immediately started rapping "Chanel Tricks" to him. He asked her to leave the station with him. They went straight to his uncle's record label and got her a deal on the spot.

Fingering the necklace, Platinum Pizzazz purred, "Is this real, honey?"

"You bet your sweet ass, it's real. I want you looking like the star you are onstage in Jamaica when you perform on Wednesday night. Now take that thong off and show daddy how thankful you are for your new bling."

Pizzazz, as she was called for short, did a slow striptease, first peeling off the Los Angeles Wildcats tee shirt that D.O.D. had also given her. It was all she was actually wearing other than the red thong. Saving it for last, she waved the thong back and forth under his nose, before diving in the bed on top of him. Still wearing the fabulous jewels, she would thank him every way that she knew how to.

Chapter Fourteen

Sunday Morning
Rome

As usual, Rome awakened at five a.m. He started every day by meditating, then working out. Not wanting to wake Turquoise, Rome eased out of the bed and into the bathroom. Victor Dumas didn't leave anything to chance. Aside from the suit that Rome had found hanging in the closet, there were also two track suits and a pair of sneakers and socks. He slipped into the bottoms and his tee shirt, put on the sneakers, then headed down to the gym on the second floor of the suite. He turned on the TV and got on the treadmill. As he got going, he heard the anchorwoman on Fox 5, Monica Jackson, say, "His wife, Andrea, was found brutally murdered yesterday on the city's West Side, but billionaire Victor Dumas already seems to have moved on. He was photographed kissing celebrity journalist Valerie Rollins at the Palms Casino late last night. Fox 5 obtained this photo exclusively of the two new lovebirds."

Plain as day, there was a photo of Victor and Val kissing that covered the entire television screen. What the hell had happened when he left the two of them last night? Had Val lost her mind? This definitely made Victor look like a suspect in his wife's murder. Without turning off the treadmill, he jumped off it, and, ran up to Val's room.

Rome banged on the door. "Val, Val, open this door at once. You've got some explaining to do."

Val was saying her morning prayers. She hadn't had a chance to get dressed yet. However, she opened the door for Rome.

"Calm down. You'll wake the dead. Let me guess. There's a report about Victor kissing me on the morning news."

"Calm down? You want me to calm down. Forget just a report. A picture of you two is plastered all over the TV. What were you thinking? You meet a billionaire and lose your mind. Does he realize he looks like he may have had his wife killed?"

Val took a deep breath before speaking. "I have already issued a statement from Victor and me saying that he leaned over to kiss me on the cheek to thank me for giving you the heads-up about his wife's death. I then heard someone calling my name, so, I turned my head to see who it was. And, that's when his kiss of gratitude landed on my lips instead of my cheek. Maybe if you would have watched Monica's report a little further, you would have heard my explanation. Of course, that's not the truth. The man kissed me out of nowhere after hiring me to handle the press for all of this. Now, you have known me for a long time and never have seen me act inappropriately with any man that I'm working with, including you. Victor assured me that he did not have anything to do with his wife's death. However, considering how she lived and obviously couldn't care less about him, if he had, I wouldn't at all blame him."

"I'm sorry, Val. I was so shocked when I saw your picture on TV. He just up and kissed you? I have to admit I saw the way he looked at you all night, but I didn't think he would make a move on you the same day his wife was found dead."

"You saw more than I did. I don't think he looked at me any differently than he looked at everyone else in the restaurant."

Rome didn't believe her. Val had an uncanny knack of figuring out someone's complete modus operandi with just one glance.

"I'm a man and I think differently. He is definitely interested in you. I'm glad you already have the problem taken care of."

"Don't I always? I'm going to get some more sleep. I mentioned to Victor that I needed to pick up some things for Jermonna at Victoria's Secret, and all these bags mysteriously appeared in front of my door overnight. He's a very thoughtful guy. What time are we shipping out of here? I am so ready to go home."

"I meet with Victor at eight. The briefing should take about an hour. But, I want to see if we can have lunch with this girl, Evelyn, who works at In-N-Out Burger. I was supposed to meet her last night at the Ballard, but got too tired. She may know something about the guys who either own or hang out at the Three Points. I'll call her when I finish with Victor. If she can't meet, we'll get out of here at noon. We can stop off at the hospital on the way to the airport."

"Okay. Listen, my friend Rebecca told me Andrea's death was definitely a drug hit, that she and some young boy were running drugs for some syndicate and owed close to $1 million. We need to find the boyfriend."

"Yeah," agreed Rome agreed. "Yesterday, a reporter told me that Andrea doesn't have any money in the bank. Thanks. I'll tell Victor all of this. I'm going to finish my workout. Get some more sleep."

Victor

Victor never actually went to sleep. It was now two a.m. in Vegas, which would make it five a.m. in Kentucky. Vance would be getting ready to go feed the horses. Even though they had groomers and trainers to take care of chores like that, Vance still insisted on caring for Wildin' Out and Full Spectrum himself.

He called his son's cell phone. Vance picked it up on the first ring. "Hey, Dad. How are you this morning?"

"I'm fine. How are you making out?"

"Not too good," Vance replied. "I don't know why, but I can't stop crying. I don't know if it's because I'm sad that Mom's gone, or if I'm sad that she never told me she loved me, never called me on my birthday, or that we haven't seen her on Christmas or any other holiday for years. What the hell happened, Dad? Why did she hate me so much?"

"She didn't hate you, son. Your mother had problems."

Changing the subject, Vance asked, "What's going on with you, Dad? I saw a picture of you and that gossip columnist Valerie Rollins kissing. Are you dating her?"

"No, son. It really wasn't how it looked. I've hired Miss Rollins to do some damage control in the media in regard to your mother's murder. I was aiming for her cheek to give her a thank-you kiss when she turned her head after someone called her name. I will admit that I she's a wonderful, gorgeous woman, but there's nothing going on between us."

"Okay, Dad. Even though it looks like she's doing more damage than controlling it, I believe your story."

Aside from wanting to make sure his son was handling the grief over Andrea's murder, Victor was also calling to ask about the marriage information that Val had given him.

"Vance, Valerie tells me that you are married to the reality star Roshonda Rhodes, and have been for at least a year. Is that true?"

Vance realized he couldn't lie to his father. With all of his resources, he was surprised it had taken him this long to find out.

"Yes, it's true. I've kept it a secret for several reasons. The main one is I very foolishly married her with no prenuptial agreement. The second one is I wanted to see if she really loved me, and didn't marry me for my fame or money. She seems to really love me. I was going to tell you at the race on the fifteenth, and let the world know then that she's my wife."

All Victor heard was the "no prenuptial agreement" part of Vance's answer. "I also strongly suspect that one of the reasons you've kept this marriage a secret is that you're still involved with Violet. If your relationship with her is over and you really love this Roshonda, and, want to stay married, we need to get a post-nuptial agreement drawn up as soon as possible. I want to meet her right away. We're going to have your mother's services after the race. I don't want you to cancel that. Do you want to be here in Vegas for your mother's cremation?"

"Yes, I do."

"All right. Call Roshonda and tell her to meet you here in Vegas tomorrow. I'll have a suite reserved for you two at the Palms. We'll make everything okay. I love you, son."

"I love you, too, Dad. I'll see you tomorrow."

Victor hung up the phone with a tear in his eye. No matter how badly Andrea had treated him and Vance over the years, like his son, there was something about her he would always love.

Valerie

Val wanted to fall back asleep, but her mind was racing in a hundred different directions. She had actually lied to Rome about not noticing how Victor looked at her. She didn't want to make too much of it. In the past she had dated younger men because they were whom she seemed to attract. At fifty-seven, Victor was a few years older than her. She realized it was too soon for him to start seeing anyone right after his wife's untimely death. However, Rome was right; she could tell that he really liked her. She had some mighty fine new clothes and a check for $50,000 in her wallet to prove that.

Smiling to herself, she turned on the television. Thank God, a shooting on the strip had knocked her and Victor right out of first place position in breaking news. Sad news for some, but welcome news for her and Victor.

The newscaster was reporting, "Las Vegas Police are still on the scene of a shooting that took place last night not far from the Ballard Casino. Twenty-three-year-old Evelyn Figueroa was shot and killed while walking to her car. Sources say Evelyn worked as a counter girl at a fast-food restaurant on Dean Martin Drive. Police are looking for the shooter. There was also a jail break at police headquarters. A suspect, Joseph Savoldi, that was also arrested yesterday on the city's West Side following a shooting incident in a police chase that left one man dead, escaped last night while awaiting arraignment on an attempted murder charge. This has been Joan Price reporting live from the Las Vegas strip."

Rome had just told her he was supposed to meet some girl named Evelyn last night at the Ballard who worked at In-N-Out Burger, which is on Dean Martin Drive. Could this be the same girl? She also wondered if this Joseph Savoldi could be the driver that Dedra arrested. If so, how did he escape? Even though Rome was somewhere in this gigantic suite, Val was still in bed. So, instead of going to look for him, she picked up her phone and dialed his cell number.

He picked up the phone on the first ring. "Too lazy to come to the gym one floor down to talk?"

"Listen, I'm watching the news. You mentioned an Evelyn that you were supposed to meet at the Ballard. A girl named Evelyn Figueroa was killed near there last night. You think it could be the same girl? They said she worked at a fast-food restaurant. Also, some guy named Joseph Savoldi escaped from jail last night. I'm thinking he could be the driver that Dedra hauled off so fast."

"Damn...damn...damn. She was Hispanic. I purposely gave her a false name, so when she mentioned me to her friends, no one would make a connection. I was sure, that way, she would be safe, and so would all of us. She knew a lot about Andrea's murder, and the guys she was running around with. Someone must have seen her talking to me. Can you get a hold of Dedra and see if the girl worked at In-N-Out Burger?"

"No problem. What happened when you met her yesterday?"

"I went back over to the Three Points to nose around. When I arrived, the cops were still there, so I went next door to In-N-Out to wait for them to leave. On a hunch, I asked her if she had heard about the shooting. Then she proceeded to fill me in on Andrea owing money to drug dealers. She said her friend knew a guy that hung out with her."

"Turn on the TV in the gym. Her picture is back up on the screen."

"Yeah, that's her." He sincerely hoped his brief encounter with Evelyn hadn't made him indirectly responsible for the girl's death. This was a bad, bad scene.

He instructed Val, "Call Dedra and find out about this Joseph, but don't ask her anything about Evelyn yet. She hasn't called you to tell you anything about Amir's fingerprints, has she?"

"No, I haven't heard from her this morning."

"It's kind of weird that my guy at the Bureau hasn't gotten back to me yet, either. And, Victor still can't find his guy, Claude. All of this is connected somehow. I have to connect the dots so that we can find out who killed Andrea, as well as the identity of Amir's killer. I'm going to get ready to meet with Victor now. I want you and Turquoise to stay put right in this suite."

"What about Jermonna? I need to get these clothes to her."

"We'll have a couple of Victor's people take them to her. As soon as I finish with him, I think we all need to head back to L.A. Jermonna has twenty-four-hour security, so she's fine. This town has gotten a little too hot for you and me right now. I'll find out what Evelyn's story was and try to get a grip on Amir and Claude when we get home. Be ready to leave for the airport in an hour and a half."

"You got it."

With those words, Val was up in a flash.

Chapter Thirteen

Dedra

"Deputy Chief Thorne speaking."

The voice on the other end of the phone barked, "I thought you had that Rollins bitch and her man Rome under control. They have found out a little too much information. Maybe I should ease up on your pay."

"That won't be necessary. Please don't call me here again. How many times do I have to tell you that?"

"Look, you don't tell me anything. I do the telling. You do the listening and what I tell you to do. You would think they would have hightailed it out of here yesterday after almost being shot. But no, not those two. They act as if they are Superman and Lois Lane. Inform her that both Andrea's and Amir's deaths are Las Vegas Police Department matters and to get out of town. Otherwise, you are going to have to take this matter into your own hands, like I had you do with that little stupid snitch, Evelyn."

"What about Victor Dumas? Do you want him to leave, too? I heard that he's going to be here until his wife is cremated tomorrow."

"No, I don't want him to leave. We're leaving him alone. We need all that sweet money Andrea left Rolondo in her will. And, the only way to get it is through Victor."

"When are you coming back to Vegas?"

"You don't need to worry about when I'm coming back to Vegas. My little rapper is performing in Jamaica later this week. I have to make sure she gets there safe and sound. When I am back in Vegas, you will definitely know it. Just get those two pests out of the way. No one is fucking up this big score for me, not even the great Rome Nyland and Valerie Rollins. The only thing you've done worthwhile in the last twenty-four hours is to get Joseph out of lockup. No one is indispensable in my world. Not even you!"

With those last words, the boss hung up on Dedra. Following their conversation, Dedra stared at the phone in her hand. How did she let greed, coupled with her addiction to cocaine, do this to her? Her out-of-control drug debt to these guys is what had gotten her into this position. As of now, she could not see any clear way out of this trouble she had gotten herself into. Buying a new home, expensive furnishings and partying had gotten her in deeper and deeper into this black hole. She pretended that she was able to afford her big house and two cars because of an inheritance from a fictitious grandmother. Every day she lived in fear that someone in the department would learn she was on the take from one of the biggest drug syndicates in the world, and hopelessly hooked on their product.

She slowly dialed Val's number. Val was her girl. They had been thick as thieves in school. She didn't like deceiving her, but she couldn't risk blowing her cover. She had actually known since yesterday that Amir Lockett's real identity was George Rich, a drug dealer who her guy had pose as one of Victor's drivers to keep tabs on Rome and Valerie. He was killed because he was supposed to hand over the $50,000 in the envelope that Victor left for Rome to her. How the dumb fuck made the mistake of actually giving it to Rome was a mystery to her. She had sent the shooters herself on the orders of the boss, who said he would give her a cut of the money. Her boss was Victor's right-hand man who had been screwing Andrea for years. They were supposed to kill George, then rob Rome and Val without hurting them. But, she had underestimated Rome being such a good marksman, as well as Val dialing nine-one-one so fast. Dedra was beginning to realize that she was doing way too much blow. She had to slow down so she could start thinking more clearly. She had always heard that Rome Nyland was no joke. Both the FBI and Los Angeles Police Department wanted him to join their forces.

But, he liked doing his own thing. Boy, she sure could use a line or two of blow right about now. She couldn't wait until this shift ended.

Val picked up her phone as soon as she saw Dedra's name on the caller ID.

"Hey, Dee Dee. I was just getting ready to call you. We're getting ready to head back to L.A., but I was wondering a couple of things. Did you find out who Amir really was?" Then, deciding to go against Rome's advice, she asked her, "What do you know about that girl, Evelyn Figueroa, who was shot last night?"

Well, at least, she didn't have to worry about getting them out of town. Lying, Dedra told Val, "For some reason, Amir's prints aren't back yet. My detectives are still piecing evidence together on the Figueroa girl. Why are you interested in her?"

Val detected something strange in Dedra's voice.

"The television said she worked at a fast-food restaurant on Dean Martin Drive. There's an In-N-Out Burger right next to the Three Points Sports Bar. I was wondering if there's any connection. Also, that guy who escaped isn't the same guy who was driving that Escalade who was shooting at us, is he?"

"Unfortunately, he is. When I left for the night, one of the guys on duty somehow left his cell unlocked and went to the bathroom. Savoldi slipped out a window, but we'll find him. Don't worry. As for Ms. Figueroa, I doubt if there's any connection to Rome,"

Dedra lied. "She was probably hooking or something on the side. I guess I'll see you the next time you're in town. If I don't speak to you again soon, Merry Christmas!"

"Merry Christmas, soror."

As she hung up, all Val could think was something with Dedra wasn't adding up.

Rome and Victor

The first thing Rome wanted Victor to know when he got to his suite was that he felt Las Vegas had become too dangerous for all of them.

"I really wish you could leave Vegas and head back to Kentucky today, Victor. I don't think it's that safe here for you."

The two men were going over all of the information Rome had gathered over the past day and this morning. Rome had given him a copy of the contract with the security firm that was guarding Jermonna, as well as the receipt that Ephraim had put in the envelope.

Victor shook his head.

"I can't. The funeral home is going to have my wife's body ready for viewing tomorrow for my son and me, his new wife, as well as Andrea's sisters, nieces and nephews. They are all flying in from Chicago. I've reserved an entire floor here for them. They'll all be arriving tonight. Valerie was right. Vance has been secretly married for a year. After the viewing, the cremation will take place. We'll leave after that. I have a lot of security. We'll be fine. I'll meet you on Tuesday in Los Angeles."

"I want to get Val and Turquoise out of here as soon as possible. Val has some packages that need to be delivered to Jermonna. Can one of your guys take them over to the hospital? I'll leave them with the concierge in your name."

"Of course."

"Why are you coming to L.A.? I figured that you would head home to Kentucky from here."

"I actually live in New York eighty percent of the time, then spend two months of the year in Kentucky preparing the horses for the Derby. Being under the same roof in Los Angeles just watching Andrea destroy herself was too much for me to bear. So, I rarely went to my own estate. But, my lawyers and accountants are in Los Angeles. This paperwork that you've presented to me states that Andrea didn't have any money in her bank account. I deposit a quarter million dollars every month into that account, plus put a lump sum of $2 million a year in there. In addition to all that, I pay all of her credit card bills directly. It makes no sense that her accounts are empty. All of the drugs in the world can't cost that much money. I also need to take a look at her will. Coming there on Tuesday also makes sense because I retained Valerie to do some public relations work for me. I would like to be available for whatever she needs."

I'll bet you would, Rome thought to himself.

Aloud, he asked Victor, "You're pretty taken with Val, aren't you?"

"Is it that obvious? After watching her career blossom, I've actually wanted to meet her for years. But, I knew her type of woman, regardless of what my financial circumstances are, would never go for a married man. If this tragedy wouldn't have befallen Andrea, I would still have had to be in Los Angeles for the next two weeks. We're running three horses at Hollywood Park on the fifteenth. So, a portion of the horse business in Kentucky will shift there for the next two weeks."

That took Rome by surprise.

"I didn't realize you own three horses. I was only aware of Wildin' Out."

"We actually own twelve race horses and about thirty horses that we are training. However, we're running three races that day. There's going to be a filly named Très Jolie. Vance is introducing his protégé, a Black female jockey named Violet McLean, who will ride her. Then, in addition to Wildin' Out, Vance is also going to ride a two-year-old colt named Full Spectrum."

Rome looked at Victor with admiration. "You continue to make history. A black female jockey on a filly. That is amazing. I'll have more information for you on Tuesday. I'll see you in L.A."

As Rome walked out, Victor told him, "I always thought Vance was in love with Violet. They have been pretty inseparable over the years. I can't wait to meet this new daughter-in-law of mine. She must be pretty exceptional to have taken Vance from Violet. It's too bad that you have a girlfriend. Violet is a fine little thing. She's very smart and independent, too."

"I've never met Roshonda. But, but I've seen her on television. I can tell you how your son got hooked. I don't know how good Violet looks, but, man to man, Roshonda is the finest woman that I have ever seen. I can't wait to meet her, either."

The men shook hands and Rome left to get Turquoise and Val to head to the airport.

Chapter Fifteen

Roshonda

It was almost ten a.m. in Los Angeles. Like most Sunday mornings, Roshonda was watching Joel Osteen. She loved the smiling television pastor's words of wisdom and perspective on life. She had spent most of the night in tears after finding out that Andrea had been killed inside of the bar that she had sped away from. She had been trying to reach Vance to tell him what she had overheard Royale saying. She was praying that Royale wouldn't figure out why she had taken off so fast or where she headed. She was pretty sure she didn't have to worry about that, though. The only person that knew about her connection to Vance was Rebecca, and she had been silenced to the tune of half a million dollars. Oh well, she needed to get up and head to the gym. She had to work later in the day. The show was going to film her having an early dinner at Philippe with another one of the judges.

Her thoughts were broken into by the ringing of the intercom. *Who could that be?*

It was Sunday. She wasn't expecting any deliveries or company this morning.

"Yes?" Roshonda asked the doorman.

"Mr. Vance Dumas to see you."

"Please send him up."

Roshonda dashed into the bathroom, threw some water on her

face, then brushed her teeth. She ran a quick brush over her hair, and put on her blue cashmere wrap robe. The bell rang. She opened the door to see her adorable little husband standing there looking so sad. Grabbing him, she pulled him into the living room.

"I'm so sorry about your mother, sweetheart. I'm so glad you came home to me."

Instead of calling Roshonda as his father had suggested, Vance had decided to hop on his plane and fly to L.A. to pick her up. His mom's murder was really starting to get to him. He collapsed against Roshonda, crying. She didn't know what to do. She had never seen a man cry like this. Leading him to the couch, she sat him down and whispered, "Hush now, honey. It's going to be okay."

"No, it won't. I didn't even get to say goodbye to my mother. And, I feel terrible because there has always been part of me that wished she was dead. This is all my fault."

Roshonda told him, "No, it's not. You must not think like that." Vance dried his eyes.

"I actually came here to get you to take you to Las Vegas. My father found out that we are married. He wants to meet you. We're going to view and cremate my mother tomorrow. I want you to be with me. My maternal aunts and cousins will be there, too. No more secrets. I want everyone to know that you're my wife. All my life I have watched how badly my mother treated my father. I was afraid you might do the same thing to me, especially since we got married so fast. That's why I wanted to keep us a secret. But, over the past year, I have learned that you are a wonderful woman."

Roshonda couldn't believe her ears. She kissed Vance deeply. He returned her kiss and then stroked her long hair. Leaning her back on the sofa, he undid her robe. His mouth found her breasts and he began to suckle them as if he were a baby looking for milk. His hand found her vagina, and he slowly finger-fucked her. Roshonda reached for his dick. It was already hard.

Vance stood up and undressed quickly.

"I have to have you now, babe. I can't wait."

With no further foreplay, he entered her. This was the first time in the year that they had been together that he didn't use a condom. She was his wife. He wanted to fill her with his sperm, and hopefully, his baby.

He pounded his dick into Roshonda. With the first thrust, he expunged the first time he caught his mother fucking his horse trainer in a stall. Vance plunged deeper into her, letting go of the pain he endured when his mom brutally whipped him for accidentally spilling a bag of her cocaine. Then, with a final stroke, he exorcised the ghost of loving his mother no matter what, emptying all of his juices into his gorgeous wife's womb. Afterward, the two of them lay still on the couch for awhile. Vance finally spoke.

"You need to get dressed and packed. My dad is expecting everyone for dinner tonight in Las Vegas."

"I'm supposed to tape the show this evening, but I'll tell them I have a death in the family and will have to shoot the scene later this week."

Vance repeated after her, "A death in the family. Ever time I see this story on television or look at a newspaper, I feel like this is happening to someone else, not my family. It's unbelievable."

Roshonda sat up, then kissed him on the lips. Vance had stated that he didn't want any more secrets between them. "I have to tell you something."

"What is it, baby?"

"I was in this hotel suite on Friday night waiting to meet with Royale Jones. He told me he had an endorsement deal for me. He went into the bedroom to take a phone call. I overheard him say he was about to make a big score with Andrea Dumas. He gave whomever he was speaking with an address in Las Vegas. Then he told me he had to make a fast run and to wait there for him to return. I wrote down the address, left him a note saying that I had a pressing appointment, then left. I kept trying to reach you on your cell phone. When you didn't pick up, I drove to Las Vegas. I got there around three in the morning. When I pulled up to the Three Points Sports Bar, I heard gunshots, so I hightailed it out of there."

"What made you drive all the way to Las Vegas in the middle of the night?'

"I believed your mom was in danger and I wanted to help. Unfortunately, I was right. I've had several messages from Valerie Rollins since then, and from Royale, but I haven't returned either of their calls. I don't ever want to speak to him again. However, I think Valerie knows I was there. You know, there was a photo on the news a little while ago of her kissing your father."

"I know. My mother was full-figured like Miss Rollins when my father first met her. I think he likes her, but he claims there was nothing to the kiss. I have to tell my father everything you told me so he can tell his private investigator. They may also insist that you give this information to the police."

"All right. I hope they don't think I had anything to do with her murder because I didn't. You know that, don't you?"

"I know you could never hurt anyone."

Roshonda was relieved that Vance felt that way.

"Good. Let me make my call and pack. Do you want me to drive us to Las Vegas?"

"No, sweetheart. I have my plane. We're no longer a secret. It's time for you to start living Vance Dumas-style."

Chapter Sixteen

Los Angeles

Valerie, Rome and Turquoise landed back in Los Angeles around noon.

"Are you ladies hungry?" Rome inquired.

Even though Val was dying to get back to her house, change out of her new dress and matching Marc Jacobs shoes and get to work, she didn't have any groceries at home. Plus, it was too late for her to go to church.

"I wouldn't mind going somewhere and getting a bite."

Rome turned to Turquoise, "How about you, baby? Do you want to continue celebrating with a birthday brunch at the Four Seasons in Beverly Hills?"

Turquoise, who was looking quite chic in just about Burberry's entire London collection, including a leather jacket, yarn-dyed checked shirt and boot-cut jeans, not to mention her Burberry Brogue Alkerden patent leather and canvas pumps, was ecstatic. She had never had brunch at the Four Seasons.

"I'm starving and would love to keep celebrating. But, can we get in that place without a reservation?"

Rome pointed to Val. "Ms. Rollins can get us in. Isn't that right, Ms. Rollins?"

"No problem. I'll call them as soon as we get in the car."

Victor had sent a new Bentley SUV to pick them up. The driver told Val, "Mr. Dumas would like you to keep the car for the time being so he knows that you're safe. There are two of us drivers and we change shifts every twelve hours. I am Dwayne."

With a smirk, Rome asked, "Where's my car? Doesn't Mr. Dumas care about my safety?"

Once again, Val was speechless. As a young chick, she would have refused all of this man's generosity, but as a seasoned hen, she recognized she had better accept whatever he was offering and enjoy the perks while they lasted.

"Okay, Dwayne; the Four Seasons, please."

Remembering that the last driver that picked them up for Victor hadn't been who he claimed to be, Val took the card he had given her out of her purse to call him. But, Dwayne was way ahead of her.

"Ms. Rollins, please pick up the phone back there. Mr. Dumas would like to speak to you."

Victor was already on the other end of the phone that was in the back seat.

"I thought you might want to make sure this is my real driver. He is and he's a good man. I'll see you on Tuesday."

"Okay, thanks. The car is lovely, but it really isn't necessary."

"It's really no trouble at all. I have a fleet of cars in L.A. just sitting in garages, complete with drivers just hanging around with nothing to do. When Rome told me that we were paying for around-the-clock security for your friend, Jermonna, I wanted to make sure that you also are well protected with all that's going on. Remember, you were also shot at too yesterday. I just found you. I don't want to lose you quite yet."

Val blushed and got quiet as they ended the call. She immediately dialed the restaurant where they were headed.

Val had no trouble securing a reservation at the restaurant for them. The concierge told her to come right over.

As they pulled onto Doheny Drive, then into the Four Seasons hotel's driveway, a red Ferrari was entering in front of them with the license plate "Sweet4U."

Rome pointed to the car. "Val. I saw that car in front of the Three Points in Vegas yesterday. I could never forget those plates."

As he spoke, a young girl in a tight green Emilio Pucci strapless dress emerged from the car. She had gorgeous, ebony-colored skin and bright red hair. Even though it was a cool, L.A. December morning, she wore no wrap and sky-high, silver cutout boots.

Val took a good look. "That's the new rapper, Platinum Pizzazz. She has a hot new single called 'Chanel Tricks.'"

A short, fat little guy with an afro got out of the driver's side of the car.

Rome asked, "Do you know him?"

"No, but I'll find out who he is. Let's go in."

Turquoise's jaws were beginning to get tight, watching the exchange between Rome and Valerie. *I mean, I guess she is pretty, as well as youthful looking for her age, but what is with this fat old bitch?*

Rome couldn't seem to make a move without her and Victor Dumas was obviously mesmerized by her. It was Turquoise's big birthday. She was supposed to be getting all of her man's attention, not Val and Victor's dead wife. She had never realized Rome worked so hard. This was going to have to change. Sucking her teeth, she took his hand and exited the luxurious vehicle.

The Four Seasons looked gorgeous as they made their way to a table. The Christmas decorations were already up and the restaurant looked like a winter wonderland. Val spotted Vivica A. Fox having brunch with her publicist, B.J. Coleman, at one table, Jamie Foxx eating very quietly on the outside terrace, and, Tichina Arnold, enjoying brunch with her husband and friends. She heard someone call her name. She turned around and saw her friend, Adrienne Lopez, eating with Cathy Hughes, the grand doyenne of media, who owned Radio One, TV One, Syndication One and Interactive One.

Val leaned down and hugged both Adrienne and Cathy. Adrienne was sharp wearing a Helmut Lang dress and Jimmy Choo black and white color block shoes. She was carrying a vintage Black Louis Vuitton purse that Val had given her for Christmas years ago. Adrienne smiled at them as she sipped Billecart-Salmon Brut Rose champagne.

Val introduced Rome and Turquoise to the ladies. Turquoise promptly handed her card to Cathy, telling her, "Ms. Hughes, I admire you so much. Call me if you need my help with any real estate."

All Val could think was, *does she ever stop promoting her business?*

Aloud Val told Adrienne and Cathy, "I'll see you two later. Enjoy your brunch."

Sunday brunch at the Four Seasons Hotel Los Angeles at Beverly Hills was the place in town to be. The buffet included a dim sum station, omelet station, quesadillas station, eggs benedict station, sushi, salads, pastries, a carving station and much more. People loved it because you could eat all you want.

When the three of them sat down, Rome ordered Turquoise a bottle of Cristal. He saw Platinum Pizzazz and her escort heading toward the omelet station.

"Let's go, Val. Do your thing."

Val almost ran to catch up with them. "Platinum Pizzazz, right? I'm Valerie Rollins. I love your work. I would love to do a piece on you."

Pizzazz had been watching Val on TV her entire life. She couldn't believe she was hearing correctly. "You want to do a piece on me? That would be a dream come true. This here's my manager, D.O.D."

Rome stepped in. "D.O.D. Nice meeting you, man. I'm Rome Nyland."

D.O.D. was just as stunned as Pizzazz was. Rome was a personal hero of his. "Pleased to meet you, man."

"That's a nice toy you're driving," Rome remarked to D.O.D. "We were in Las Vegas yesterday and I saw the same car. But, I thought a woman probably drove it with those vanity plates *Sweet4U*."

"Aw, naw, man. That's my uncle's ride. He moves around a lot. No telling where he was yesterday. He let me hold it to bring Baby Girl here to eat. My uncle's Sweet Lyrics. You know, him, my dad and their cousin had a group back in the day."

Together, Val and Rome exclaimed, "Sweet4U!"

"That's the group. Here's my card. Call me when you want to git wit us. Good lookin' out."

Val handed him her card. "Thanks. Let's try to make this interview happen soon."

At that point, Turquoise had reached her limit. "All right, you two. No more shop talk."

Once again, Rome kept hearing Val's words *"You've never mixed business with pleasure before.*

He kissed Turquoise on the cheek. "No problem, baby. Let's eat."

He would find out exactly what position Sweet Lyrics and his nephew played in this scenario later on. They went about the business of filling their plates and, one by one, arrived back at the table. Val was busy on the phone when Rome and Turquoise sat down.

She announced to them, "I have my day cut out for me tomorrow. I'm going to do *Good Day L.A.* at seven in the morning to discuss Jermonna's plight, then follow that up with Fox News Channel at ten. Then, I'll head home and get a statement for Victor out on the web, and do my radio show in between all of that. This is going to be a busy holiday month."

From his and Platinum Pizzazz's nearby table, D.O.D. studied the three of them as they chatted. He may have only been twenty-two years old, but, he was no fool. He had been in Las Vegas the night before. However, D.O.D., whose real name was Ashton Oaks, was not going to let Mr. Football Player turned Private Dick and his little celebrity snitch sidekick know that. He and his family had turned a lucrative pimping and drug-dealing side hustle into a huge syndicate that had taken over the entire West Coast. While on the surface, people thought he was just another fledgling rapper, while his crew, the Bugatti Blades, were entertainment entrepreneurs, the real deal was they recruited women to run drugs and turn tricks for them.

The Blades were able to lure the broads by pulling up to clubs and strip joints as they were closing up for the night driving Bugattis with trunks filled with Louis Vuitton, Gucci and Chanel bags. The guys would offer the hottest broads coming out a luxury purse. They then informed them that they could get them into a late-night party where they could easily make $2,000 in a few hours. They would lie to the women and swear that there was no sex involved, convincing them all they had to do was talk to the high-rollers. Then, once they arrived at the club, they slipped ketamine into their drinks. When they came to, none of those chicks remembered what actually happened. All they knew when they woke up was they had two g's to put into their new designer bags.

From then on, they were hooked. When he met Platinum Pizzazz and heard her record, D.O.D. figured he would make her his woman, then turn her into a superstar. He soon planned to turn her out and make some real money. Nothing was going to stop that. That old broad, Andrea Dumas, shouldn't have tried to play him. He didn't like the fact that Rome recognized his uncle's car. That was not cool. He needed to find out how much Nyland and Rollins knew about her murder.

Wiping his mouth, he told Platinum Pizzazz, "Finish your brunch, baby. I'm going to go over and see if I can get your interview set up with Valerie."

"Thank you, daddy."

D.O.D. approached their table. "I see you all are celebrating something. I thought I would come over and offer you a bottle of champagne."

Turquoise took the lead. "It's my birthday, and I would love some more champagne."

D.O.D. kissed Turquoise's hand. "It would be my pleasure, pretty lady."

As he motioned for a waiter, he said to Rome, "So, you were doing a little gambling in Vegas yesterday?"

Before Rome could answer, Turquoise interjected, "Oh no, he never gambles. He had business there, but we mainly celebrated my birthday."

For once, Rome was grateful for her interruption. He told D.O.D., "Yeah, we just hopped down and back."

The waiter arrived at the table.

"A bottle of Cristal for the lady. Just put it on my bill." D.O.D. looked them all over one last time, deciding he could not ask any more questions without raising too many flags. "Well, I'm out. You'll be hearing from us, Valerie."

Val nodded. "Okay. By the way, what does D.O.D. stand for?"

D.O.D. stared Val directly in the eyes:. "Double O Deadly."

That piercing look he gave her made Val realize she needed to get the cash Rome had given her, along with Victor's check, home. For some reason D.O.D.'s vibe sent a chill through her entire body.

"I think it's time we got out of here, too. Are you guys ready?"

"Yeah," Rome agreed. "After yesterday, you and I definitely deserve a day off."

"How about my champagne?" Turquoise asked.

Val quipped, "I'll have them cork it and you can take it with you."

Chapter Seventeen

Royale

It was a typical Sunday evening in the City of Angels. The traffic was light as Royale drove his Bugatti Veyron Grand Sport Vitesse down Wilshire Boulevard. The $2.5 million car had been a gift from Andrea Dumas. All he had to do was give one good lick of his tongue to that bitch's pussy and push a couple of hits of cocaine up her nose, and Andrea bought the car in cash for him the next morning. He then figured out a way to get nine more Bugattis for his crew to drive using the monthly funds that Andrea's husband deposited into her account. Unfortunately, the Bugattis, which were so splendid that they altered the way Royale viewed the world, had emptied out the dope fiend whore's bank account. Even though her old man deposited $250,000 a month into the account, Andrea's drug and shopping habits, coupled with D.O.D.'s and Royale's needs, easily exceeded those funds.

The final straw came when they were shopping at Gucci one day and her Black Card was declined. So, Royale dumped Andrea, took the cars, then turned her over to D.O.D. and his boys. But, as usual, the bitch fucked up again. This time she smoked up more dope than she sold. Her fate was automatically out of both his and D.O.D.'s hands. The big boys wanted her dead. She was of no use to them alive anymore. So, they had devised a scheme that once the bitch was dead, Rolondo Jemison would inherit all of her assets. She signed them over to him one night, thinking she was signing a joint bank account that D.O.D. had opened for the two of them, never realizing that Rolondo Jemison even existed.

Royale pulled the Bugatti up to Blair House, Roshonda's apartment building. He had almost forgotten he required all talent that signed up with his agency to fill out a form with their addresses on it. He had been trying to get in touch with her since he found her note on Friday night, to no avail. The way she ran out of there like a bat out of hell was bothering him. He wondered if she had overheard any of his phone conversation. If she had, he would have to deal with her.

He looked around the lobby of the high-rise building. He knew for a fact that condominiums there went for around $1.3 million. *How could Roshonda afford to live like this on that little reality show salary?*

He also definitely knew for a fact that it only paid a few grand an episode.

"Can I help you, sir?" the doorman asked.

"Roshonda Rhodes, please."

"I'm sorry, sir. Ms. Rhodes left this morning with luggage. I don't think she'll be back tonight."

Royale took a hundred-dollar bill out of his pocket and handed it to the guy. "Did she say where she was going?"

Discreetly pocketing the bill, the doorman told Royale: "No, sir, but she left with that black jockey whose mother was killed in Las Vegas. You know, Vance Dumas."

"Thanks, my man."

What the fuck was she doing with Vance Dumas? This wasn't looking good at all. Royale's phone rang as he got back into the car.

"Yo, man. It's Sweet. I have a few things I need to run past you. Where you at?"

"In Century City, on Wilshire."

"How soon can you meet me over by the Baldwin Hills Crenshaw Plaza? I have to run through a restaurant adjacent to it called Post and Beam to speak to this background singer real quick. It's at 3767 Santa Rosalia Drive."

"I can head there now."

"Cool, see you in a few."

Royale turned the car around and headed toward Baldwin Hills, which was the home to the largest middle- and upper-middle-class, African-American community in Los Angeles. Baldwin Hills Crenshaw Plaza, a shopping mall, sat at the northeast foot of Baldwin Hills. The mall maintained its cultural roots with a Museum of African Art.

The restaurant was owned by Brad Johnson, an innovative restaurateur that had started out at the Cellar Restaurant in New York, which was owned by his late father, Howard Johnson.

Sweet Lyrics was already seated at a table when Royale walked in. As soon as he sat down, Sweet asked him, "Are you hungry? I ordered the grilled beer brine pork chop with charred onions."

"That sounds good to me, man. Order that for me and a shot of Ciroc."

Sweet motioned for the waiter to come to the table and gave him Royale's order. When the waiter left, Royale asked Sweet, "What up?"

Sweet leaned in so no one could hear them. "D.O.D. ran into Rome Nyland and that gossip chick, Valerie Rollins, earlier today at the Four Seasons. Rome told him he saw my car in Vegas yesterday. D.O.D. played it off, but we could have a problem. You know he's a private dick these days."

"We do have a problem. The big guy called me yesterday from Vegas. Rome is working for Victor Dumas. He was already trying to find Andrea when she got murked. I need to find out what he and the gossip columnist know and fast. "

"It looks like we may have some help. D.O.D. also said the pretty black real estate lady whose picture is on all the billboards around town was with them. Her name is Turquoise and she was celebrating her birthday. He had to mean Turquoise Hobson. Didn't she sell you the spot over in Compton?"

"She sure as hell did, and I paid her in cash. I'll drop by her office tomorrow and make like I need to buy another property. Then, I'll find out what she knows. We'll nip this one in the bud real fast."

Changing the subject, Royale asked Sweet, "Does D.O.D. have everything under control with Platinum Pizzazz for Wednesday?"

"Yeah, he's ready. All she knows is she's performing in Montego Bay, Jamaica. She won't have a clue as to what's in her suitcase. Have you found Roshonda yet?"

"No, but her doorman said she left this morning with Vance Dumas. I have to get to the bottom of that, too."

"D.O.D. has Valerie's card, so he can also call her. We need to find out what's going on with Jermonna Bradley, too."

Royale nodded. He didn't like the way things were spiraling out of his control. He needed to get in touch with Dedra, but since the boss was so furious, he didn't think it was a good idea to call her until the boss told him to. He was going to wait a few days and then send an attorney representing Rolondo by Victor's attorney's office here in town with a copy of Andrea's will.

"Have D.O.D. call Valerie tomorrow. I have come too close to being a billionaire to let Rome Nyland and that talking head bitch stop me." The waiter arrived with their food and the two men ate in silence.

Rome

Even though Rome had told Val he was taking the day off, he was hard at work. Instead of heading home after dropping Turquoise off at her townhouse in Ladera Heights, he stopped by his ex-girlfriend, Davida's, house nearby in Baldwin Hills on Don Tomaso to see his son, Romey. He gave his son his weekly allowance, then watched the football game with him.

At the end of the game, Rome told him, "Okay, man. It's time for me to go to work. I'll pick you up for school in the morning."

"You got it, Dad. Soon, though, very soon, I'll be driving myself to school."

Rome laughed. Romey was fifteen and had his learner's permit. He would be able to drive alone as soon as he turned sixteen.

"Yes, you will, son. I know you can't wait."

Rome left there and drove down the hill to Crenshaw to see an old friend of his, Tyler Townsend. If anyone could shed some light on what this D.O.D. and his uncle were up to, she could. She might even know the real identity of Amir Lockett. His boy at the bureau still hadn't gotten back to him, and Dedra claimed the fingerprints weren't back yet. His gut told him she was lying. He had to figure out why.

Rome pulled into the tiny strip mall in front of Tyler's video store. The first time he came here years ago, one of her workers had pulled a gun on him. Once he let Tyler know he had been referred to her by his man, Ivan Rostropovich, they had gotten along. He rang the bell and was buzzed in.

Tyler was behind the counter in deep conversation with a customer. The store actually sold a lot more than videos. A drop-off point for half of the stolen goods in Los Angeles, Tyler sold everything from clothing to shoes to big and small appliances to weapons. "I see you're as beautiful as ever."

Gorgeous and tall, with skin the color of hot chocolate, Tyler, turned around when she heard Rome's voice. "And, you are still fine as wine in the summertime."

She stepped from behind the counter and hugged him. "It's been too long, man. How the hell are you?"

"Great."

Tyler knew Rome had to be there for business. He was never one for social calls.

"What can I do for you? I know you didn't pop in here after all this time to say hello."

Rome looked at Tyler standing before him in a black cashmere dress with a silver fox collar. Looking real funky, with her hair in a huge curly afro, she had on studded, high-top wedge sneakers. He thought to himself that, *maybe I should start dropping by more often.*

"You never were one to waste time. I was wondering if you know anything about the singer, Sweet Lyrics, and his nephew, D.O.D.? I saw his Ferrari yesterday in Las Vegas pull away from the spot where Andrea Dumas was murdered. Then, I ran into the nephew driving the same car earlier today at the Four Seasons Hotel in Beverly Hills. I need to get a grip on what their deal is."

"Are you paying?"

Rome handed Tyler ten hundred-dollar-bills.

"You know I am."

"Then, I'm talking. There's a place near here called Post and Beam. We can grab a bite to eat and shoot the breeze at the same time."

Tyler grabbed her Louis Vuitton Sunshine Express North-South handbag from behind the counter and headed out the door with Rome following her. "Let's take your car."

He opened the door of his gray Cadillac SRX Crossover for

her. He planned to give the smaller SUV to Romey for his birthday next month. Post & Beam was only about five minutes away. There were two Bugattis parked out front.

Tyler glanced at the cars and told Rome, "Well, well, well. You may have already solved your problem."

"What do you mean?"

"Those million-dollar babies belong to Royale Jones and the one and only Sweet Lyrics."

It was finally coming together for him. Jermonna had said she was on a booking that Royale set up for her. Royale used to play for the Los Angeles Wildcats. Val said some gang that wore Wildcats gear called themselves the Bugatti Blades. Royale drove a Bugatti, and, in addition to his Ferrari, apparently so did Sweet Lyrics. But, Royale and Sweet being part of some international drug gang did not make any possible sense. Plus, how did Andrea, Amir and possibly that poor girl, Evelyn's, murders fit into this scenario?

Rome let Tyler take the lead as he followed her into the restaurant.

"Let's eat at the bar. That way we can scope out whatever moves the fellows make."

They sat down.

The bartender placed napkins in front of them.

"What can I get you?"

Tyler told him, "I'll have a shot of tequila with a side of ginger ale."

"How about you, sir?"

"Cranberry juice mixed with orange, and, we'd like to see a couple of menus."

Settling their check after finishing dinner, Royale and Sweet Lyrics almost jumped out of their skin when they saw Rome walk in.

"Do you think he's having me followed?" Sweet asked.

Royale studied Rome before answering. "I don't know, man. We have to say hello, though. He and I are fellow retired athletes, you know. I also know that chick he's with. That's Tyler Townsend. She ain't no joke in the streets."

"Don't I know it," Sweet stated. "I bought a few burners from her myself."

Tyler saw the guys looking at her and Rome, so she smiled and waved. They waved back.

As the bartender placed their drinks in front of them, RomeTyler motioned to Rome to turn around.

"Just roll with it. Royale and Sweet are coming this way."

Both Royale and Sweet Lyrics gave Tyler a kiss on the cheek. Rome extended his hand to Royale.

"Man, it's been a long time. I haven't seen you since we did that autograph session in San Diego several years back."

Royale didn't have the foggiest idea what autograph session Rome was talking about, but he went along with it, saying, "That's right. It's good to see you. This is my man, Sweet Lyrics."

"Sweet," proclaimed Rome proclaimed, shaking his hand. "It's an honor to meet you. This must be my lucky day. I met your nephew this afternoon at the Four Seasons and his fine little rapper, Platinum Pizzazz."

"It's an honor to meet you as well, man."

Looking at Tyler, Royale quipped, "So, you're looking gorgeous, Miss Tyler. What are you two up to tonight?"

"Rome is an old friend. We decided to have dinner to catch up."

"All right now. Tyler, it's always a pleasure. Rome, as I said, it's nice to make your acquaintance, man," Sweet told them.

"I've been a fan for a long time," Rome told him. "You two stay cool."

When Royale and Sweet got outside, a light bulb clicked on in Royale's head. "Call one of the boys and tell him to get over here. When Rome leaves the restaurant, he knows what to do. Mr. Mister Nyland walked right into a trap. This hit couldn't have gone any better than if we had pre-planned it."

Chapter Eighteen

Rome

After Royale and Sweet Lyrics made their exit, Tyler proceeded to give Rome the rundown on the two guys.

"Look, those two are more than friends. They are in business together. Sweet Lyrics' ex-wife has a whole lot of kids. Her son with him is locked up in Pelican Bay State Prison in Crescent City for murder, drug trafficking, extortion, kidnapping, and all sorts of stuff. The word on the streets is that even in prison, he's controlling multi-million-dollar drug organizations. The rest of the brood, along with the mother whose name is Shaquida Pitts, sell drugs all over the country. They torture people and will shoot you if you look at any of them the wrong way.

"Now, Royale has to be mixed up with them some kind of way because they all wear Wildcats gear. I don't know how Andrea Dumas fits into this, though. A socialite like her wasn't exactly on my little lesbian clique's radar, but I know she copped dope from them, so her death may be connected to the Bugatti Blades. Oh, Sweet's nephew, D.O.D.'s main man's name is Sincere. His girl, Nicole, has sold clothes to me in the past. She somehow brings me top couture stuff from Neiman Marcus. I think she has someone on the inside of the store working with her."

"Are you two ready to order?" asked the bartender.

Tyler went first.

"I'll have the long cooked greens with smoked ham hock to

start and the boneless beef short ribs with fresh horseradish as my main dish. How about you, Rome?"

"Let me get the orecchiettte asparagus, roasted cauliflower, braised garbanzos, nettle pesto as an appetizer and the grilled organic chicken breast with poached garlic, lemon and thyme."

The bartender took their menus.

Rome made no comment as to what Tyler had just said. He listened and absorbed all the information that she was giving him. However, he did take a special note that Jermonna had mentioned that a guy named Sincere had taken her and Andrea to the Three Points Sports Bar.

Tyler continued, "Be careful. These guys are real dangerous. Maybe you should let the cops in Las Vegas handle this one."

At that suggestion, Rome shook his head. "For some reason, they seem to be moving slowly. Val's soror is the Assistant Deputy Police Chief, but she's had this guy Amir's body since yesterday, and has yet to give me any info on his prints. I also still don't have the identity of the guy that I shot. She never even asked for my gun. And, the fool who was driving the car that the guy shooting at us was in yesterday escaped from jail overnight. I've never seen such haphazard police work in my life."

"Dedra Thorne's the Las Vegas Assistant Deputy Police Chief, right?" asked Tyler. "I know her. She used to date an old girlfriend of mine."

Although Rome had suspected Tyler's sexual preference was women, he had never known for sure until now.

"I wonder if Val knows that about Dedra. She never mentioned that Dedra is a lesbian to me."

"Of course she knows. Val's best friend in New York, Irene Gandy, used to kick it with Dedra a long time ago. In fact, Val introduced them. Irene is fabulous. She's still the only African-

American publicist that has ever been a part of the certified Broadway Press Agents Union."

Rome was in deep thought as he listened to Tyler.

"You realize that it's been at least twenty-five years since Sweet4U had a hit, so I'm not surprised that he may be dipping and dabbing in illegal businesses. Royale retired around 2004 or 2005. That baseball money could be getting short, too. Yet, they're both pushing million-dollar cars. It's kind of funny, Royale doesn't look the same to me. His features haven't changed. But, I remember him being darker and more muscular. His voice even seems a little different. It used to be heavier and kind of Midwestern. I think he's from someplace in Illinois near Chicago. Tonight, he sounded Southern."

Their food was arriving. Laughing, Tyler commented, "Maybe he's using bleaching cream on his skin and went on a diet. Seriously, word on the streets is these Bugatti Blades are into some heavy stuff, so be careful. Let's eat. This food looks good."

As soon as they finished dinner, Rome took Tyler back to her shop. He was glad to be heading home to downtown L.A. where he lived on the top floor of a building he owned in Chinatown. He headed north on Crenshaw, then turned on Slauson. It was when he hit Sepulveda that he noticed the Bugatti behind him. This wasn't one of the cars that had been in front of Post & Beam, but a navy blue one. The Bugatti sped up, pulling up alongside Rome. Before the driver could get his window down, Rome reached into his side panel, pulled out his gun and fired once, hitting the guy right at the center of his forehead.

The Bugatti veered off the road, smashed into a tree, flipped over, then exploded. A car behind it was able to veer to the other side of the road missing the fire. Rome never even got a look at the driver. He eased up the road a little more, then called nine-one-one.

"Nine-one-one. What is your emergency?"

"I was riding North on Sepulveda and saw a car burning pretty badly."

"Okay, thank you, sir. We'll get somebody there right away."

Both Val and Tyler were right about one thing. These guys were definitely deadly stuff players that meant serious business. This was his second close call with death in two days. Rome had never been a quitter, but he wanted to be around for his son. *These guys must really be after something big from Victor.* They were looking for something far bigger than some measly $1 million that Andrea allegedly owed them. Once he found out what it was, he would resign from this case. Victor was paying him $10,000 per day. It was damn good money, but it wasn't worth his life. The ringing of his phone jarred Rome out of his thoughts.

"Are you okay?" Val yelled into the phone.

"I'm fine. I was involved in a little car accident."

"I wouldn't call that a little car accident. Rome, you have to call in your guys to help you with this. You shouldn't be riding around town alone."

He didn't even want to ask her how she knew he had been involved in tonight's incident so fast. Val's phone never stopped ringing. She had eyes and ears everywhere. That, and her loving ways, made her invaluable to him.

Rome yawned.

"I'm almost home. Get some sleep. I'll talk to you in the morning."

He pulled into his underground garage and headed upstairs. He was glad to be home. Today had wound up being another day from hell.

Chapter Nineteen

Valerie
Monday

In the aftermath of the frightening weekend she had experienced, the week was starting out really good for Valerie. While she would never admit it, she loved having Dwayne drive her around in the fabulous Bentley SUV. Plus, after what happened to Rome the previous night, having a driver with her at all times now seemed to be a good idea. He had picked her up promptly at five that morning and driven her to the Fox Studios where she did two shows. From there, he drove her to the credit union where she deposited Victor's check. That had been so exciting. With her windfall, she could do some much needed maintenance on the house and have a great Christmas. She would even shock her relatives by making it home to Michigan for their annual Cousins Luncheon and be able to buy everyone lovely gifts.

Val had put a statement for Victor out on the Public Relations Newswire saying he would be establishing the Andrea Dumas Foundation with an initial $5 million donation. In addition to adopting five families and getting them housing and clothes, the money would also go to women who were trying to get off drugs to get them detoxed, counseling, homes and schooling. Val had spoken to Victor for a long time on the phone the previous night. She volunteered to head up the foundation until they could find someone to take the job permanently.

At the Santa Sleigh Ball, which followed the race on the fifteenth at Hollywood Park, Val planned to present the first check to a young woman who held down a full-time day job, then went to college classes every night. Val had met the ambitious young woman at a seminar on Careers in Journalism that she recently taught. Very courageous, she was a single mother of two young children.

Currently surfing the Internet for stories to report on her radio show, Val was on *TMZ's* website when she came across a photo of Platinum Pizzazz. The caption read:

Platinum Pizzazz Heads To 92.3 The Beat Wearing One Million-Dollar Necklace! Platinum Pizzazz is wearing a St. John Emerald wool and rayon dress with paillettes. Although the rapper wouldn't tell us who gave her the black and canary diamond necklace, she did say that it is a one-of-a-kind piece. Next up for Platinum Pizzazz is a performance in Montego Bay, Jamaica on Wednesday night.

Val looked closely at the picture. The necklace matched the exact description of the one that Jermonna said Andrea was wearing on Friday night. Rome said he saw that Ferrari D.O.D. was driving yesterday in front of the Three Points Bar in Las Vegas on Saturday. Oh My God!

She picked up her phone and called Rome immediately.

"Well, hello," he answered. "I was beginning to think you had ridden off into the sunset with your new Bentley and driver."

"Rome," Val practically yelled into the phone, "I'm on *TMZ's* website looking for stories for tomorrow's radio feed and I came across a photo of Platinum Pizzazz wearing a necklace that looks exactly like the one that Jermonna said Andrea was wearing."

"Forward the photo to both Victor and me right away. No, on second thought, send it to me and over to Dedra. Tell her to print it out and take it up to the hospital for Jermonna to identify. I know we told Jermonna not to do any more talking to the police, but this is a different situation. I'll call the security at the hospital and tell them to let Dedra speak to Jermonna. Victor is busy with Andrea's cremation today. He doesn't need anything else to deal with."

"You got it. Where are you anyway?"

"In my office putting pictures up on my bulletin board of all the players we're dealing with so far. I need to figure out exactly how each of these people are connected to each other and to Victor and Andrea, and what the pay-off really is. When I finish with this, I'm going downtown to file a missing persons report on Victor's guy, Claude Hoskins. It's been forty-eight hours and he still hasn't surfaced. Are you free for dinner so we can compare notes on today's events?"

"Yes, I'm free."

"Okay. I'll call you back when I make some headway with this stuff."

"Got you. Bye."

Used to multitasking, Val forwarded him the picture and then called Dedra to tell her to also expect it.

Seeing Val's name on the caller ID, Dedra answered with a chipper, "Hey, soror."

"Hey. I'm emailing you a picture taken this morning of Platinum Pizzazz. She's wearing a necklace that looks like the one Jermonna says Andrea was wearing before she was murdered. Rome was wondering if you can take the picture over to the hospital to see whether or not Jermonna says it's the same one. Rome saw the same red Ferrari this guy D.O.D., who's her manager, was driving in L.A. yesterday, in Las Vegas in front of the Three Points Bar on Saturday. We ran into the two of them at the Four Seasons."

Dedra thought to herself, *This Rome never misses a trick. Now he is telling me how to do my job.*

Aloud, she told Val, "No problem. I'll do it as soon as I check my emails."

"Oh, Dee Dee, one more thing. Rome is filing a missing persons report on Claude Hoskins this afternoon."

"All right. I'll talk to you later."

Dedra opened up her email too look at the photo. This was definitely the same necklace that the boss was looking for. Those fools were supposed to give her the necklace so she could give it to him to fence. Humph! There would be hell to pay for this. D.O.D. had lost his mind since the boss had to go underground.

She punched up her guy's number. He answered on the first ring. "What's up?"

"What's up is that D.O.D. gave his little rapping bitch the necklace that you're looking for. She had the nerve to be photographed in it this morning on the way to a radio station. My soror, Val, saw the photo. Apparently Jermonna Bradley described the necklace that Andrea was wearing the other night to Val and Rome. Then, Rome saw Sweet Lyrics' red Ferrari here in front of the Three Points Bar. He saw the car again yesterday, with D.O.D. driving it, in Los Angeles."

"You listen to me and listen to me good. I'll get the necklace back from D.O.D. and Platinum Pizzazz. Then, after they complete the job for us down in Jamaica on Wednesday, I'll deal with them, too. But, you have to deal with your little sorority sister and her buddy, Rome. It's time for both of them to bid this world farewell."

"Are you saying what I think you're saying?"

With venom in his voice, the boss growled, "Yes, I am. It's time for you to kill both of them. I don't care if you have to lure them back to Las Vegas or go to L.A. I want those two busybodies dead by the time Rolondo collects the money and property Andrea left him in her will. You hear me? I want them both dead!"

With those words, he disconnected the call. Dedra put her head on her desk. How could she kill her best friend of thirty years?

But, if she didn't follow the boss's instructions, he would release damaging information about her to the Las Vegas Police Department and her stellar career in law enforcement would be over. It was only Monday. She had a few days to figure this all out. There was one thing that she had already come to a conclusion about, though. Jermonna was never going to see this picture of Platinum Pizzazz wearing Andrea's necklace.

Royale

Right after Dedra got chewed out, the same thing happened to Royale. His ears were almost ringing from the yelling coming out of his phone.

"Are you crazy?" asked his boss. "I told you to leave Rome Nyland to me. That guy has smoother moves than Kobe Bryant. Now a $2 million car is gone up in smoke, not to mention that one of our best men is dead. Please leave Rome to me. It's been a long time since he and I have crossed paths, but I can handle that motherfucker. To add insult to all injury, I get a call that Platinum Pizzazz is wearing a necklace that I have someone ready to pay us millions for. But, don't you worry, I will handle those two myself. Royale, you are treading on thin ice. It's time for these mistakes to stop! Goodbye. I'll be in touch."

Royale had been on his way out the door when the phone rang. He had dressed extra carefully that morning in a brown Armani suit and beige cashmere turtleneck sweater. He put on a pair of dark-gray, crocodile-stamped leather Prada driving shoes. Instead of his diamond Rolex, he put on a Victorinox Swiss Army watch. He was headed over to Turquoise Hobson's office. Even though he didn't want to look flashy, it was important for him to make sure he was dressed to impress. He didn't know the nature of her relationship with either Rome Nyland or Valerie Rollins, but he sure intended to find out.

Killing Rome seemed impossible, but he had to get him off of his tail until Rolondo could get a hold of Andrea's money. A $500,000 payment was due to their Bugatti connection. The connect needed it to satisfy the crooked banker that was working with them to buy the cars. The ten Bugattis that they rotated driving had all come from an Italian connection who worked closely with a bank in Italy that was able to rig paperwork. Instead of costing almost $20 million, they had gotten the fleet for about $5 million. The one he originally had belonged to his deceased cousin. Once he met Andrea, she gladly coughed up the cash for the rest. However, he had to get his guy the money. If anything was ever suspected, they could all go to jail for international fraud and bank robbery, not to mention car theft. Before heading out, Royale dialed Roshonda for the tenth time since Friday. Her phone went straight to voicemail again. Her silence and his knowledge that she had been seen with Vance Dumas was not setting well with him. He had to deal with her, too. Royale jumped in his car to make his way to Beverly Hills.

Chapter Twenty

Turquoise

Sitting in her office on North Canon Drive in Beverly Hills, wearing a St. John beige and red silk color block top with stretch cotton Emma pants and Phillip Lim Diamond snakeskin and leather d'Orsay pumps, Turquoise was ready for business. The only problem was she hadn't had any business in several weeks. With everything going on with the economy, people weren't exactly running out and buying multi-million-dollar mansions every day.

She glanced at the Breitling watch on her wrist that Rome had given her for her birthday. It was worth at least $20,000. What she wouldn't do for the money instead of the watch. She had been hoping for an engagement ring from Rome. She needed to get him to the altar fast and become his wife before she had to close down her business.

Since Rome was fifty-two years old, but had never been married, most of her girlfriends didn't think that he had any intentions of settling down with a wife. She didn't care what they thought. She had been married in her early twenties to an aspiring actor. He never landed anything other than television pilots that were never picked up and occasional bit parts in movies. Back then, Turquoise was working for Century One Real Estate. She spent every dime of her commissions on desk fees and her husband's photos. Then, one day she arrived home early to find him in bed with his acting teacher. Not even bothering to kick the son of a bitch out, Turquoise packed her clothes, moved in with one of her girlfriends and never looked back. The day that she ran into Rome at Ralph's Market, she had recognized him immediately. Having perfected the art of flirting, she engrossed him in a conversation about football that led Rome to suggest she join him for dinner if she didn't have any immediate plans. Dinner led to a quick cocktail at her home where they ended up in bed. That was seven months ago and they had been together almost nightly ever since. She refused to let this fish off of the hook.

She was on a mission to make him her husband. At that point her assistant, Sylvia, buzzed her. "There's a Mister Royale Jones to see you, Turquoise."

Royale Jones! He had spent $250,000 in cash with her the year before, buying an old building with a bar on the bottom floor over in Compton. She could use another sale like that right now. She hurried out to her reception area.

Giving him a kiss on the cheek, she exclaimed, "Royale, how nice to see you. What can I do to help you?"

He stood back and assessed her. She was one classy, good-looking broad.

"It's good to see you, too. I'm thinking about moving out of my apartment and buying a house. I wanted to see if you have anything in a brother's price range in Beverly Hills."

"Of course I do."

"In that case, if you don't have any plans for lunch, let me take you out for a bite and I can tell you exactly what I'm looking for."

Smiling, Turquoise assured him, "My afternoon is free. We can walk over to Caffé Roma. It's just a few doors down. Let me grab my purse."

As they walked out the door, Turquoise told Sylvia, "If Mister

Nyland calls, tell him I'm at lunch with a client and I'll call him when I get back."

At the sound of Rome's name, Royale perked up. He was on the right track.

"Will do," Sylvia told her employer.

Caffé Roma was practically next door to Turquoise's office. The trendy upscale restaurant transformed into a nightclub at night. It was frequented by many celebrities and had been a favorite lunch spot of Mayor Antonio Villaraigosa before he got into politics. Since Turquoise was a regular, she and Royale were seated quickly.

"May I get you two something to drink?" the waiter inquired.

Turquoise never drank while out with clients unless closing a deal, so she answered, "Still water is fine for me."

Royale told him, "A shot of Ciroc straight up."

Observing Turquoise's necklace and watch, Royale commented, "That's some impressive ice you're wearing."

"My boyfriend gave me the necklace and watch for my birthday on Saturday."

"He must be pretty serious about you. You're wearing almost fifty grand worth of diamonds. Of course, if you were my woman, I would have thrown in at least a five-carat ring with the watch and necklace."

Turquoise grinned from ear to ear. "You may know him. He used to play football. His name is Rome Nyland."

When he walked into her office, Royale didn't have an actual plan. Unwittingly, Turquoise had just delivered one to him on a silver platter. He may not be able to exterminate Rome Nyland. So, he would hit him where it always hurt any man he had ever known the most. Rome's woman was about to become his.

"That's a coincidence. Not only do I know Rome, but I ran into him last night."

"Really, where?"

"We both had dinner at this place near the Baldwin Hills Plaza called Post and Beam. My boy, Sweet Lyrics, and I were kicking it, and your man was eating with this chick I know. Her name is Tyler."

Hearing that Rome had been out with another woman, Turquoise immediately tensed up.

"He's never mentioned anyone named Tyler to me. He dropped me off after we had brunch at the Four Seasons and told me he was going to spend some time with his son, then go home and get some rest. I can't believe he would lie to me like that."

"I wouldn't worry about it, beautiful. I'm sure he has a good explanation for his actions. "

"Can I take your order?" the waiter asked.

Almost too upset to eat, Turquoise told him, "I'll have the Insalata Mista Di Mare and a Grey Goose Martini straight up with a lemon twist."

She suddenly needed a drink.

The waiter turned to Royale. "And you, sir?"

"You can give me the spaghetti with meatballs."

Although she didn't know Royale all that well, Turquoise felt like confiding in him.

"I don't get why Rome has to have so many women around him. I had to spend my birthday with his nosy partner, Valerie Rollins. She was bad enough. Now here's another chick. I don't mean to sound like the desperate girlfriend, but what does this Tyler look like?"

"No doubt about it, she's fine, but she can't hold a candle to you, baby."

Satisfied with his answer, Turquoise changed the subject.

"Well, we're here to talk business. What is your price range and what kind of house do you want?"

Royale felt like the cat who just swallowed a canary. This was going to be a piece of cake. He would have this naïve bitch eating out of his hand soon, as well as sucking his dick. Then she would tell him every move that Rome was making to find Andrea's murderer.

Chapter Twenty-One

Rome

Glancing at his watch, Rome saw it was a little past one. He had been on the phone and computer all morning. His intercom rang and his boy Alan told him Romey was on the way up. His son had told him that morning ,when he dropped him off, that he only had a half-day at school. They rarely got the chance to have lunch together. So, Rome suggested he catch a cab from Sherman Oaks where he attended the Buckley School to Chinatown for lunch at his crib. Michael Jackson's three children, Prince, Paris and Blanket, also attended the exclusive private school.

"I'm back here, son!" he called out when he heard Romey come through the front door.

Romey set his backpack on the floor of Rome's office.

"Hey, Dad." Observing the pictures on the wall, Romey pointed to Platinum Pizzazz. "Why do you have a picture of Jo Ella on your wall?"

"What do you mean, Jo Ella? That's Platinum Pizzazz."

"Platinum Pizzazz is her new rap name. But, her real name is Jo Ella Conrad. Some of my boys I play football with went to elementary and junior high school with her. Then she went to Dorsey High. But one of my boys told me that she dropped out last year."

"Isn't she a lot older than you, son?"

"No. I read online where she claims to be eighteen, but she's only sixteen."

Well…well…well…Not only was Rome going to try to get a warrant on this D.O.D. for possibly the murders of Andrea, Amir or whoever he was, and attempted murder for shooting at him and Val, along with grand theft of Andrea's necklace, but now he could also get him on statutory rape. He hated to disturb him, but he had to call Victor now and email him a photo of Platinum, or Jo Ella, wearing the necklace.

"You haven't answered me, Dad. Why is her picture on the wall?"

"I'll explain it to you in a minute, son. Let me make one call. Go on in the kitchen. I already have pasta, bread and all the trimmings on the stove out for your lunch. Start fixing your plate and I'll be right with you."

As soon as Romey left his office, Rome punched up Victor.

His client picked up right away. "Good afternoon, Victor."

"Good afternoon. I'm sorry to bother you. I think we've located Andrea's necklace. I'm going to email you a photo right now of a new rapper wearing a necklace that fits the description."

"Hey, Rome. You aren't bothering me. I'm in my room catching up with some work on my laptop. We finished with the cremation. Everyone is kind of resting now until dinner. I rented out a private room for the repast. Send it over now."

"Okay, if it is the necklace, I'm going to need someone to email me the receipt, appraisal or whatever paperwork you have to prove you purchased it. Then, I'll take it down to police head-quarters here and get arrest warrants for the rapper and her boy-friend for theft and Andrea's murder. I saw his car on Saturday in Las Vegas and then again yesterday here in L.A."

"Your email just came through. Yes, it is her necklace. I'll call my assistant right now. She can also fax you photos of Andrea wearing the necklace. Man, you work fast."

"Once again, thank Val. She was surfing the web looking for stories for her radio show and saw the photo on *TMZ*."

All Victor could say was, "She is some kind of special. I'll be in Los Angeles first thing tomorrow. I have to meet with my attorneys and go over Andrea's will. Then, why don't we all have dinner? I'll call Val and have her make a reservation at Mr. Chow. I hear the Chinese food is very good there. My son and his wife also have some information for you. There was also another $50,000 wired into your account today. I thought you might need it to pay some more bills related to your investigation."

"Thanks, man. It is a pleasure working with you. I'll see you tomorrow."

"Good bye, Rome."

Following his conversation with Victor, Rome went into the kitchen to join Romey. As soon as they finished eating, he was going to drop him off, then go to police headquarters.

Romey barely gave his dad a chance to pile the pasta on his plate and sit down at the table before asking, "So why do you have Jo Ella's picture, Dad? Is she in some kind of trouble?"

Rome didn't want to lie to his son, but this was a very serious, confidential matter. He chose his words carefully. "Now, Romey, you understand I can't discuss my work. I met her yesterday at the Four Seasons. Valerie is supposed to be doing an interview with her and I was doing some background work for her. When is the last time you spoke to this Jo Ella?"

"I never really talked to her. My crew was always a little too slow for Jo Ella's kind of girl. The other day, one of my teammates was saying he heard she's shacked up with some older dude in a house on Rodeo across from the Village Green. He lives in Village Green and has seen her getting out of the dude's Ferrari. She may be a big rap star now, but she's still a slut."

"That's not cool, son. I've never heard you talk like that."

"It's true, Dad."

"That may be, but I always want you to behave respectfully toward any woman."

Out of the mouth of babes. Thanks to his son, he now knew where to steer the cops to pick Pizzazz and D.O.D. up. His phone rang.

"Rome, it's Wilson Rivera."

"Wilson, my man. What's happening?"

"I wanted you to know there's an Internal Affairs Bureau investigation going on with our Assistant Deputy Police Chief, Dedra Thorne. I know that you've been working with her, but maybe you should refrain from giving her too much information. One of my sources told me that the Internal Affairs Bureau thinks she may have let that guy Joseph Savoldi escape from his cell the other night, even though she wasn't on duty at the time. The man vanished into thin air, so it had to be an inside job."

"Thanks for the tip. My gut has been telling me something isn't right with her. Check with Western Union tomorrow afternoon. I'll have something there for you."

"Good looking out. We'll talk again soon."

"Later."

"Okay, Romey. I have to go back in my office to finish a couple of things and call Val. You finish your lunch and I'll drop you off at home."

"Dad, are we going to have Christmas dinner at Miss Valerie's again this year? I'll spend Christmas Eve with mom and then she's heading out Christmas Day to go to Reno with her friends. I had so much fun with Miss Valerie last year. I couldn't believe she had all those gifts for me."

Rome hadn't even thought about Christmas dinner. He hadn't introduced Romey to Turquoise yet and he didn't know what her plans were for the holidays. Whatever they might be, he and Romey would have to go to Val's first. Then, his son would spend the whole week with him until his mother returned from skiing. Christmas was coming fast. He had to get Val over here to decorate.

"Of course we are, son. As much as Val loves Christmas, she's probably already started wrapping gifts. I'll be right back."

Rome sat down at his desk and punched up Val.

She answered by telling Rome, "You're going to live a long time. I was getting ready to call you."

"You have some new information?"

"A crime reporter friend of mine just called me. The police haven't been able to identify the body that was in that Bugatti that tried to kill you last night; it was burned beyond recognition, along with everything in the glove compartment or any wallet he may have had on him. But, here's the kicker. My friend saw me on TV earlier today. Since I'm working with Victor he called me because they were able to piece together the license plate and the car was registered to the dear departed Mrs. Andrea Dumas."

"You've got to be kidding."

"I wish I was. He wanted a statement from Victor, but I asked him to hold off, if possible, until tomorrow and I could give him an exclusive."

"That's good looking out. I'm getting ready to drop Romey off at home, then head to the police station. Listen, Val, keep all of this under wraps. If you hear from Dedra, do not, I repeat, do not, mention this to her. She may be your soror and all, but I got a tip that she may be on the take."

Val simply listened to him. She had been getting strange vibes about Dee Dee ever since Saturday when she didn't take Rome down to the police station for formal questioning after he shot and killed that man.

"I've got you."

Looking at the clock on his wall, Rome told her, "It's two-thirty now. Why don't we meet for dinner at seven o'clock?"

"Make that eight o'clock at Mastro's Steakhouse. One of my sources there told me that Beyoncé and Jay-Z have a reservation for six people tonight. I can pick up some scoop, enjoy some delicious food and feed you information at the same time."

"You're a triple threat woman. See you at eight. Mastro's is right next door to Turquoise's office. I'll still get there at seven and treat her to a cocktail before you arrive."

He hung up with her, then printed out the photo from *TMZ* of Platinum Pizzazz wearing Andrea's necklace and Victor's receipt for $5 million, along with the $10 million appraisal. The price of this necklace was ridiculous. You could feed entire small countries for less. I guess when money was no object and continued to flow in the way it did for Victor's empire, $5 million for one piece of jewelry was no big deal.

He threw everything into his briefcase, and then called out to Romey, "Son, let's go."

It took Rome about forty-five minutes to drop Romey off, then head back downtown to police headquarters. It was busy as usual. Rome told the officer at the front desk, "I'd like to see Lieutenant James Pace, please. My name is—"

Finishing his sentence, the officer stated, "Rome Nyland. I'm a big fan of yours. Let me see if the lieutenant is in."

He rang James on the phone. When James answered, he nodded his head. "Okay, I'll tell him." He looked at Rome. "He'll be right out."

Rome and James had played football together at UCLA. James only did two years in the NFL before he was sidelined with an ankle injury. He opted to join the police academy after he retired, following in the footsteps of his father and grandfather.

As soon as he saw Rome, James engulfed Rome in a bear hug. "My man!"

Laughing, Rome told him, "L.T. You're looking good, man."

"You are a sight for sore eyes, my brother. But, I know you didn't come all the way down here to give me some compliments. What do you have for me?"

"I have a few things to lay on you, man."

"Okay, come on back."

As they sat down, James told Rome, "You know we don't have any herbal tea here, but I can send someone out to get you a cup if you like."

"No thanks, man. I'm cool. I'm working for Victor Dumas. You know his wife was found murdered in Las Vegas early Saturday morning. One of the cats who works for him has been missing ever since. His name is Claude Hoskins."

Rome opened up his briefcase. "Here's his file. He's a bachelor with no family. Victor last spoke to him by telephone on Friday afternoon when he hired me. He doesn't know if he was here in L.A. or in Las Vegas. His main residence is here. He has a house out in Tarzana, but he hasn't been seen there in a couple of weeks. His office was in Las Vegas. I need to file a missing persons report on him."

"No problem. I'll get that done right away."

Handing James the photos of Platinum Pizzazz and Andrea, along with Victor's receipt and appraisal for Andrea's necklace, Rome continued, "Andrea Dumas was wearing this necklace when she was killed. It went missing, but this rapper, Platinum Pizzazz, whose real name is Jo Ella Conrad, was photographed wearing it this morning over at 92.3 The Beat. I saw her boyfriend's red Ferrari with the license plate Sweet4U in Las Vegas in front of the Three Points Sports Bar where Andrea was killed, then again yesterday at the Four Seasons in Beverly Hills. He goes by D.O.D. I don't know his real name. He told me he's the singer Sweet Lyrics' nephew. Victor wants to press charges against the girl for stealing the necklace."

"I'm going to make your day... I do know this son of a bitch's real name. It's Ashton Oaks. He's twenty-two years old and has been in and out of trouble since he was a juvenile. He has been hauled in on suspicion of murder, armed robbery, drug dealing, even assault and battery. I know that gang of his is responsible for half the murders in this town and around the country, but he has never done any hard time."

"I'm pretty sure you can also charge him with statutory rape. My son says Platinum Pizzazz is really only sixteen."

"Okay, since Mr. Dumas is pressing charges on the necklace, I can get a warrant for grand theft and I can get him on endangerment of the welfare of a minor. The murder charge is going to be hard, though. Even though you saw his car near the Three Points, we don't have a murder weapon or even probable cause or a witness linking him to Mrs. Dumas. Plus, the crime was committed in Las Vegas."

"I hear you. I guess two out of three isn't bad."

The lieutenant reassured him, "And, hopefully, once we get in his house, we'll find some clues to the murder that I can pass along to the Las Vegas authorities."

"How soon do you think you can get a warrant for his arrest?"

"I'll take all of this to the District Attorney's office right now. I would like to be able to raid his house by the morning. Do you want me to call the Las Vegas authorities in on this?"

"Not yet. I got a tip that there's an Internal Affairs Bureau investigation being done on Dedra Thorne, the Deputy Assistant Chief of Police. My source thinks she may have something to do with Andrea's murder and that guy trying to shoot Val and me. For now, I don't want to tip her hand."

"Okay. Let me tell you, if any of this information can get this D.O.D. and some of his gang members off the streets, I will give you a special commendation."

Just to be sure they were talking about the same crew, Rome asked James, "What's the name of the gang?"

"The Bugatti Blades. They terrorize all of South Central and have moved into Las Vegas, Chicago and New York."

Rome hesitated for a moment, before saying, "On the Q.T., I have one more tidbit to lay on you."

"You know you can talk to me."

"I'm the person who called in the burning Bugatti downtown last night. The driver tried to kill me. Val got a tip from one of your guys that the car was registered to Andrea Dumas. She was mixed up with these guys in a big way."

"This info will stay with me. I'm just glad you got out of there alive last night. I'll make sure no one questions what or who caused the accident."

"All right, man, I'm out. Hit me as soon as you get the warrant."

"Will do. It's always a pleasure. You make my job easy."

Rome shook his hand, then headed out.

Chapter Twenty-Two

Valerie

Feeling uneasy and a bit restless due to another attempt to kill Rome last night, Valerie decided to get out of the house and hit Mastro's a little early. Just in case she did run into her favorite celebrity couple, Beyoncé and Jay-Z, she had dressed up for dinner. She was wearing a Jessica Simpson Cold-Shouldered burgundy draped dress and Manolo Blahnik d'orsay pumps that matched the dress perfectly.

The moment she stepped into the restaurant's bar area, Val heard a familiar voice yelling, "I just don't understand you, Rome. I have never been so embarrassed in my life as I was today. My client complimented me on my jewelry, so I very proudly told him that my boyfriend gave it to me for my birthday. When I revealed who *my boyfriend* is, my client proceeded to tell me that he saw you at a restaurant last night with some woman. You told me you were going to spend time with your son, then go home to get some rest. What kind of fool do you think I am?"

Oh, no. That was Turquoise. Val approached the bar right away to try and diffuse whatever the situation was.

"Turquoise, Rome. How are you two doing tonight?"

"Not good," answered Turquoise replied. "Your partner here played me yesterday."

Rome couldn't believe this was happening to him. Neither public nor private scenes were his thing. He calmly told Turquoise,

"That was a business associate of mine, Tyler. She was a friend of my cousin Charlie's."

Val stepped in.

"Look, lower your voice. I could hear you all the way outside. You don't have to worry about Rome and Tyler." Val whispered to Turquoise, "Tyler thinks that her dick is bigger than Rome's."

Turquoise looked at Val like she was crazy. "What do you mean?"

Rome gave Val a light punch on the shoulder. "I wouldn't say all that. What Miss I've Got Jokes here means is Tyler is into women. I would never just lie to you. I was heading home to get some rest, but the case I'm working on was on my mind. So, I decided to go see Tyler for some help. Who's your client anyway?"

Turquoise just rolled her eyes at him.

"That doesn't really matter. You're a famous guy. People are going to notice you. I just don't understand why you didn't call me and let me know you were still out. I thought we had something good going here."

"We do have something good going, but I'm a private detective. I make a lot of moves that I can't tell anyone about."

Turquoise pointed to Val.

"Well, she certainly seems to know your every move."

Val laughed. "That's because we work together. But, don't be so sure about that. I didn't know he was out with Tyler last night either."

The three of them laughed. At that point Magic and Cookie Johnson walked past them.

He shook Rome's hand, then kissed Val on the cheek.

"It's nice to see both of you," Magic told them.

"It's good to see you two also. Enjoy your dinner."

Val turned her attention back to Turquoise. "I was looking forward to having a glass of wine in a calm atmosphere when I got here. I guess that idea went out the window. Are you two cool?"

"Yes, we're cool," Turquoise reluctantly answered. "Bartender, please give the lady a glass of chardonnay on me. I'm sorry, Rome."

Rome kissed Turquoise lightly on the lips.

"No problem, baby. When Val and I finish here, I'll pass by your crib. You don't have to worry about me and other women. Cheating on someone I care about has never been my style."

The hostess approached them. "Valerie, your table is ready. Do you need to make it for three instead of two?'

Turquoise answered for Val.

"No, I was just leaving." She turned to Rome.

"I'll see you later, my love."

When Val and Rome sat down, Val started in on him.

"It's none of my business, but that chick is a little off-kilter. How did you meet her anyway?"

"At Ralphs Market. She picked me up in the produce section."

"Are you serious?"

"As a heart attack."

"Well, maybe that's why she makes you act a bit fruity when you're around her."

"May I take your drink order?" asked the waiter.

"I'll have a cranberry mixed with orange juice, and the lady will have a glass of chardonnay."

"I haven't finished this one yet."

"I'm not worried about that. I know you soon will. Let's have a look at the menu. I have a lot to tell you."

When the waiter returned with their drinks, Val was ready to order dinner.

"I'll have the Iceberg wedge to start and the bone-in rib eye with creamed corn and a baked potato. I haven't eaten all day and can take what I don't eat home."

Rome spoke up, "I'll have the seared ahi tuna as an appetizer and the Chilean sea bass with the gorgonzola mac and cheese and sautéed spinach."

The waiter collected their menus.

"So how did you make out at the police station?" Val asked Rome. "Were they able to execute a warrant to arrest Pizzazz and D.O.D.?"

"Yes, my man sent me a text saying they are going to raid the Bugatti Blades' bar over in Compton as well as D.O.D.'s house on Rodeo between La Brea and La Cienega in the morning. It turned out they have a huge file on D.O.D., whose real name is Ashton Oaks. James has been wanting to put him away for a long time, but never could make anything big stick."

"I feel sorry for Platinum Pizzazz, getting mixed up with a guy like that. She's just getting started in the entertainment business."

"I know. Romey knows her. He says she's only sixteen, but he also said she always hung out with rough guys. Listen, once this arrest goes down in the morning, I want you to be extra careful. These guys may retaliate if they find out the lead on the necklace originated from you."

"I'll be fine. The world saw that necklace on *TMZ*. No one will suspect me. Besides, I've got my two drivers who I suspect are heavily armed."

All of a sudden they heard a commotion with everybody in the restaurant "ooohing" and "ahhing." The King and Queen of the entertainment world, Jay-Z and Beyoncé, were walking right past their table. They both smiled and waved at Val and Rome as they were ushered to a private room.

Val glowed with excitement.

"Well, I've got my story for tomorrow. Seeing them out at dinner is every gossip columnist's dream."

Not impressed, Rome nodded.

"Did you make the reservation at Mr. Chow for tomorrow night?"

"Yes. Victor told me to make the reservation for six. I think he's including your overzealous girlfriend. He says Roshonda has some important information for you that she doesn't want to discuss on the phone. You know she's a little shady. She used to be one of Rebecca's girls. Vance gave Rebecca a huge check to pay off Roshonda's 'debt' to her. Maybe she wants to tell you why that guy swore he saw her in front of the Three Points at the same time Andrea was killed."

"I guess we'll find out what she has to say tomorrow night. It will be very interesting to meet her in person."

Their food arrived and Val dug into her steak. She hadn't taken time to eat anything today. The two of them hadn't noticed, but Turquoise had never left the restaurant's bar area. She wanted to hear what Valerie and Rome were actually meeting about. She sat close enough so that she could hear their conversation, but on the side of the bar where the two of them couldn't see her.

Rome brought up Christmas to Val.

"By the way, my son asked me if we were having Christmas dinner at your house again this year."

"Of course you all are. I'm finally going to try to get started decorating tomorrow. In fact, since I have extra money from working with Victor, I'm going to order two live trees to go along with my pink tree and a lot of poinsettias and wreaths. It's going to look gorgeous."

"Can you order some for my house, too, and decorations for the front of the building and hallways on the other floors?"

"You know I will, but I think you should ask Turquoise to help you. She doesn't trust you or us."

"You have a good point. I'll ask for her help tonight."

After overhearing that exchange, Turquoise decided she had better head out before they discovered her spying on them. And, even though Val had called her "overzealous," she liked that she suggested to Rome to ask her to help him decorate his building. She had never been that crazy about Christmas, but she would put on a good front. Plus, she was excited about getting another chance to break bread with Victor Dumas. You never know what the future holds. Becoming Mrs. Rome Nyland might save her financially, but taking on the title of Mrs. Victor Dumas was equivalent to Jesus Christ being resurrected from His grave. Her money might be short, but she was definitely getting her hair done, a mani/pedi and a new outfit for tomorrow night's dinner.

She glanced at her watch. It was only eight-thirty. She still had time to pop into Rite-Aid to pick up a few Christmas decorations for her condo. She would impress Rome by already having a wreath on her door and a few other holiday knick-knacks around the house when he arrived later.

Back at the table, Rome and Valerie were digging into their food. In between bites, Val mentioned, "When I spoke to Victor earlier, he told me the first thing he's going to do tomorrow when he gets into town is head straight to his attorney's to look at Andrea's will. It's blowing his mind that she didn't have any money in the bank. I also told him about the Bugatti that burned up last night being registered to Andrea. He said he would try to locate the title for it and inform his insurance company. I can't believe all of the shady stuff she was mixed up in."

"What's going on with you and Victor? You seem to be getting pretty tight very fast."

"I don't know. I never expected someone of his status to be so down-to-earth and kind. I would be lying if I was to tell you that I'm not interested in him. But I've only known the man for two days. What do you think?"

"I think that you are the most beautiful, kindest, generous woman that I've ever met. I must be crazy for not snatching you up myself. You deserve someone like Victor. You know I believe in love at first sight. I saw Davida cheering on the sidelines when I rolled into the end zone after catching the ball when I was nineteen and was with her until last year. I say go for it."

"Are you sure? The man just lost his wife."

"Yes, I'm sure. That marriage was dead a long time before Saturday. I know your track record with men has never been too good, but this is fate. It's time for you to snatch your little bit of happiness and stop worrying about everyone else for a change."

"But, I'm old, Rome. A man like that could snag any of these beautiful young starlets or a gorgeous doctor or lawyer in her twenties or thirties. He's out of my league."

"First of all, you still look like you're in your thirties. And, I've been observing him. He's a pretty grounded guy. The man has billions of dollars, so of course women are going to throw themselves at him every day. But, he had too tough of a time with his wife. He's looking for somebody that also wants to take care of him, not a carbon copy of his wife that's just in it for the money and wants to party all night and spend all day shopping at Louis Vuitton and Chanel."

"Count me out, then. I don't see anything wrong with shopping every day at Louis Vuitton and Chanel."

They both laughed. Before she could say anything else, the waiter was back at their table. "Would either of you care for dessert?"

"She'll have a glass of wine for the road and I'll have the fresh seasonal berries. Then, I'll take the check."

"I can get the check."

"No, we'll expense this one to Victor. If you get him back a necklace that he paid $5 million for that was appraised at ten, he'll owe you a lot more than a measly forty-dollar steak!"

Chapter Twenty-Three

Tuesday Morning

The Streetz of Compton
Where they actin a fool and they carry the tool
Them sick dudes in the streets of Compton
Where I found The Game, he was stackin his change
to maintain in the streets of Compton
—The Game

Without flashing lights or sirens, four unmarked LAPD units slowly made their way past Nickerson Gardens along Compton Avenue. The 1,054-unit public housing apartment complex at 1590 East 114th Street in Compton was the recognized birthplace of the Bounty Hunter Bloods gang. Now the entire area was run by the Bugatti Blades.

In the lead car, Lieutenant Pace signaled to the detectives behind him as they approached the Beer Garden Sports Bar. It was four a.m. The early hour was planned so that they could take the suspects who were inside by surprise.

With helmets, shields and bulletproof vests on, they ran up to the front and back doors, yelling, "Police! We have a warrant! Open up!"

Instead of opening the door, a shot was fired through the window. Pace waved his arm, giving a signal for everyone to move in. They took the battering rams and forced the doors in the front and back of the bar in. Another shot was fired. One of Pace's officers fired back, hitting the shooter twice in the leg. When he fell down, the officer grabbed his gun and continued through the house. Before they could even look for D.O.D. or Pizzazz, the officers sniffed a strong odor of something burning coming from the kitchen. They moved cautiously toward it. Two women were standing over an entire methamphetamine laboratory. One of them pointed a gun at Pace. An officer snuck up behind her. As the action was transpiring, the other woman somehow dropped the glass pot she was cooking in, causing it to explode! Flames immediately shot into the air. She caught on fire. An officer snatched off his jacket, wrapped it around her head, picked her up and ran out of the back door.

"Move it out!" shouted Pace. He grabbed the other girl and bags of dope on the counter and ran out of the door. As they reached the pavement outside, there was a loud explosion that blew out all of the windows in the bar and the floors on top of it. They all dove for cover. Yelling into his radio, Pace exclaimed, "We have a fire at One Hundred Fourteenth and Compton Avenue. We also need several buses."

Never in his wildest imagination did he ever think they were walking into a methamphetamine laboratory. There had to have been over three hundred pounds of meth stacked up in there. Rome was his hero.

At the same time, Lieutenant Pace raided the Bugatti Blades headquarters looking for D.O.D., another group of officers were knocking on the door of a modest house on Rodeo between La Brea and La Cienega. This was the Rodeo at the foot of Baldwin Hills, not the famed street lined with designer stores in Beverly Hills. The telltale red Ferrari was parked right in the driveway.

"Police! Open up! We have a warrant!"

Half asleep, D.O.D. grabbed for his gun and his phone at the same time, and quickly dialed the boss's number.

"What?" barked the voice on the other end of the phone.

"The pigs are at my door," whispered D.O.D.

"That's what you get for letting that dumb bitch have that necklace. You were supposed to hand the necklace over to Dedra. Whatever you do, they had better not get my product or my cash!"

D.O.D. felt the butt of a gun in his face. He looked over on the other side of the bed and saw a gun was also pointed at Pizzazz, who had actually fallen asleep wearing her new necklace. The cop told her to get out of the bed.

"Take off that necklace. We have a warrant to recover it."

The other cop snatched D.O.D. up. He was naked. It didn't matter. He cuffed him and told his partner, "Read them their rights."

The man on the other end of the phone didn't waste any time making another call. Shrieking into the phone, he yelled, "That asshole D.O.D.'s house just got raided! He was supposed to transport that product to Jamaica tomorrow! Now that's not going to happen! I am losing money by the hour! Get some men over there as fast as you can and make sure he and that girl don't make it downtown alive. You had better get my product and my money!"

"I'm on the way, boss. We have bigger problems, though. The bar was infiltrated. The building is on fire. Everything is gone. Amanda and Savoldi have both been taken to the hospital. Amanda was burned and he was shot. And, Yusef and Sheila have been arrested."

The boss couldn't believe what he was hearing. A half-million-dollar-a-week business had gone up in smoke. Dedra was supposed to have taken care of all this.

"Just get over to Rodeo fast!"

The detectives over at D.O.D.'s were busy searching the house. So far they had uncovered twenty bags of heroin, fifteen bags of cocaine, around $15,000 in cash, along with an armory of guns.

A detective held a gun on D.O.D. as he took the handcuffs off him, so he could get dressed. As soon as he laced up his sneakers, he slapped the cuffs right back on him. He was waiting for a female officer to arrive to handle Pizzazz getting dressed.

"I think I found the rest of the jewelry Andrea Dumas was wearing," announced another detective. He walked into the room holding a velvet drawstring bag that held at least a six-carat diamond solitaire ring, a matching band, what looked like an eight-carat cocktail flower ring, diamond studs that had to be at least five carats apiece and a diamond Rolex watch.

The female detective arrived and took Platinum Pizzazz into another room so that she could get dressed. The young girl was in shock. She had no idea that D.O.D. was in the drug business or that her beautiful necklace had been stolen off the body of a rich dead woman. By now Lieutenant Pace had made it from the Compton bust over to Rodeo.

"Let's move them out."

They put both D.O.D. and Pizzazz into the back of a squad car and proceeded down to La Brea, where they turned to head downtown. It was around five-thirty in the morning, so the traffic was still light. A black Yukon Denali pulled up out of nowhere. The car's passengers fired shots into the backseat of the police car, first striking D.O.D. in the neck, then shooting again, hitting Platinum Pizzazz twice in the neck and shoulder. The driver hadn't noticed Pace and his partner in an unmarked car right behind his Denali. Both men quickly shot at the tires of the Denali. The back tires blew out, causing the huge SUV to skid and veer off into the strip mall on the right side of the road. It hit three parked cars before smashing into the front of a McDonald's. Pace and his partner waited until three squad cars surrounded the Denali. All of a sudden both men in the Denali jumped out shooting. Pace's partner shot back, hitting the one guy in the stomach. He went down. The other guy tried to get a shot off, but Pace was too fast for him and shot him in the arm and leg. He dropped the gun and went down. The cops in the other squad cars jumped out, grabbed their guns and cuffed them. As they did, three ambulances showed up. These two guys weren't that bad off. They would definitely survive. However, D.O.D. was dead and Platinum Pizzazz was critically wounded.

The EMS workers got them into the ambulances while two cops rode in each of them, accompanying them to Cedars-Sinai Medical Center.

Chapter Twenty-Four

Seven o'clock the same Morning
Valerie

"This is Gossip On The Go With Your Girl Valerie Ro. Mastro's Steakhouse in Beverly Hills was the place to be last night. The posh eatery was crawling with A-Listers and chicsters. The whole place took a pause when the King and Queen of show biz, Jay-Z and Beyoncé, made their grand entrance. Other chicsters in the house included Magic and Cookie Johnson, and I bumped into Eddie Murphy with his two brothers, Charlie Murphy and Vernon Lynch on my way out the door. This has been Valerie Ro With Gossip On The Go."

The phone rang as soon as Val hung up the phone with WDKX in Rochester, New York. The voice on the other end of the line was whispering.

"It's me. I'm here at work at the hospital. That new female emcee, Platinum Pizzazz, came in here about an hour ago. She's been shot twice and is in critical condition. The guy with her didn't make it. I'll call you later with an update."

The phone disconnected. Val had been on the radio since four a.m. She turned up the sound on the television right away. The report on Platinum Pizzazz wasn't on yet, but the newscaster was saying there had been a shootout between police and suspected gang members in Compton. There was footage on of a burning building. She dialed Rome right away.

Rome and Turquoise were finishing up an intense lovemaking session when the phone rang. In fact, he was still inside of her.

"No, don't answer it," Turquoise begged him.

Rome glanced at the phone and saw it was Val, then slowly pulled out of his woman. "This better be good."

Hearing how husky his voice sounded, Val was positive that she had interrupted Rome and Turquoise in the middle of a morning romp in the sack.

"I don't understand when you became a sex maniac. Listen, Platinum Pizzazz is at Cedars-Sinai with two gunshot wounds. I think D.O.D. may be dead. Nobody knows this yet. And, there's a report on the news that there was a shootout early this morning in Compton between the cops and a gang. They've got at least one fatality there, too."

"When do you go back on the air?"

"Not until ten-thirty, but I have to write tomorrow's radio feeds and call my editors and tell them about Platinum Pizzazz."

"Okay, I'm going to call my man, then head over to the hospital. By the way, just because I didn't spread my body around doesn't mean that I haven't always been a sex maniac. Maybe you should take my lead and get your cobwebs dusted."

"Kiss my ass, Rome. I'll talk to you later."

Turquoise had overheard Rome's entire conversation with Valerie. "Why does she care how much sex you have? I think that fat heifer has the hots for you."

"No, she doesn't. Val is definitely the sister I never had as well as my best friend. And, it's not fair for you to call her names. She is gorgeous!"

"Well, why doesn't she have a man?"

"She made a lot of bad choices. She spent ten years with a boxer who had a lot of other women. She wasted time with another guy who was a restaurateur. Victor likes her, though. Maybe she can finally hook up with the right guy."

Turquoise thought to herself, *Not if I have anything to do with it.* Rome sat up.

"Let me jump into the shower. I need to be at an appointment soon. I'll pick you up around seven for dinner. We're going to Mr. Chow with Victor, his son, Vance, and, Val."

"That sounds very nice. I'll head over to the Beverly Center and get something to wear so I can look nice and sexy for you."

Reaching into his wallet, Rome handed her his Black American Express card.

"Here, have a good time shopping on me. I noticed that you've already started decorating for Christmas. Why don't you just hold on to the card and pick up some Christmas trees, poinsettias and wreaths for my building? I already have lights and ornaments. Do you mind?"

"Thanks, honey. You are too good to me. Of course I don't mind. I'll be glad to get your building decorated. I'll get right on it today."

Exposing herself, Turquoise pulled back the covers on the bed, letting Rome have another glimpse of her goodies. "Are you sure you don't have time for another round?"

"Why not? Since Val says I've become a sex maniac, I might as well act like one. Let me start by putting kisses all over your body."

Royale

Watching television, Royale couldn't believe that his entire building was gone. Thank God he had been smart enough to put the deed in Rolondo's name so that no one could connect him to the Bugatti Blades. Rome Nyland had to have tipped the cops off while investigating Andrea's death for Victor Dumas. He wanted that bastard dead really badly, but it was way too hot out there now to make moves that might draw the authorities' attention to him.

He would have to bide his time. He only had one more day before Rolondo could get his hands on Andrea's millions. He was also supposed to be inheriting her house in Bel Air. He would have to be patient. In the meantime, he still needed to find Roshonda to make sure she hadn't overheard him on the phone last Friday. He would call Turquoise in a little bit to try to find out what Rome was up to.

Rome

When Rome left Turquoise's condominium in Ladera Heights, he headed straight down to police headquarters. He dialed James on his cell phone on the way. The police lieutenant picked up on the first ring. He greeted Rome with, "My man! That was some kind of collar you got me this morning. Thank you. I have all of Victor's wife's jewelry for you. Since it's you, and you gave me the receipts, you can pick it up now. It's a little too pricey to leave in an evidence room."

"I'm on my way there now. I wish you could have gotten a confession out of D.O.D. before your guys had to shoot him, but I'm sure Victor will be happy to get the jewels."

Lieutenant Pace told Rome, "I'll see you when you get here."

Rome hung up from James and dialed Victor.

"Hey, Rome. I was just getting ready to call you. I saw on the news that Platinum Pizzazz has been shot by the police and her companion is dead. Does this have anything to do with Andrea's murder or jewelry?"

"Yes, it does. I'm on my way down to police headquarters to pick up the jewelry now. Unfortunately, the kid D.O.D. is dead and they didn't get a confession for Andrea's murder first."

"That doesn't matter. I can't believe you recovered the jewelry so fast."

"Where are you going to be in about two hours? I'll drop it off to you."

"At my lawyer's office. Why don't you meet me at the Cochran Firm at 4929 Wilshire Boulevard at eleven? Are we all set for dinner tonight? My new daughter-in-law really wants to speak to you and Valerie."

"Yes, Val told me that everything is set up. I'll see you in a couple of hours."

Chapter Twenty-Five

Turquoise

Standing at the counter of Gucci on Rodeo Drive in Beverly Hills, watching the salesgirl bag up her new goodies, Turquoise was admiring her purchases. She was like a kid on Christmas morning. Making good use of Rome's credit card, she had purchased a black silk dress with tulle and puff sleeves for $2,850, a pair of new Hollywood high-heel, open-toe platform sandals for $640 and a bright bit black python clutch for $1,900. She would make a great impression on everyone who laid eyes on her tonight.

As she walked out of the door with her shopping bags, her phone rang. She saw that it was Royale. "Hi, Royale. How are you?"

"Hey, gorgeous. I called your office and your assistant told me you're not in yet, so I thought I would try your cell phone. Anything up yet?"

"Actually, yes. I found two properties that I would like to show you. They're both in the $2 million range."

"That sounds good."

"Would you like to talk about them over dinner?"

"I can't tonight. In fact, I'm not even going in the office until much later today. I have to accompany Rome to an important dinner tonight at Mr. Chow."

"Oh yeah? I was thinking of having dinner there myself tonight."

"We'll be there at seven. Maybe we can all grab a quick cocktail together."

"Maybe we can. Hopefully, I'll run into you tonight. Talk with you later."

"Bye, Royale."

Hanging up from her, Royale could barely contain his glee over getting that little nugget of information. He would scoop up one of his honeys and head to Mr. Chow tonight, do a little ear hustling and beat Rome at his own game. This had been a rough morning. His building was gone. Some of his employees were either dead or in jail. He had to put a hit out on his protégé and then inform his main partner that his nephew was dead. He needed the tide to turn in his favor ASAP.

Victor

At the same time that Royale was plotting against Rome, Victor was meeting with his attorneys at the Cochran Firm. Although the renowned and esteemed Johnnie Cochran had been dead since 2005, his law firm continued to flourish. Overlooking the grand estates of Hancock Park, with the Hollywood Hills and legendary Hollywood sign in the background, the Cochran Firm's victories are unlike any other firm. That was why Victor chose to stay with them.

The front desk rang as he was looking over Andrea's paperwork.

"There's a Mr. Nyland here to see you, Mr. Dumas."

"Please have her escort Mr. Nyland back here."

As soon as Rome walked through the door, Victor introduced him to his attorney.

"This man has to be the fastest and most efficient private investigator in the business. You guys need to hire him to help with some of your cases."

The attractive female attorney smiled at Rome.

"It's a pleasure to meet you, Mr. Nyland. May I have your card? I'll leave you two in here alone so that you can speak in private."

Rome handed her his card.

As soon as she left the room, Rome opened his briefcase and handed the cache of jewelry to Victor. "It's all here. I've never seen anything like this necklace before, or the rings, for that matter."

"Some of it was done by Raju Rasiah of Beverly Hills and some by Lu Willard Jewelry. She's a very beautiful Black jewelry designer in New York."

"Yes, I've heard of her. She's very close to Val. You do realize that Val has really been instrumental in this case. She's not so sure that D.O.D. killed Andrea, so I'm going to keep tracking clues."

"It sounds good to me. I also need you to look into a Rolondo Jemison. Andrea left him $100,000 in an account that had about $300,000 in it. So, she wasn't totally broke. His lawyer contacted the firm today. He already knew this guy was in her will. I need to find out who he is and what he was to my wife."

"No problem. Put that jewelry someplace safe. I'll see you tonight."

"See you tonight and thanks again."

Dedra

Staring blankly at the report on her desk, Dedra didn't know what to do. She knew the right thing to do would be to file an extradition order to bring the girl Platinum Pizzazz to Las Vegas once she was well enough to travel and also charge her for grand theft in this jurisdiction since the jewelry was stolen in town. *How could that D.O.D. be so stupid to keep all of that stuff in his house?*

Her phone rang. "Assistant Deputy Chief Thorne speaking."

The voice on the other end growled, "Your time is up. That bitch has cost me too much money. I want her dead by tomorrow night or you'll be pushing up daisies by Thursday."

The phone went dead.

Dedra knew it was either Val or her. It was going to be hard to say goodbye to one of her oldest friends, but, self-preservation was everything.

Chapter Twenty-Six

Valerie

Walking into Mr. Chow wearing the sequined Karen Kane dress Victor had given her along with the Swarovski crystal Louboutin stilettos, Val was the first person in their party to arrive at the gourmet Asian restaurant. Started in London in 1968 by world famous restaurateur Michael Chow, this outpost opened in 1974. According to the *Los Angeles Times*, "Mr. Chow defies all odds and remains an impossibly chic spot that still draws the rich, famous and well-heeled decades after."

Val's favorite dish here was Ma Mignon. She needed a moment alone to collect her thoughts and reflect upon another terrible day filled with death. Although that D.O.D. character had given her the creeps, she was very sad that he had been killed. This was only Tuesday. Just two days ago, he had been like any other twenty-two-year-old, full of life and looking forward to the future. Who knows? Maybe if the future would have played out differently for him, D.O.D. could have given up the street life and formed a legitimate entertainment company. He would never have that chance now. His life had been snuffed out, like a melted candle. That poor child Platinum Pizzazz was in the hospital clinging to life. And, all over a bauble. Grant it the bauble was worth several fortunes, but not someone's life.

"Your usual glass of Chardonnay, Valerie?" asked the bartender.

"Yes, thank you."

Val took a few steps over to the hostess. "Is our table ready? The rest of my party should be arriving in about twenty minutes."

"We'll be ready for you, Val."

"Hi, Val."

Val turned around and saw her dear friend, La Toya Jackson. They were wearing identical pink mink jackets. They both started laughing.

La Toya hugged Val. "You are so funny. First, you tweet how much you like my jacket, but I didn't expect you to go out and get one."

"No...no...I didn't go out and get one," Val explained, "My client bought me this jacket. And now I know how he knew I loved it so much. He told me his secretary saw our tweets to each other."

Approaching Val and La Toya, Victor assured them, "That is precisely what happened. And, I must say, you both look gorgeous in it. Miss Jackson, you are a lady that I have always wanted to meet. I am a huge fan of yours as well as your entire family."

"Thank you. My condolences on your loss."

Val introduced La Toya's companion.

"Victor, this is Toy's business partner, Jeffré Phillips."

Victor shook Jeffré's hand. "It's a pleasure to meet you."

"It's great to meet you, too."

La Toya hugged Val. "Our table's ready. Take care of the jacket, Val. Let's get together soon."

The two ladies gave each other two air kisses on the cheek.

Vance approached the bar. "Dad, we're here."

This was the first time Val had ever seen Vance up close. He looked like a little boy. Roshonda, who looked stunning in a Louis Vuitton brown and white checkered dress with a matching purse, towered over him.

"I'm Valerie. Hi, Roshonda; we've met before."

Vance kissed Val on the cheek. "It's nice to meet you, Valerie. Ever since my father met you, he's become a real news junkie."

Val smiled. She was saved from having to make a comment by Rome and Turquoise's arrival.

Rome kissed her on the forehead.

"Victor, Val."

"I'm sorry we're running a little late. You must be Vance. Your father has told me a lot about you."

Shaking Rome's hand, Vance told him, "I hope it was all good. This is my wife, Roshonda."

"It's nice to meet both of you. This is my lady, Turquoise."

Dressed head to toe in the Gucci ensemble she had purchased that morning, Turquoise was almost speechless. Not only was she once again in the presence of Victor Dumas, but now she was meeting his famous son as well, not to mention that Roshonda was her favorite reality star. She loved *Diamond in the Rough*.

"Well, we're all here," Val told the hostess. "Let's sit down and eat."

Even though Val now knew that Victor didn't have anything to do with Andrea's murder, she still didn't think it was a good idea for the general public to think he was celebrating anything. Keeping that in mind, she had reserved Mr. Chow's private room upstairs for them.

Platters of food were already on the table when everyone sat down. The head waiter informed everyone, "Since there are six people in your party, Valerie took the liberty of ordering communal-style. So for the first course you have here: chicken satay, Beijing seafood salad and Shanghai cucumbers. The second course dishes are Ma Mignon, which is Valerie's favorite, green prawns, Beijing chicken and scallops tofu. They will also be putting fried rice, chicken fried rice, shrimp fried rice and vegetables on the table. Merlot, chardonnay and champagne will be served, as well as any juice of your choice or water. Bon appétit."

Rome marveled at Val's skills. She never left anything to chance.

"It all looks good to me. I don't know about everyone else, but I am ready to get my grub on."

As the wait staff started pouring the drinks and serving food, Victor informed the group, "I asked Val to get us all together to-night for several reasons. The first one is sadly I lost my wife a few days ago, but I also gained a beautiful daughter-in-law. God never closes any window without opening a door. I also want to thank Val and Rome for such efficient and speedy work. I know you will be able to put closure to my wife's murder as fast as you were able to recover her jewelry."

Motioning to one of his bodyguards, who sat at a nearby table, Victor continued, "So, I have brought a few things for each of you to show my gratitude."

The guard handed him an oversized briefcase. Victor took several boxes out of it.

He handed the first one to Roshonda. "Welcome to the family, my dear. May you always remember Vance's mother when you wear this."

Roshonda opened the box. Inside of it was the $5 million black diamond necklace. She couldn't believe her eyes.

"Thank you, Mr. Dumas. It's breathtaking."

"Please, call me Victor."

Vance put the necklace around his wife's neck.

The next box was from Van Cleef & Arpels.

"For you, Val. Without your work we wouldn't have recovered the jewelry so fast. So, I want to wrap a ribbon of diamonds around your wrist, so you won't forget how much my son and I value your devotion."

Val opened the box to find a huge diamond bracelet in the shape of a bow. She gasped and stared down at it with awe.

"Victor, This is too much. It is exquisite. I love it, but I can't accept this. I was merely doing my job."

Taking her hand, he clasped the bracelet around her wrist.

Victor turned to Rome and Vance.

"Lastly, to the two men at the table; at this point in my life, I can't make it without you. Continue to use your time well."

Rome and Vance both opened their boxes which held Breitling diamond watches.

Rome gave Victor a pound.

"Thanks, man."

"Dad, as always, thanks."

Val held up a glass of champagne. "To Victor, Andrea's memory and to Vance and Roshonda. I know this is a very difficult time. However, I wish you a future filled with sunshine!"

The group started eating, enjoying the sumptuous food.

At the same time that Victor was saying thank you to everyone, Royale had entered the restaurant. After asking the hostess for Rome Nyland's table, she directed him upstairs. Observing the scene unfolding in front of him, he couldn't believe what he was seeing. First, he had hit pay dirt because sitting right before him was Roshonda. Secondly, he had stumbled upon the necklace that the boss wanted. All he could think of was calling some of his crew to rob them of all that bling as soon as they walked out of the restaurant. He knew with all the security that Victor and Vance traveled with, a robbery wouldn't be possible tonight.

Turquoise looked up and saw him standing there. Jealous that she hadn't received anything from Victor, as well as of Valerie's bracelet, she jumped up and hugged him.

"Royale, you said you might be eating here also tonight. Everyone, this is my client, Royale Jones."

Val noticed that Roshonda looked like she had seen a ghost. Rome now knew who blew the whistle on him and told Turquoise about his dinner with Tyler, and Vance glanced at his dad's body-guard with a "watch this guy" look in his eyes.

Royale approached Roshonda.

"Hey, baby. You ran out on me the other night. I've been blowing up your phone trying to reschedule to talk about that job. Your phone keeps going to voicemail."

"Hello, Royale. Let me introduce you to my husband, Vance Dumas. And, this is his father, Victor Dumas. We had a death in the family. I've been dealing with that. I'll call you tomorrow."

Feeling the need to explain how she knew Royale to everyone, Roshonda continued, "Royale is working on a clothing line deal for me."

Royale was still digesting Roshonda's introduction to Vance as her husband.

"Your husband?"

He shook Vance's hand.

"Congratulations. I see you have as much luck with the fine ladies as well as you do riding fast horses. You are one lucky dude."

Royale turned his attention to Victor. "It's an honor for a bud-ding entrepreneur like myself to be in your presence, sir."

Placing himself between Victor and Royale, Rome stood up. "What's up, Royale? Are you stalking me, brother? I haven't seen you in years and now I run into you twice in a few days."

"No, man. I'm just out trying to get a good meal like everybody else."

Val stood up next to Rome, and extended her hand to Royale.

"I'm Valerie Rollins. We've met before, years ago down in Florida. Oh boy, it was at a baseball player's house. I can't think of his name. One of my main girls, Carolyn, was dating him at the time."

"I remember. There is no way I could ever forget a woman as fine as you are."

Val chose to ignore his obvious flirtation. "My friend, Jermonna Bradley, also told me that your talent agency is currently representing her."

Summing Val up from her perfectly coiffed long blonde hair to her stylish outfit, Royale understood why Turquoise was so intimidated by her. She was a little too old and thick for his normal tastes, but he hadn't lied by telling her she was fine. He certainly wouldn't throw her out of his bed. And, there was something about her that made you want to fuck her and confide all of your deepest secrets to her at the same time.

"How is Jermonna doing? I hear she caught a bad break over the weekend."

"The doctors won't let her have contact with anyone while she's detoxing, but I spoke to one of her nurses today and she told me that she's getting better."

Something about this man didn't seem right to Valerie. His features were the same, but she remembered Royale Jones as having a much darker complexion. And that night she met him, his demeanor had been very different. This guy came off like a street hustler instead of a retired professional athlete. She was going to Google him as soon as she got home to see if she could gain some insight into his real story.

Rome spoke up.

"I heard what happened to that kid D.O.D. who we met on Sunday. That's a tragedy. Please give Sweet Lyrics my condolences."

Royale wanted to make sure this group would never know that it was his decision to have D.O.D. killed.

"Thanks, man. I had no idea the young blood was so deep into the street life."

"Are you dining alone, Royale?" Turquoise asked.

"I sure am. I don't know what happened to my date."

"Then, please join us. I don't think anybody would mind. Right, guys?"

Once again, Val noticed how frightened Roshonda looked. This Turquoise had some kind of nerve, but before she could protest, Victor piped in, "Of course, we don't mind. Waiter, please add another chair and place setting."

Once Royale was seated, as the waiter continued to pour wine and champagne, Victor continued his conversation. "As Rome knows, I visited my attorneys today to put my late wife's affairs in order. Vance and Roshonda, you two may have thought your marriage was a secret, but, somehow Andrea knew all about it. Although her bank accounts were just about depleted, she still had two accounts, one with $100,000 in it that she left to someone named Rolondo Jemison. After you left my lawyer's office, Rome, we discovered a new will. Andrea left $1 million in it to you, Roshonda, and to her yet-to-be-born grandchildren. She also left the two of you a letter. Stop by the Cochran office tomorrow, so you can pick up the check and the correspondence."

Taking a bite off her plate, Roshonda cringed. She had never told Vance that she actually knew his mother and that was the reason she drove to Las Vegas to make sure she was okay.

As if she was reading Roshonda's mind, Val told her, "Andrea ran in the same circles as your former mentor, Rebecca Fuqua. The other night, Rebecca told me that you two were married. I'm sure she also told Andrea."

Listening to Val, all Roshonda could think of was that not only did everyone at this table most likely know that she was a former call girl, but, by now, Royale had to have figured out why she ran out on Friday night. She knew he wouldn't think twice about killing her to keep his secret. He might even drop the bomb about how well she knew Andrea. She no longer had an appetite. Putting her fork down, Roshonda suddenly stood up.

"I'm sorry. I don't feel so well. Thank you, Mr. Dumas. I mean, Victor, for the necklace. It's the most beautiful piece of jewelry that I have ever laid eyes on. Vance, can we go home?"

Between his mom's death and Roshonda confiding to him that she had actually heard the shots that may have killed her, Vance was starting to tear up again. Plus, he was still in training for his race. He pushed back from the table.

"That's a good idea, sweetheart. Dad, I'll call you tomorrow. I'm going to stay over at Roshonda's apartment until after the race. Once we get past it, I've decided to look for a house out here so that Roshonda can continue with her career."

Never missing an opportunity, Turquoise immediately dug a card out of her purse and handed it to Vance.

"Please call me. I'm sure Turquoise Hobson Realty can find you a fabulous estate to fit your needs."

At that point Val wanted to strangle Turquoise. She shot Rome a deadly look. Sensing Roshonda needed to get something off of her chest, Val also handed the young woman her card.

"Call me later tonight and let me know how you feel. Also, I'm sure *TMZ* is outside of the restaurant. Although I would love to break the story myself, I'll do Harvey a favor. As you leave, tell his cameras that in the wake of Andrea's murder, Vance does still have some joy in his life. Then, introduce Roshonda to them as Mrs. Vance Dumas."

Vance told her, "We'll do that, Valerie."

Victor spoke up. "Vance, the horses will be here on Thursday. Make sure your staff is ready to meet them."

"I got you, Dad. Good night, everyone."

Royale couldn't believe what he was hearing. Andrea had left Rolondo only a paltry one-hundred g's? That had to be a mistake. And, what about the house in Bel Air?

Rolondo was expecting at least $100 million. *What happened to that will?*

He had to cautiously get some answers. As the waiter passed around the plates of food, he casually remarked, "My condolences on the death of your wife, Mr. Dumas. It's surprising a woman of her means didn't leave more to her family."

"Thank you. I hate to talk about it, but she had a drug problem. I switched the deeds to all of our properties back into solely my name and corporations years ago. Then, last Wednesday, she walked into the office unannounced, informed them that she wanted to change her will, and left that $1 million to Roshonda."

Val and Rome exchanged glances. That guy in Las Vegas had been very persistent about seeing Roshonda driving away from the scene. They both silently realized that it was definitely time to question her. People have murdered for a whole lot less than $1 million. Valerie decided to change the subject.

"Victor, you mentioned your horses are arriving on Thursday for the $750,000 Cash Call Futurity race. Is someone driving them cross country from Kentucky?"

"No, that would be too much wear and tear on them. They're actually coming by FedEx."

His answer caught Val by surprise. "FedEx?"

"Yes, the horses are loaded into specialized jet stalls, which look like the horse trailers you see driving down a road, but are designed for air travel. Two horses go into each stall, which is then loaded on a palette and onto the prescribed upper deck of a FedEx cargo plane. They have hay and water and someone stays with them the whole time to make sure they have everything they need.

And, the horses are accompanied by a veterinarian and groomers who know the animals well."

Rome was impressed.

"That's amazing," he commented. "And, you have three horses coming, right?"

"Actually, there will be six horses arriving. Wildin' Out, Très Jolie and Full Spectrum, who are running, along with their lead horses. I may have to hire some extra help here, though. My guy who normally coordinates all of the racing activities for me, Claude, is still missing."

Royale flinched at the mention of Claude's name. Deciding to come here tonight had been a good decision. Listening to everyone's conversation, he had formed Plan B. Even though that bitch Andrea had outsmarted his crew from her grave, he had just figured out another way to get $100 million out of her husband. He also had to get a handle on this Roshonda situation. Why hadn't he known that she was married to Vance Dumas? Now, he was positive that she had overheard him talking about Andrea on the phone, and that's why she had taken off so fast. He was going to have to hang around her apartment building to catch her when she was on her way to work to find out. The boss wasn't going to like any of this. But this Turquoise was sure coming in handy.

The waiter was back at the table. "Does anyone need anything else?"

There were still platters filled with food left on the table.

Turquoise sighed.

"I am stuffed. I have to watch my size six figure, but I'm sure Valerie has room for more. She doesn't seem to be on a diet."

Victor spoke up.

"I don't see anything wrong with Val's weight."

Smiling gratefully at Victor for coming to her defense while ignoring Turquoise's dig about her weight, Val asked, "Does anyone want to take any of this food home? I would love the Ma Mignon and some fried rice to go."

Rome didn't hesitate.

"I'll take whatever's left to go. It will save me from having to make lunch tomorrow. And, I will invite the guys downstairs up to have the rest."

The bus boys started clearing the table as the waiter asked if he should put out a dessert tray.

Everyone shook their heads. They were full.

Victor took his credit card out of his wallet.

"I'll take the check."

The waiter refused the card. "That won't be necessary. Valerie already took care of the check. Your takeout bags will be by the door. Thank you."

Valerie just continued to take Victor by surprise. He scolded her.

"Val, you shouldn't have done that."

Rome agreed with him.

"No, you shouldn't have."

Val held up her wrist to show off her new bracelet.

"Believe me. I was more than happy to do it. It's fine."

Always plotting, Royale was thinking it wouldn't be a bad idea to get close to Valerie. "Thank you, Valerie. I didn't mean to intrude upon you nice people tonight, but dinner was delicious. Turquoise, I'll look forward to your call tomorrow."

"You'll be hearing from me first thing in the morning. I have two houses to show you that I know you are going to love. It will be hard to choose which one you'll want to make your home."

Royale told everyone good night, then left.

Victor suddenly had an idea.

"Turquoise, expect a call from my assistant, Charmion, tomorrow.

I'd like to buy my son and daughter-in-law a house as a wedding gift."

"Thank you, Victor."

Val stood up.

"I'm going to step across the hall to the ladies room. I'll meet you all downstairs.

When she got down there, Victor was waiting for her with her mink jacket. "I didn't want to ask you this in front of the others. Can you join me for a nightcap at the Polo Lounge? I have one more thing I need to discuss with you."

"No problem. I'll meet you there."

"Why don't we let your driver go for the night? You can ride with me and then I'll take you home. Rome and Turquoise just left. He said to tell you he'll call you later."

What was that about? Rome had never left anyplace before without telling her goodbye.

"Okay, did Rome say where he was going?"

"No, but I'm sure you'll hear from him soon. Come on. My driver's out front."

Val told the hostess "good night" on the way out, then picked up her take-out. Victor opened the door to his white Rolls-Royce for Val, then spoke to Dwayne, who was in her car behind them. He then got in next to Val.

"Okay, Andre, take us to the Beverly Hills Hotel."

"I needed to talk to you alone, but I also have one more present for you that I didn't want to give you in front of the others."

"Victor, I don't need any more gifts. I'm riding around in a chauffeur-driven Bentley SUV, I'm wearing this beautiful bracelet. You're paying me more money than I've ever earned for such a short period of work in my life. I am fine."

"Yes, you are. And that is why I want you to have this. I noticed the flower ring that you wear. When Rome brought me Andrea's jewelry today, I thought this flower would look nice on your other hand. Plus, Rome told me you were a big fan of her modeling career. Take this to remember her by. You may be the only person aside from me that even remembers she once lived a positive life. It would be an honor to her memory for you to wear this ring."

He reached for Val's hand and placed the largest diamond flower she had ever seen on her middle finger that was bare. It fit perfectly.

"Don't say a word. In fact, if you want all of her jewelry, you can have it. Over the years I've given my assistant and the girls who work in my various businesses such an abundance of jewelry and designer bags that I'm sure they're not interested in any of it. The same goes for her family. They told me in Las Vegas that they didn't want anything. Far too many bad memories came with it."

Tears formed in Val's eyes. She loved diamonds, and actually had a nice collection. But, there had been periods in her life between pay checks over the years that she had to pawn her jewelry in order to survive. More often that not, she could never afford to redeem the pawn tickets. So, she lost the jewelry.

"Thank you. I may never take this ring or my new bracelet off."

The Rolls pulled into the driveway of the Beverly Hills Hotel.

Chapter Twenty-Seven

Vance and Roshonda

Just as Val had predicted, as Vance and Roshonda walked out of Mr. Chow, the waiting paparazzi descended upon them. They stopped and posed. Then, taking Val's advice, Vance spoke directly to *TMZ*'s cameras.

"As you know, with my mother having been murdered just a few days ago, this is a very difficult time for me. I am grateful to have my wife of one year, Roshonda Rhodes, by my side to help me get through this. Thank you for all of your outpouring of love and sympathy."

Before they could ask him another question, Vance pushed Roshonda into the waiting limousine.

Roshonda was still in a tizzy.

"Vance, I'm sorry to run out on your dad like that, especially since he gave me this exquisite necklace, but I couldn't sit there and eat with Royale. I know he knows that I overheard him talking about your mother. I don't want to go straight home. Can we stop at the Polo Lounge for a nightcap?"

"No problem. Driver, can you take us to the Beverly Hills Hotel, please?"

Vance pulled Roshonda close to him.

"Listen, you are going to have to tell my dad and Rome about that tomorrow. If we wait any longer, they may start suspecting you of killing Mom."

"I'm scared to go home. I'm sure Royale is staking out my building."

They headed into the Polo Lounge and were escorted to a booth. Vance looked around him as they were seated.

"I'll tell you what. When we finish, I'll get us a bungalow here. I can have someone go to your apartment and get my luggage as well as pack a bag for you. I'll have them go in and out the back way so no one will see them. Stop worrying."

"Well, that was certainly a speedy recovery."

Vance and Roshonda looked up to see Victor and Valerie standing at their table.

The first thing Vance noticed was that Valerie was wearing his mother's flower diamond ring on the same hand as the $300,000 bracelet that his father had just given her. *What was going on with these two?* His father never went anywhere and now he was at two places in one night. Vance hated it took his mother being murdered to get his father to move on. But it was about time. Maybe the old man was getting some pussy from Valerie.

"Dad, Valerie. What are you two doing here?"

Easing into the booth with them, Victor told his son, "We could ask you the same thing. Do you mind if we join you?"

"Please do."

"It's my fault. I wasn't really sick. That Royale gives me the creeps," Roshonda admitted.

Val told her, "I noticed how you tensed up when you saw him. "What was up with that?"

Vance decided to tell them what was going on.

"Actually, Roshonda has something she needs to get off her chest about Royale and Mom's murder."

Val stopped him from going any further.

"Before you start, let me call Rome. He needs to hear whatever you have to say."

She took out her cell phone and immediately punched him up. "What's up?"

"First of all, why did you leave without saying goodnight?"

"Your boyfriend told me to. And, I do work for the man."

Val ignored his snide reference to Victor as her "boyfriend."

"Where are you? Victor and I are in the Polo Lounge with Vance and Roshonda. She wants to tell us some things about Royale. I need you to come over here."

"I'm actually still in Beverly Hills. Turquoise wanted me to drop her off at her office instead of at home since she wasn't there long today. She wanted to go through some listings and prepare for an open house that she's having tomorrow. She told me that she'd take a cab home. I'll be there in five minutes."

"All righty-dighty. See you when you get here."

"He's only over on North Canon. He should be here shortly."

"Dessert and coffee for anyone?" asked the waiter. Val had been so busy digesting all that went on at the table at Mr. Chow, that she had barely touched her wine.

"I'll have a glass of chardonnay."

Vance told him, "I'll take the warm milk chocolate bread pudding, please."

Roshonda decided to join her husband and also order dessert. "The raspberry sorbet sounds good."

"And, I'll have the same bread pudding that my son is having, along with a brandy."

True to his word, Rome walked in five minutes later just as Val and Victor's drinks were being served.

"I'm not going to even ask how you all ended up here, but hit me with whatever you've got." He motioned for the waiter to come over.

"I'd like a cup of herbal tea, please."

Val spoke up first. "Roshonda, before you get started, I think you should know that an eyewitness swears he saw you driving away from the Three Points Sports Bar in Las Vegas between Friday night and Saturday morning, around the same time that Andrea was killed."

"That is true. I was there. But, then I heard shots. So I drove off."

"What were you doing there?" asked Rome.

"I actually have known Royale for about three years. I'm not proud of my background, but since Vance knows what I used to do and Valerie has made it clear tonight that she is also aware, I may as well be honest. I used to turn tricks for him behind Rebecca's back. I mean, he was a big baseball player. Like me, though, now he seemed to have gone legit. I ran into him a few weeks ago at Greystone Manor in Hollywood. He told me he was so proud of me and *Diamond in the Rough*. He said he was sure that he could get me some endorsements. But, when I got to his so-called office and saw that it was really a hotel suite, I knew he was up to no good. Then, I overheard him say he was about to make a huge score with the billionairess Andrea Dumas. He gave whomever he was talking to the Three Points address in Las Vegas and informed them that Andrea would be there about two in the morning. I tried to call Vance, but I couldn't reach him. I chose to hightail it out of Royale's hotel suite. I then hopped into my car and drove straight to Las Vegas."

She broke down crying.

Val wasn't finished with her questions.

"Rebecca told me your marriage to Vance was a secret. Why did you feel you had to go to a location that Andrea was supposed to be at?"

By now Roshonda was sobbing.

"I don't know. I wanted to protect her since she was Vance's mother. But, when I pulled into the parking lot and heard the shots fired, I panicked and drove back to L.A. I swear I didn't have anything to do with her death."

Vance put his arm around his wife.

"Royale is also now ruled out as the murderer. If what you're saying is true, he was still here in Los Angeles during the time frame the murder occurred. He also told you at Mr. Chow right in front of all of us, that you ran out on him the other night," Val reasoned.

Rome spoke up.

"I hate to say this, but, I'm still going to need you to go down to the police station with me tomorrow and give your story to the lieutenant. I'm sorry, Victor and Vance, but with that mysterious windfall of $1 million that Andrea left Roshonda without ever meeting her, she is looking like our prime suspect."

Valerie interjected, "It's not exactly cut and dry. I still believe that Royale and the Bugatti Blades are involved in Andrea's murder somehow. But your past connection to him makes it look like you could have all been in this together. I'm sorry, honey."

Rome turned to Victor.

"You'll need to get an attorney to come with us to represent Roshonda in the morning."

Vance told Rome, "I'll take care of the attorney's fees. She's my wife and I know she didn't kill my mother."

Victor couldn't believe what he was hearing. Had this woman who his son had married with no prenuptial agreement just said she used to "turn tricks for Royale," a man he had sat down to dinner with?

On top of that, Val and Rome obviously believed she may have killed Andrea. He had also been quite surprised and wondered why and how Andrea left $1 million to a woman she had never met. *How had he allowed this to happen to Vance?*

His son was just like him, a fool, who fell for a beautiful face and knock-out body. By him staying married to Andrea, Vance had no idea what a real relationship with a woman consisted of. Before he could stop himself, Victor started choking on his brandy.

Val yelled, "Victor, are you all right?"

He kept choking and couldn't breathe. Val immediately stood him up and raised his arms over his head. He was still choking. By now everyone in the restaurant was watching. Rome pushed Val out of the way, placed his arms through Victor's and did a Heimlich maneuver. The brandy spouted out of his mouth. Victor collapsed back down in the booth with a sigh of relief. Val handed him a glass of water.

"Sip this slowly."

Vance was scared out of his wits. "Dad, are you okay?"

"Yes, son. These last few days have been a little too dramatic for me. I think it's time for me to head home."

Valerie thought that was the best thing she had heard him say all night. "Why don't you try to get some rest tomorrow? You haven't stopped to take any time for yourself since you found out Andrea was dead. A day in bed isn't going to kill you."

"I think you might be right. If you're ready, I'll take you home."

"If you don't mind," Rome told him, "I'd like to take Val home. I have a few more things I need to run by her."

"No problem."

With his father looking ill, Vance decided that he and Roshonda should accompany Victor home. "Dad, I would feel a lot better if we stayed with you tonight. That way I'll know that you're okay and I can watch out for Roshonda at the same time."

Victor didn't really want Roshonda under his roof and would have liked to snatch Andrea's necklace off her neck, but told him, "Fine."

He turned to Val and Rome. "I'll talk to you both in the morning."

Val kissed Victor on the cheek. "Can you have your driver bring the bags I left in the car in to the concierge? Call me if you need to talk tonight. Thank you for the beautiful gifts. I'll be home soon."

The Dumas Family walked slowly out of the Polo Lounge. Without even asking, the waiter brought Val another glass of wine.

"Thank you."

"What do you think?" Rome asked. "By the way, that's a nice ring."

"We'll talk about the ring later. If Roshonda didn't kill Andrea, I'm willing to bet that she knows who did. I'm also not buying the story that she and Andrea never met. From what I've heard about Andrea, she was anything but charitable. I don't think she would have changed her will suddenly to prepare for her unborn grandchildren. Both Rebecca and Victor told me that she never gave a damn about Vance."

"Plus, Vance is a millionaire many times over in his own right. There was no need for Andrea to give her any money."

Val drained the last of her wineglass. "I need to get home. It's almost midnight, which is almost three in the morning on the East Coast and I start my first radio report at seven-twenty East Coast Time. Let's pick this conversation up tomorrow."

Chapter Twenty-Eight

Turquoise

She didn't want to let Rome know her real reason for wanting to stop by the office. The property that she previously sold to Royale had been on Turquoise's mind ever since she saw reports on the morning news that a building in the same block had exploded during a police drug bust. She needed to check her records to see if it was Royale's building. Then, when Victor mentioned the name Rolondo Jemison during dinner, she was almost positive that was the name Royale had the deed to the building put in. She needed to check the files for 2011.

The deed to the building was also on Royale's mind. After listening to Victor, it was only a matter of time before Turquoise would put two and two together and realize that Rolondo owned the building. So, he decided to break into her office and steal whatever records she had of the sale. The minute he pulled up in front of her office, he spotted the lights on. His sixth sense told him she was way ahead of him and was searching for the files. He didn't want to kill her. But, he was going to have to find a way to stop her from telling Rome. The boss thought they should lay low on the Bugattis until it cooled down in the streets, so he was driving a bright red 2014 Chevrolet Corvette. Royale got out of the car. Surprisingly, the door to Turquoise's office was open.

"Turquoise," he called out, "Are you here?"

Damn. It was Royale. She could have sworn she had locked the door. She located the file that she was looking for, but didn't dare take it out of the file cabinet. Instead, she grabbed a gun that she kept in the cabinet and slipped it into her briefcase.

"I'm back here. I'll be right out."

She headed out into her reception area. "Royale, it's almost midnight. What are you doing here?"

"I was passing by and saw your lights on. I didn't know you worked this late."

"I had to prepare for an open house first thing in the morning," Turquoise lied.

"Cut the crap. The moment the billion-dollar man mentioned the name Rolondo Jemison, you remembered that's the name on the deed to my building."

"According to the news, that building no longer exists."

Royale moved so close to Turquoise that there lips were almost touching. "My question to you is are you going to tell your boyfriend?"

Looking at him, all Turquoise could think about was how fine Royale was. Maybe all baseball players favored each other. He looked a lot like Halle Berry's first husband, David Justice. She could feel herself getting wet. The action in her life had certainly picked up. A football player, a baseball player, a top jockey and a billionaire. Her life was raining successful men! "If I don't, what's in it for me?"

Royale thrust his tongue into her mouth and French-kissed her hard. Turquoise kissed him back. Coming up for air, he told her, "We're both adults. I'm sure we can work something out. I already told you, if you were my woman, you'd be wearing a huge rock on your finger to match the necklace and watch."

He locked the door behind them, leaned Turquoise back on the receptionist's desk and lifted up her dress over her head. She wore no bra. Pulling her panties down with his teeth, he slowly fingered her vagina, then ran his tongue slowly up her stomach until it reached her breasts. Gently caressing one nipple with his hand, he began to suck the other one. Turquoise started to moan. She very cautiously touched his penis, unzipping his pants. Not missing a beat, Royale used his free hand to pull his pants down. He wore no underwear.

Turquoise slowly stroked his rock-hard penis, then cooed, "Please put this in me."

"I got you, baby," Royale whispered, licking her ear. He entered her gently, then began to ride her hard, in and out, in and out, until she screamed out in ecstasy, and he came like a waterfall, emptying out into a lake.

Royale eased up off of her and looked her in the eye. "I own this pussy now."

Turquoise coyly looked up at him. "Rome who?"

Heading into the bathroom in her office to wash up, Turquoise told Royale there was a second bathroom in the hallway. When she came out, she fixed him a cognac from the bar she kept in the office to celebrate closings. Clients loved that special touch.

Realizing that a man like Royale was no one to play with, Turquoise asked him, "So, what now? Rome would get very suspicious if I upped and left him. I'm also supposed to start looking for a house for Vance and Roshonda tomorrow."

Royale made a true pimp move. "I don't want you to leave him. I want to know his and Valerie's every move. You do this for me, baby, and, I'll make sure you stay nice and healthy."

Shivering at his thinly veiled threat, Turquoise nodded her head. "Okay, I'm out. I'll see you tomorrow."

He gave her a long kiss again, squeezed one of her nipples, then headed out the door. Confused, Turquoise didn't know whether she should be ashamed of herself for cheating on a wonderful guy like Rome or flattered that, at forty she had two retired athletes lusting after her. Turquoise decided to choose the latter. Rome was probably fucking Valerie on the sly anyway. Those two were far too close not to be intimate. She picked up her phone to call a cab to finally head home. There was a knock on the front door.

"Did you forget something?"

Rome strutted through the door.

"Only you. I had to drop Val off in Hollywood. You didn't answer your cell phone, so I dropped by here to see if you were all right and still needed a lift home. Who did you think I was?"

"Sylvia. I called her and told her to come back to the office so we could go over some last-minute plans for tomorrow's open house. Why were you with Val? Victor told us that he was going to see her home."

"She called me after I left here and asked me to meet them at the Polo Lounge. Roshonda had some information for me. Then, Victor wasn't feeling well, so I took Val home. Listen, babe, I know you can use all the sales you can get right now, but I think you need to steer clear of Royale. The man's not to be trusted and is dangerous. He's nothing more than a common pimp."

"You really think that? He seems harmless to me."

"He is anything but harmless. Give me the price of the house you're planning to show him, and, I'll give you whatever commission you were going to earn. It's late. Let's get you home."

Chapter Twenty-Nine

V al couldn't believe it was already the fourth of December and she didn't have one Christmas decoration up. All this drama surrounding Andrea Dumas's death, coupled with now doing public relations work for Victor, as well as her regular work load, had totally slowed her down. She hadn't even had a chance to go shopping and spend some of her newfound wealth. She dug into the closet to pull her decorations out. She had an hour and a half break before she had to get back on the radio. She pulled her pink tree out of the box. The tree was her pride and joy. She had seen a pink Christmas tree in a store window in Harlem while visiting there a few years ago, and fell in love with it. Pink was her favorite color. But, when she went back to get it, they had sold out. One of her dearest friends, Helen Shelton, had found one online for her. Val loved it. As she dragged it into the dining room to set it up, the doorbell rang. It was only nine-thirty in the morning.

Val looked through the peephole. Dedra was standing on her porch. She unlocked and opened the door right away.

"Dee Dee, what are you doing here?" Val gave her soror a big hug. "Why didn't you call me and tell me you were in town?"

"I decided to drive in last minute. I have a few things to talk to you about that I thought would be better said in person."

"Okay, sit down. Can I get you some cranberry juice or tea?

The only coffee I have is instant. Have you had breakfast yet? I can order something in."

"It's been a rough morning." Glancing at Val's bar, Dedra pointed to a bottle of bourbon. "I'll have a Jack and Coke."

Val thought it was a bit early to start drinking. But, she was a gracious hostess. "Hey, I suppose it is cocktail hour in Paris. Your wish is my command. Let me go get you a glass, some ice, and a bottle of Coke."

While working from home during the day, Val always carried her cell phone around with her from room-to-room. Back in the kitchen, she sent a text to Rome:

Dee Dee here acting weird. Come over.

She returned to the living room to find Dee Dee doing lines of cocaine on her coffee table. She was taking sips from the bottle of Jack Daniel's in between.

"What are you doing?"

"Some of the finest cocaine around. I told you I wanted Jack and Coke."

"Dee Dee, what's going on?"

"Oh, loosen up, Val. I've been doing blow since we were in school. But, I guess your little goodie two shoes ass wouldn't know that. As I remember, you never even smoked a joint. Well, you don't know what you're missing."

"Stop it, Dee Dee."

Dedra mocked her. "Stop it, Dee Dee. No. You need to stop it, Val. Why can't you be satisfied with simply being a gossip columnist?"

"What do you mean?"

"What I mean is you and that fool, Rome, live your lives like you're in some kind of seventies blaxploitation movie. He thinks he's *Shaft* and you think you're *Foxy Brown*, *Cleopatra Jones* and *Get Christie Love* all rolled into one."

"Oh, come on, Dee Dee, you know that's not true."

Dedra did the last line of cocaine that she had. She had been snorting it all morning. She was high as hell, as well as horny. She stared at Val's size forty-two triple-D breasts.

"Why don't we have a little bit of quick fun since I'm here? I'm feeling very sexy and horny, and you never age. You still look so beautiful."

Swallowing another gulp of whiskey, Dedra reached out her hand and touched Val's breast. Since it was early and she was at home, Val wasn't wearing a bra under her cashmere sweatshirt.

Dedra's eyes got big. "Oh, shit. I've wanted to suck these big titties from the minute I laid eyes on you freshman year in the dorm. My chance has finally come."

She pulled up Val's top and put her mouth on Val's nipple. Val pushed her away. "Dee Dee, have you gone completely crazy?"

Dedra reached into her pocket and pointed a gun at Val. "No, I'm perfectly sane. But I'm sick and tired of you getting in my way. I had to kill Amir, whose real name was George, by the way. Then, I had to get rid of that dumb bitch, Evelyn, for running off her mouth to Rome. Even my boy D.O.D. was killed because you are in my way. It's over. Now, I'm going to kill you."

"Come on, Dee Dee. Put the gun down. We can talk about this. We've been friends for over thirty years. I'm sure we can work this out."

"No, we can't. It's too late to work anything out. The boss wants you dead. It's either you or me."

"What boss are you talking about? Did you kill Andrea, too?"

"Not that it makes a difference since you won't live to talk about it, but no, I did not kill Andrea. I don't know who killed that ho. She owed millions of dollars to the big boys, including real Italians, who live in Italy, so it could have been any number of people."

"But, Dee Dee, why are you doing all of this?"

"For the money, you stupid bitch. You're the only person I know who doesn't care about having a big bank account. "

Dedra didn't hear Rome quietly enter the room and take up position behind her. "Drop your gun, Dedra."

Dedra spun around to face him. "Oh, it's the great Black Hope. I'm not surprised at your ass showing up trying to save Val. All the rumors must be true. Maybe she's been giving you all the loving I've been longing for all these years. You drop your gun or I'll kill your girl right here."

From the back of the house, Dwayne came up behind Val.

"Drop the gun, Miss. We can all sit down and talk about this. No one has to get hurt."

Rome had called the police the moment he received Val's text.

The sound of sirens approaching the house suddenly filled the room.

"It's over, Dedra," Rome told her. "You know you don't want to really hurt Val."

Tears were now streaming down Dedra's face.

"No, I don't."

In one swift move, she brought the gun up to her temple, then pulled the trigger.

"No, Dee Dee!" Val screamed. She tried to reach her, but Dwayne held her back.

The police came rushing through the door as soon as they heard the gunshots. Rome grabbed Val in his arms as a cop knelt down, took Dedra's gun out of her hand and checked her neck for a pulse. He looked up at Rome, Val and Dwayne.

"She's gone."

Val collapsed on the floor next to Dedra's body. She continued to cry hysterically, "Dee Dee!"

Several paramedics entered Val's living room. As they lifted Dedra's head, part of her brain came pouring out in a fountain of blood. Val screamed again.

Rome pulled her off of the floor.

"Come on, Val; let me take you to your bedroom."

Val fell back to her knees in front of Dedra's body, still wailing at the top of her lungs. She refused to budge. Rome realized that Val never took any sedatives, so there were none in the house. He turned to the paramedic.

"Miss Rollins needs to be checked out, too. Can you give her something to help calm her down?"

Before the paramedic could answer, Val screamed, "No, I don't want anything!"

At that point James Pace walked into the house. Rome had also immediately telephoned him to explain the situation. As a fellow police officer, he had hoped to get there in time to reason with Dedra. He had also wanted to discuss the jewelry theft since it had taken place in Las Vegas. He was shocked to see Dedra lying dead on Val's floor with her gun still in her hand.

He took one look at the distraught Valerie.

"Okay, men. Let's move the body out of here now."

As Valerie's address was broadcast on police monitors in newsrooms around the city, with a bulletin that there was a hostage situation and gunshots fired there, her colleagues all rushed to her house. There were now television crews from every network as well as radio and print reporters stationed out in front. Her colleagues from the tabloids like Pat Shipp from the *National Enquirer* and Kevin Frazier from *OMG: The Insider* were also there, as well as Lee Bailey from *EUR Web*, Lisa Collins, the publisher of *LA Focus*, and reporters from *TMZ*.

Traveling with no security in a burgundy Cadillac Escalade,

Victor came to a screeching halt in front of Val's house. He jumped out and ducked under the yellow police tape that now surrounded her lawn. Not dressed in one of his usual tailor-made suits, Victor was incognito, wearing a black Sean John sweat suit and Gucci sneakers.

As reporters yelled his name, a police officer stopped him.

"You can't go inside the house."

Victor didn't care what the officer told him.

"The hell I can't. One of my employees called me and told me to come over here and Miss Rollins also works for me."

The front door opened and the EMS workers pushed the body bag on a stretcher through the door. Rome saw Victor standing in front. He waved to the officer.

"Let Mr. Dumas in."

At the sight of the body bag being carried out of Val's house, Victor and the rest of the crowd outside didn't know what to think. *Was Valerie dead?*

"Who is that?" he asked the paramedics. They ignored him and loaded the body into the ambulance. Victor rushed inside. To his relief, Val was alive and well, sitting in a chair, cradling her cat and weeping. He knelt down beside her and put his arms around her. She put her head on his shoulder and kept crying.

Victor looked at Rome and Dwayne. "What happened here?"

Rome shook his head. "Dedra came here to kill Val, but shot herself instead."

A cell phone on the floor rang. James picked it up. "Hello."

"Who is this? I'm looking for Dedra."

"This is Lieutenant James Pace of the LAPD. Who am I speaking with?"

The phone went dead.

Rome wanted Val to leave her house.

"Victor, I want to take Val over to my house until we can get this living room cleaned up. Can you help me get her out of here?"

Val looked at him.

"Stop talking about me like I'm not sitting here, Rome. I don't want to go anywhere. I can't go way downtown to your house."

Victor touched her cheek.

"Then how about you come to my house? I have a full staff there. They can take care of you. Just come for today. We need to get you out of here for now so the police can do their job."

Val sounded like a little girl. "I have to bring Lucky. She's scared."

"I have four entire guest suites and a guesthouse out back. There's room for Lucky. Come on; let's go."

Val reluctantly got up. "I need to put on some real clothes and get my purse. I can still see Dee Dee standing there pointing that gun at me."

When she left the room holding the cat, James spoke. "Here's the deal. I'm going to call Deputy Thorne's superiors in Las Vegas and tell them what happened. I have to turn her phone over to them. As soon as they inform her next of kin of her death, then we can release the details to the media."

Val came out with Lucky in her pet carrier, catching the tail end of James's sentence. "I don't have a number for Dee Dee's mom or brother. They should be in her phone, though. They live in Tulsa, Oklahoma."

She turned to Rome. "I need to take my laptop with me. I have to send out an email to my stations and let them know there won't be a feed for tomorrow."

"Okay, I'll go in your office and get it for you. But, when you get to Victor's, I want you to rest. We've been dealing with unexpected death due to gunfire since Saturday. All of this would be hard to take, even for the most seasoned soldier stationed in the Middle East."

"Mr. Dumas and Valerie, we haven't formally met. I'm Rome's friend, James Pace. Do you want to speak to the reporters out there when you walk out?"

Val nodded her head.

"I am one of them. I'll make a quick statement."

Rome came out with her laptop. "All right. Let's get Val out of here."

It seemed like hundreds of flashbulbs exploded in their faces as they walked out. When they saw Val, everyone started clapping and cheering that she was alive. The KTLA reporter stepped right up to Valerie and hugged her.

"As you can see, we are all grateful that wasn't you, Val, who came out of here in a body bag. We love you. Can you tell us who it was and what happened?"

"I can only say that someone I thought I knew very well threatened to kill me this morning, but took her own life instead."

With those words Val collapsed against Rome. Holding her up, he, Victor and Dwayne, rushed her to Victor's truck.

"Rome, follow my car to Victor's house," Dwayne said.

The three trucks sped away.

Chapter Thirty

The Boss

Damn! Damn! Damn! If Dedra's phone was in the hands of a cop, that meant she had either been arrested or was dead. He was going to have to get a new, clean cell phone right away. His phone rang.

It was Royale.

"Man, what's going on? Some fucking cop answered Dedra's phone."

"Val Rollins was on the news. She said someone who she thought she knew tried to kill her, but killed themself instead. It had to be Dedra."

"Where was this report done?"

"In front of Val's house. She had Rome and Victor Dumas on either side of her, and a lot of cops behind them. Then they got into an Escalade and left."

"This is not good. Our lawyer called me this morning and backed up the story you heard last night about Andrea's new will. He also says that all Rolondo is getting is $100,000. I told him to have them send it to Rolondo and gave them a post office box number. You are going to have to get that necklace from Roshonda. I don't care if you have to kill her to do it. With the meth lab gone, we are down at least $300,000 a week in income. Your guys also didn't get the product D.O.D. was taking to Jamaica. We need millions fast for the Italians."

"We can get it. I have a plan to get at least $100 million out of Victor Dumas."

"I'm listening."

"His horses will be at the FedEx hangar tomorrow at LAX. They're coming in for the big race at Hollywood Park on the fifteenth. All we have to do is snatch Wildin' Out and some filly named Très Jolie. Dumas ought to cough up money real quick for them."

"It sounds good, but where would you take them?"

"I've already found a small horse farm down in Temecula, about eighty-nine miles from here, that boards horses. I spoke to them and I can hire them to meet me at LAX tomorrow. I told them I worked for Vance Dumas. I have it all figured out. I need to detain Vance and his people so we can get in and out with the horses before they get there. I have this new bitch that I'm pretty sure can help me with that."

"Okay, also put some pressure on Roshonda. Send her a text and explain to her that unless she gives up that necklace, you'll tell her hubby and daddy-in-law about that little sex tape that she and Andrea made, and that she and Andrea have been eating each other's pussies for years and that's why she left her $1 million."

"I got you. I'll check back in with you when I have the horses and the necklace."

Valerie

All three cars pulled up around Victor's circular driveway on Stratford Court in Bel Air. Dwayne opened the door of Victor's truck for Valerie. She suddenly realized that Victor was driving himself with no security following him. She also noticed his casual attire. He must have left here in some hurry.

She told him, "Thank you for coming to see about me. I didn't think you ever drove around alone and not dressed up."

"No problem. I was actually getting ready to work out when Dwayne called and told me you were in trouble. It's often a lot faster when I move around alone."

They stepped into his foyer. Val had been in many fine homes including Neverland when Michael Jackson was alive, but Victor's house was magnificent. The floor and walls of the foyer were all matching marble. As they walked in, they heard live classical music coming from a piano.

"Who's that playing the piano so beautifully?" Val asked.

Victor shook his head.

"I don't know. Let's find out."

The group followed the sound of the music into the first room on the right. There, amongst beautiful red and gold furniture, with matching drapes, was Roshonda sitting on the piano bench playing her heart out. When she saw them standing there, she stopped.

"Oh, hello. Rome, are you here to take me to the police station now? Vance is in the library with the attorney. I'll let them know that you're here."

With Val's life suddenly being in jeopardy, Rome had forgotten all about his appointment with Roshonda. Plus, Jim was still back at Val's house. Their meeting would have to wait.

"No, Val was almost killed this morning. My friend, the lieutenant, is occupied with that investigation right now. We'll have to postpone your meeting with him until tomorrow or maybe even Friday."

Val told Roshonda, "You play the piano beautifully."

"Thank you."

Roshonda knew she should ask under what circumstances Val

was almost killed and if she was all right, but the truth was, she really didn't care. She was grateful the heat was off of her for a minute.

Instead, she told everyone, "I'll go tell Vance that the appointment's off for today."

Victor reached for Val's arm.

"Let's get you and Lucky upstairs."

"I'm sorry, Victor; I'm not myself. She's going to need a litter box and some cat food, even if we're just here for the day."

"Stop worrying. We'll take care of everything. Follow me. Dwayne, take Rome to my office, then have Jalilah rustle up some lunch for all of us. Tell her to serve it in the main dining room for six. I guess Vance and his attorney, as well as his wife, will be joining us. Have her send up Val's lunch on a tray and also tell her set up a tea service, juice, soda and wine bar in the guest suite with the fireplace. That's where Valerie will be."

"Will do, boss."

Val followed Victor up the winding staircase. The artwork in this house was worth a fortune. She noticed a Romare Bearden, Radcliffe Bailey, Picasso, Jacob Lawrence and two Jean Michel Basquiats lining the walls along the stairs.

Victor stopped in front of a door and opened it to a beautiful bedroom done in every shade of purple that you could imagine. The couch and chaise longue were covered in the same regal fabric as the comforter on the bed. There was also a huge terrace with a beautiful view of the mountains. She finally set Lucky's carrier down. Victor put her laptop on the desk.

"Thank you. This suite is lovely. I should have at least thought to pack something to rest in. Although I doubt that I can sleep. I keep seeing that blood gushing out of Dee Dee's head."

The tears started to flow again.

Victor put his arm around her. "I told you to stop worrying about anything. Come with me."

She followed him down the hallway. Val thought he was opening the door to another bedroom, but when she stepped in, she saw that she was inside of a closet that was bigger than her entire house. There were rows and rows of dresses, furs, coats, pants, and shelves of shoes. There was a huge dresser in the middle of the room. Many of the clothes had tags on them.

Victor told Val, "I'm sure you can find something in here. I believe most of these clothes are size fourteen and sixteen. I doubt if Andrea had even looked in this closet for years."

"I noticed when we found her that she was very thin. I don't feel right going through her things."

"As I told you last night, you are welcome to all of it. Even the maids around here are a size minus zero. That's the way of Hollywood. Now, I'll leave you here. Jalilah will send one of the girls up in a minute with some food and drinks for you."

Val smiled at Victor as he left. She wasn't up to closet shopping. But, she did need something to lounge around in and maybe some slippers. She opened one drawer of the huge dresser. She pulled out a gorgeous eggplant rayon georgette, three-quarter-sleeve tunic with embroidery. She looked in the label and saw it was a size 2X and by Johnny Was. Good, nice and roomy. She could slip into that. Now, to find a pair of leggings. She opened another drawer that was filled with leggings in every color. As she reached for a pair of black ones, a photo fell out. Val couldn't believe what she was looking at. It was a picture of Andrea and Roshonda performing fellatio on each other. Oh my God! She had told Rome that she was almost positive Roshonda knew Andrea, but she would have never guessed it was intimately. She quickly dialed Rome's cell phone.

"Are you okay?"

"Yes, can you have someone bring you up to the room I'm staying in? I have something to show you. Come alone."

"I'll be right up."

Val practically ran back to her room with the tunic, leggings and photo. When she got back, a little lady was coming out of the bathroom.

"Your kitty litter box is all set up in there, along with a bowl of food and water for her. One of the caretakers has a cat, so I borrowed some litter and a can of food from her." Val also noticed a fruit and cheese platter was on the table next to her bed, along with water, juice, soft drinks, a bottle of Kendall Jackson Chardonnay and a bottle of Dom Perignon champagne.

"Thank you. That was very kind of you."

"My name is Christine. I'll be helping you today. I see you found a couple of things in Mrs. Dumas's closet. Mr. Victor told me you might not be feeling up to looking through it, so, I'll find you a pretty robe and a few other things. Would you like me to draw you a bath?"

"A bath would be wonderful, but you don't have to wait on me. I can do it myself."

"I love you on *Life After*. I saw you crying on TV this morning. It is an honor for me to wait on you."

Just then Rome knocked on the door.

"Come in. Christine, can you leave us alone for a minute?"

"No problem. Just pick up that phone and push two when you need me."

As soon as Christine walked out, Val handed Rome the picture. "Got damn! Where did you get this?"

"In Andrea's dresser."

"Okay, I don't want Vance to see this, but I have to show Victor.

I also can't wait until tomorrow to take Roshonda downtown to talk to James. I'm calling him now. Her presence at the Three Points, the million bucks Andrea left her and this photo are all he needs to make an arrest."

He pulled out his cell phone. "Yeah, Victor, I need you to come up to Val's room."

While Val and Rome were discussing Roshonda, she was downstairs reading a text message from Royale.

Meet me tonight at six at the bar at the Four Seasons. Bring me your new necklace or hubby and daddy will know how close you and mommy were.

Was he crazy? She was not going to give him her new $5 million necklace. She had earned it, the way Rebecca had made her service Andrea. She was grateful that Vance's investigator had never discovered that little secret. She was a little uneasy about Rome and Valerie, though. They seemed to figure out everything. She would worry about them later. Right now, she had to find a way to get Royale off her back. She deleted his text without answering it and went to look for Vance. Little did she know it was already too late. The cat was out of the bag!

Victor walked into the room.

"What are you two up to?"

Rome handed him the photo. "Where did this come from?"

Val told him, "I found it in Andrea's dresser drawer when I was looking for some loungewear. I'm sorry."

"There's nothing for you to be sorry for. You're not either of these sluts. This picture does not surprise me. I knew her leaving Roshonda that money was no coincidence. My wife was always trying to get me to join her in threesomes and orgies. I am a man of God, though; not a heathen."

Rome regretted that he hadn't looked further into Andrea's daily routine and habits as soon as they identified Andrea's body.

"I'm the one who should be apologizing. I should have come over here to look through Andrea's belongings first thing on Monday. There are probably a lot more clues other than this picture buried in there that could lead me to her murderer. I was so damned focused on that necklace, that I let investigating her other property slip by me. If you don't mind, I'd like to look through her closet and bedroom now since I'm here."

"Be my guest. At least we have our answer as to why Andrea left Roshonda $1 million. My poor son."

"What about your poor son?" Vance asked, entering the room. Reluctantly, his dad handed him the picture.

Vance looked at it.

"I've always known that she and Mom were involved."

Victor, Val and Rome exclaimed in unison, "You've always known?"

"Yes. Aside from the fact that she's the most gorgeous woman that I have ever laid eyes on, her relationship with Mom was one reason I approached her when I first saw her eating alone at the Palm Steakhouse. I had seen them out in Las Vegas the night before, and Mom was rubbing her hand between Roshonda's legs under a table in a casino. They didn't see me. At first I thought I would mess with Roshonda's head to get at Mom, so I bought her an entire Gucci wardrobe to reel her in. But, when I got to her apartment for lunch, she was so beautiful and nice. I actually married her to rescue her from Mom. I probably fell in love with her that night I saw her out with Mom. I didn't want to see her go down the same path of drugs and destruction that Mom did."

Val tenderly asked him, "Has Roshonda ever mentioned to you that she was involved with your mother?"

"No, but, the day after we got married, Mom called me and told me that no little-to-nothing runt like me could hold on to a woman like Roshonda."

Rome had to ask him straight up.

"Vance, did you kill your mother?"

"No, I hated and loved her at the same time, but I could never kill her."

He started to cry. Victor grabbed his son and hugged him. Totally drained, Val sat down on the bed and started weeping again. This drama was never-ending.

"Can you guys give me a little time alone?"

"Come on," Rome told Victor and Vance. "Val is supposed to be resting. Why don't you two show me where all of Andrea's stuff is? We'll see you later, Val."

Chapter Thirty-One

Turquoise

The drama that had unfolded at Valerie's house this morning was unbelievable to Turquoise. She may have been a bit suspicious of her relationship with Rome, but she didn't want to see her dead. Turquoise was thinking how her life had taken a tremendous turn in just a couple of days. For the first time in months, it was busy at Turquoise Hobson Realty. She had two fabulous houses to show Royale. True to Victor's word, his assistant, Charmion, had called bright and early, wanting to retain her to get a house for Vance and Roshonda. In addition, Victor wanted her to find five moderately priced two-bedroom apartments to move families that he was adopting into before Christmas. The assistant told her she would have to work with Valerie on the apartments and Victor would pay all of their rent up two years in advance. Turquoise knew of an apartment building that was recently built in Inglewood that was almost totally vacant. She should be able to close that deal tomorrow. Charmion told her as soon as she gave them the exact numbers, Victor would send a check over to pay for everything in full that included her thirty percent commission. Yes, it was going to be a Merry Christmas for her!

Sylvia's voice over the intercom broke into her thoughts.

"Mr. Jones is here to see you."

"Send him back."

Looking at Royale took her breath away as he walked into her office looking very handsome. While Rome wore all black every day, this man loved colors. Today he was wearing a charcoal gray suit with a pink silk shirt and matching handkerchief in his jacket pocket.

He kissed her passionately.

"Good afternoon, gorgeous."

"Good afternoon, yourself. You're a little early for our appointments at the properties." Looking at houses was the least of things on Royale's mind. The house buying story had been a ruse to get close to Turquoise. He never had any real intention of buying a house. He did need a new building to house his operations, but, that would have to wait until he pulled this horse-snatching job off.

"I stopped by here, baby, to tell you that I have to cancel our appointment to look at houses for this afternoon. For the next couple of days, I'll be busy taking care of some important business that came up. But, I brought you a little something-something. Happy belated birthday."

He placed a blue Tiffany box on her desk.

Turquoise was afraid to see what was inside.

"Well, don't stare at it. Open it."

Turquoise pulled off the white ribbon, and lifted a ring box out of the larger box. She flipped it open. A yellow diamond heart surrounded by white diamonds practically jumped out of the box at her.

"As I told you. If you were my woman, you'd be wearing a ring to go with the necklace and watch."

He placed the ring on the middle finger of Turquoise's right hand.

She held up her hand to admire the ring.

"What do I tell Rome when he sees this?"

"I would love for you to tell him, 'Go to hell. I have a new man.' But, for now, just tell him you've always had it and decided to pull it out for the holidays. No harm done."

Turquoise knew it was wrong to take this man's ring, especially after Rome asked her to drop him as a client. However, greed won out over loyalty.

"Thank you. I love it."

"You are very welcome, and we'll celebrate later. For now, I have to run. Oh, I heard about the shooting over at Valerie's. Is she okay?"

"Yeah, I spoke to Rome earlier and they're all over at Victor's house in Bel Air."

"Who does 'they' consist of?"

"Valerie, Rome, Victor, Vance and Roshonda. Valerie is over there until they can get her a new carpet. The other one has bloodstains and brain fragments on it. Her living room walls are pretty messed up, too."

"Why are Vance and Roshonda there?"

"For some reason, Roshonda's afraid to go back to her apartment. So, she and Vance are staying there until I find them a new house. I have two properties I can show them tomorrow."

"Oh, yeah? Do me a favor, baby, and make that around three in the afternoon. Then, I'll swing by here in the early evening and we can check into the Ritz-Carlton out in Malibu for the night. I'm sure you'll find a way to get rid of Rome for an evening."

Still staring at her new ring, Turquoise told him, "I can't wait to properly thank you."

Once Royale left, she thought back to Rome telling her how dangerous the man was. She brushed his comments off as being jealous. He could probably see that Royale was interested in her. Her conscience was starting to nag at her. Royale no longer seemed interested in buying a house. Thinking back to last night's dinner, she had been a little surprised that he knew Roshonda. She wondered if he already knew she was dating Rome and had used looking for a new house as a way to get close to her so he could keep tabs on Rome. Maybe she should return his ring and stay away from him as Rome had suggested. She held her hand up again. She would pull back from him, but, she definitely was keeping the ring.

Chapter Thirty-Two

Valerie

Opening her eyes, Valerie couldn't remember where she was. It was dark outside. She looked at her watch. It said it was five, but she was very foggy and didn't know if that meant five o'clock at night, or was it already the next morning?

She turned on the light on the nightstand next to the bed and realized that she was at Victor's house in Bel Air. Dee Dee had threatened to kill her, then shot herself instead. She started to cry. All she could see was Dee Dee freshman year at Howard in their dormitory, Meridian Hill; Dee Dee standing next to her as they pledged; Dee Dee on the cheerleading squad with her. Val turned on the large-screen television on the wall in front of her. Her face, then a shot of Dee Dee's body being wheeled out of her house, stared back at her. She turned up the sound so that she could hear what the newscaster was saying.

"For the second time in four days, celebrity journalist Valerie Rollins was almost killed. Last Saturday, she was riding in a limousine in Las Vegas when shots were fired at the the car's driver, Valerie, and Hall of Fame former NFL player Rome Nyland. The driver, Amir Lockett, was killed. This morning, Valerie's longtime friend and sorority sister, Las Vegas Police Department Assistant Deputy Chief Dedra Thorne, threatened to shoot Valerie over the journalist's involvement in the ongoing investigation of socialite Andrea Dumas's murder. When Nyland, along with Dumas Electronics Head of Security Dwayne Askew, told Thorne to drop the weapon she had aimed at Valerie, the police officer took her own life instead. Apparently, Thorne was somehow involved with the murders of Andrea Dumas and Amir Lockett. Her police department was investigating her actions internally at the time of this morning's suicide."

Then, the station showed footage of Val talking to the media, then collapsing. "Valerie is said to be recuperating from both near fatal incidents at the Bel Air estate of Dot.com billionaire Victor Dumas." The photo of her and Victor kissing last Saturday night in Las Vegas flashed across the screen. "The new widower and the popular journalist appear to be romantically involved. We are all very curious to find out how long the relationship has been blossoming. This is Sarah Bush, Channel 7, Eyewitness News."

Sarah was supposed to be a friend of Val's. How could she be doing this to her?

She had to call her right away and straighten this craziness out. She looked on the nightstand for her phone. It wasn't there. She could have sworn she put it there when she came upstairs. She looked in her purse, but it wasn't there either. She was positive that she had brought the phone and its charger with her. There was a soft knock on the door. She got out of bed to open it to Rome.

"Hey, you're up."

"Yes, and I can't find my phone or the charger. On top of that, I'm no longer reporting the story; I am the story!"

Rome handed the phone and charger to her.

"I took them so I could handle your calls for you. I wanted to call your stations and Eric Faison at Superadio to let them know where you are. The phone has been ringing off the hook."

"Who called? Have you been here all day?"

"Yes, I've been here all day. First, I went through all of Andrea's belongings, which I should have done Monday. Secondly, I was not going to leave you here alone after what you went through this morning, not to mention on Saturday. Victor and Vance seem like cool guys, but we've only known them for a few days."

"Thank you. Who called?"

"It's more like, 'who hasn't called'? Your cousins Claudette, Karen and Sherrie, your friends from New York, Shelley, Helen, Irene, Adrienne, Kenneth, Angelo, Nathan, Lu, Ayanna…that list is endless, Theresa, Barbara Jean, Renell, Trent, Johnny, Charles, Jocelyn, La Toya, Janis, Cassandra, Eric, you and Dedra's line sisters Suzanne, Patsy and Chicago, your editors, your spiritual advisor Marva Lee, TV shows, everybody."

"Well, I need to go home so I can call them back. I need to call Sarah right now and tell her that there's nothing going on personally between Victor and me."

Rome sat down on the bed next to Val and put his arm around her.

"You can't go home right now, Val. That's what I came up here to talk to you about. I'm sure you were too distraught when we got you out of there this morning to really see the state of your living room, but it's a wreck. There's blood and brain residue all over the carpet and the cops knocked over furniture taking Dedra's body out. You can't live there for a few days, Val."

"But, it's my home," she cried. "I also work there."

"Hear me out. Victor feels that this morning was all his fault because Dedra wouldn't have had orders to kill you if it weren't for you trying to help him. And, I feel it's my fault since I'm the one who got you involved in this whole mess on Saturday morning. So, tomorrow we are having new leopard print carpet installed in your living room. And, we're getting rid of that old furniture in the living room and the dining room."

"You can't do that. I have the money you and Victor paid me, but I was going to use it for other things. I can't afford all new furniture right now."

"Don't worry about it. It's on Victor and me. You're getting all new MacKenzie-Childs furniture to match all your little teapots, salt and pepper shakers, bathroom stuff, and everything else MacKenzie-Childs you have in your house."

Val refused to listen to him.

"I don't want you guys to do all that."

"It's the least we can do. You almost lost your life twice this week because of us. Listen, we still don't know who gave Dedra the order to kill you. I have a reporter in Las Vegas, Wilson, who tipped me off that Internal Affairs was investigating her, looking into who may have ordered the hit. So, it's better you don't go home right away until I find that person," Rome insisted.

"I don't want to stay here, though, Rome. Everyone will think I'm some sort of husband thief. Besides, this place is too big and there are far too many people here. I'm used to solitude."

"I told Victor that's how you would feel. So, he is going to put you in a bungalow at the Beverly Hills Hotel. Dwayne will stay in an adjoining one. For now, you and Victor are going to have to suck up the heat you two are taking over that kiss. Just roll with it. Since this is already Wednesday, I suggest you take tomorrow and Friday off from the radio, and start fresh on Monday. You've been through a lot in a short time, Val. Your house should be ready by next Wednesday."

Val knew when to surrender.

"Okay. I guess you're right. I still need to get my things."

"I don't think it's a good idea for you to go to your house, and all of your friends that I've spoken to today told me they are squeamish about going into a house right after someone committed suicide in it. Make me a list of everything you need. I know you don't like Davida, but she's an ex-cop that's used to crime scenes. She can go in with me to pack things up. But, it really won't be necessary. Victor says he'll buy you whatever you need. In fact, I heard him on the phone with American Express. Your very own Black card should be here momentarily, so Rodeo Drive will be at your disposal."

"I can't believe that. He's crazy."

"Crazy about you. He told me that he's wanted to meet you since the nineties when you were on TV every day defending Michael Jackson and O.J. Simpson."

Val was silent and simply smiled.

Rome was grateful that something had made her smile.

"Let's go down to dinner. In honor of Vance being home, the cook prepared a huge soul food dinner that's right up your alley."

Val asked him, "Did you find any more evidence in Andrea's things?"

"Yes, quite a bit. At least twenty bags of heroin, fifty bags of co-caine and a whole lot of pills, maybe a thousand. I'm sure they're the drugs your friend, Rebecca, mentioned were missing. I called Jim. He's bringing the vice squad and some DEA guys over here later to pick everything up and to question Roshonda. I also found this picture of Andrea. Victor says the guy in it with her is his missing worker, Claude. He had no idea that Claude and Andrea even knew each other."

Val studied the photo.

"Is he related to Victor? He looks like him. He doesn't have the gray patch in the front of his head like Victor. But, if you take away this guy's beard, they have an amazing resemblance."

"You're right. Let's ask Victor."

Val looked at her phone. "Don't ask him yet. He has a scanner in his office, right?"

"He has an entire computer room down there, complete with four fifty-inch plasma screen computers."

"Good. Scan this picture of Andrea and Claude and email it to Prettynurse1@gmail.com. That's the private duty nurse that sits with Jermonna on the afternoon shift. I want to see if Jermonna has ever seen this Claude. You haven't been able to find a trace of him anywhere. I'm starting to think he's somewhere watching our every move."

"You have a very valid point. I'll take care of this right away."

"I'll call the nurse right now and tell her the photo is coming. I'm going to jump into the shower and change out of these sweats and put on this tunic and leggings."

Val pulled her notebook out of her purse.

"I'm going to make a list for you right now of what I need for the next few days from my house. I don't like wearing Andrea's clothes, and I don't want Victor spending any more money on me."

Rome thought she was crazy for that. The man had more money than someone could spend in three lifetimes.

"Davida and Romey should be here soon and we'll get right over there."

When Rome left the room, Val locked the door. She had acted very brave in front of Rome, but she was well aware that her life was still in danger. She called the nurse, told her to expect the email and to call her back immediately if Jermonna recognized Claude. Val suddenly realized that she was starving and hadn't had anything to eat all day. She hadn't touched the cheese plate, or even the wine, for that matter. A comforting soul food dinner was just what she needed.

She was in and out of the shower, dressed and down the stairs in no time. Looking for the dining room, Val was shocked at all the activity that was going on in Victor's house. There were television lights and a couple of cameras set up out by the pool, and at least five people mulling around that looked like a television crew. *Had Victor decided to have a press conference without telling her?*

She finally found Victor. He hugged her.

"Here you are. I was just coming upstairs to get you, in case you couldn't find your way."

"What are those cameras doing out there? Are you having a press conference about the latest developments in Andrea's murder?"

"No. Roshonda told her reality show producers that she's married. So, they are filming her and Vance here today. They've asked me to be on the show, too."

"I'm sure they did. Are you aware that the impact an appearance on *Diamond in the Rough* by the elusive Black billionaire Victor Dumas, whose wife was just brutally murdered, who also discovered an ex-hooker-turned-reality-star daughter-in-law that he didn't have a clue that he had, would cause that ignorant show's ratings to skyrocket? That would make Oprah interviewing Bobbi Kristina and Joel Osteen look like the *Ricki Lake Show*. No, I can't have them talking to you. Just let them get a shot of you having dinner with Vance and Roshonda. Where's the director? I'll speak to he or she about this."

"He is already in the dining room eating."

"Well, that's where I also need to be because my appetite suddenly has returned."

Rome was already seated at the table along with Vance, Roshonda, a few people Val recognized from *Diamond in the Rough*, and a young guy, who Val assumed was the director. Everyone was helping themselves to fried chicken, ham, pork chops, fried whiting, macaroni and cheese, collard greens, string beans, rice and gravy, steak and black-eyed peas. There was also a huge salad.

"I'm Val," she told everyone as she sat down. A bing went off on her cell phone, indicating that she had a new text message. It was from Jermonna's nurse.

Jermonna says the man in the picture's name is Sincere.

This situation was getting more bizarre by the moment. Claude and Sincere were the same person.

"Rome and Victor, can you two come with me? Can we go to your office, Victor? Excuse us for a few minutes, everyone."

Closing the door to the office, Val showed them the text message.

Rome asked Victor, "How long has Claude worked for you?"

"Not that long. I've actually never met him in person. The only reason I know that's him in the picture is because I have photos of all my employees."

"Who hired him and how did he come to run your Las Vegas office?" Rome asked.

"All the hiring is done by my human resources people. He applied for a job in the small Nevada office that I told you about."

The wheels were turning in Val's head.

"Okay, two things. Number one, since Claude, also known as Sincere, is based in Las Vegas, I'm willing to bet he's the boss Dee Dee was referring to this morning that wants me dead. Number two, are you sure you don't personally know this man, Victor? He bears an uncanny resemblance to you."

Victor looked a little closer at the photo. Claude did look a little like him.

"I don't see how he could be related to me. I'm the only child of only children. I don't even have any cousins."

Val told him, "Jennifer Sands thought she was an only child until her sister killed her and took her place, like poor Jen never existed."

Rome jumped in. "At least we've likely identified Andrea's murderer. The same person probably ordered the hits on D.O.D., Platinum Pizzazz and Val. It almost makes sense why Claude has vanished into thin air. Jermonna said that Sincere was in the bar with her and Andrea. Now, we have to lure this cat out of his hiding place before he has someone else come after Val, or, any of the rest of us. It's also time to tell Roshonda that we know about her involvement with Andrea and see if she also knows Sincere. I'm also going to call Tyler and see if she knows Sincere's last name."

Valerie was still angry that Roshonda's show was downstairs filming.

"The first thing we need to do is get these reality TV people out of here. Any one of them could be working for this guy. And, even if they're not, their lives are in jeopardy by being here. We don't know when or where he's going to strike again."

A thought crossed Rome's mind.

"I have an idea. Let's lure him out with Platinum Pizzazz. Val can call back one of these TV shows that wants to know about this morning's shooting and do an interview. Tell them that Pizzazz is out of her coma and has decided to give an interview about her life with D.O.D. They tried to kill her after she got arrested. This should make him go running to the hospital to finish the job. We'll have the cops there to grab him."

"You don't think he's still in Las Vegas?" Victor asked.

Rome didn't think that was the case.

"No. My gut tells me that Val is right. Sincere is someplace very close, having our every move watched."

Val wasn't really up to doing any interviews, but a girl had to do what a girl had to do.

"I'll call *Entertainment Tonight* and tell them I'm available to-morrow. Rome, you call Lieutenant Pace and tell him what we plan to do with Pizzazz. Victor, you go back into the dining room and tell everybody that you don't know where they're going, but they've got to get the hell up out of here. Then, let's eat!"

As the guys were leaving Victor's office, Val's phone rang. She motioned for them to wait a minute.

"Hey," she answered. "Thanks, I'm fine. Really. Okay, thanks a bunch."

"That was a source over at West Angeles Funeral Home. Both Dee Dee's and D.O.D.'s bodies are there. They're preparing Dee Dee's body to be sent home to Oklahoma tomorrow. D.O.D.'s wake is tomorrow night. If he was connected to Sincere and that guy is one of the Bugatti Ballers, he'll be there. We should hold off on me doing any interviews and get the cops and both of your extra guys and security over to the funeral home. I'll email my source at the funeral home this photo to be on the lookout for him."

Rome and Victor stared at Valerie in admiration. Her sources were always amazing. Everyone she came across loved her, so, people were always dying to tell her things.

Right now Rome knew she needed some nourishment.

"Are you finally ready to eat?"

"I've been ready. Let's hit the dining room."

Victor cleared everyone, with the exception of Vance and Ro-shonda, out of the dining room. Val didn't mince any words with Roshonda when she sat down.

"Roshonda, all of us at this table know that you had an ongoing relationship with Andrea. Your husband has always known, yet says that he loves you deeply. Why did you pretend that you didn't know her?"

Roshonda was stunned and relieved at the same time. "Because I wanted to forget that I ever knew her. Whenever I saw Andrea, it was a paid date arranged by Rebecca; nothing more, nothing less. I swear I didn't kill her."

She got up and ran out of the room. Vance ran after her.

Val looked at Victor and Rome.

"Well, that really went well. I don't think she's ever going to tell us the real story. Since Vance doesn't seem to care about his wife's past, maybe we should forget about it. I think this guy Sincere is our man."

Rome nodded his head.

"Maybe you're right. I'll tell Jim to forget about talking to her when he and his team get here."

Victor was in shock over the drugs Rome had discovered in Andrea's closets.

"I can't believe all that stuff was in my house. I could have gone to jail for a long time if the police had found those drugs instead of you, Rome. You really think those are the drugs she may have been killed over?"

Val was as shocked as he was.

"Well, if they were, the police will have them and not the bad guys. I'm going to report all of this when I get back on the air on Monday. That might bring this guy out of hiding, too."

Rome remembered to call Tyler.

"Hey, pretty lady. Remember you mentioned that someone named Sincere was Sweet Lyrics' nephew, D.O.D.'s main man? Do you happen to know what Sincere's last name is? Yeah, I know D.O.D. got killed yesterday in a shootout with the cops. That was really a bad scene. Oh really? Okay, let's hook up tomorrow and I'll lay some bread on you. As usual, thanks. Bye."

"Tyler said Sincere is this guy's street name. He bought a plasma TV from her a while back and used a credit card. The name on the card was Valerian Davidson," he told Val and Victor.

Victor suddenly looked like he had seen a ghost.

"What's wrong, Victor?" Val asked.

"My real last name is Davidson. I had it legally changed to Dumas after my mother and father died."

Val knew they had to be related.

"I knew his resemblance to you wasn't coincidental. We need to find out how you guys are related."

Rome pulled out his iPad.

"Let me Google that name."

He typed in *Valerian Davidson*, but just like when he had Googled the name *Claude Hoskins*, nothing came up. "It's a blank. This Sincere/Claude Hoskins/Valerian Davidson character is way under the radar."

Victor was still in shock.

"His first name starts with a V, just like my entire family. My father's name was Vanteague. He has to be related to me somehow."

Dwayne entered the room.

"Lieutenant Pace and his officers are here, sir."

"Send them all to the library."

Victor then called out for Jalilah.

She came in right away.

"Yes, sir?"

"Send some sandwiches, coffee, tea, juice, soda, cookies, fruit and cheese to the library. The police are probably hungry. I have a feeling that we're in for a long night."

All of these new discoveries had drained Val.

"I'll leave the police and drugs to you guys. I'm not up to all that. I'm going to make some calls and let everyone know I'm all right, then try to see what I can find out about Valerian Davidson on my computer. Victor, what was your mother's first and maiden name?"

"You really don't want to know."

"Yes, I do,"

"She had your first name, Valerie, which is very close to Valerian.

Her maiden name was Neblitt. My dad also had a store clerk whose name was Valerie Anderson. He used to call her and my mom the two Vals when I was little."

Rome wanted to get all that dope out of Victor's house.

"Come on, Victor. Let's go deal with James."

Val stood up.

"You two do that. I'll be in my room."

Chapter Thirty-Three

Thursday Morning
Royale

Normally not an early riser, Royale was up at seven this morning. He had a big day ahead of him. Setting his plan in motion to snatch two of the Dumas's horses, he had assembled a team of eight guys. They had already traveled down to the horse farm and paid the owners for the boarding of the horses, as well as for the use of their trailers today. By now, the two trailers and their drivers should already be at the FedEx Hangar at the airport. He had checked with FedEx and found out that the plane was scheduled to land at two-thirty.

Royale had asked Turquoise for the number to Vance's office. She gave it up with no questions. Then, he had one of his girls call there, telling his assistant that the flight transporting the horses was going to be late. The new fake arrival time would now be four o'clock. His plan was to get to the hangar around one, knock the workers out, tie them up, and take them to a nearby hotel. Then, some of his guys would assume the identity of the FedEx workers. When the plane came in, they planned to hold the horses' handlers at bay by gunpoint, then put the horses in the trailers and hightail it to Temecula. A ransom note would be sent by text to Rome's phone from a prepaid cell phone tonight. He had gone through Turquoise's phone while she was in the bathroom on Tuesday night and gotten Rome's numbers. This plan was money in the bank. The only thing left to do was to run out and purchase black turtlenecks, black jeans, gloves and ski masks for the guys. He didn't want to take the chance of getting any of their faces caught on camera.

His phone rang. Looking at Roshonda's name on the caller ID, he answered, "I see you finally came to your senses and decided to get in touch with me."

"Good morning, Royale. This is Vance Dumas. I thought I would give you a call, man-to-man, to tell you to stay the fuck away from my wife!"

Surprised that it was Vance on the other end of the phone, Royale told him, "Brother, if you knew as much about that little slut you're married to that I know, you wouldn't be so quick to defend her honor."

"I'm not your brother, and you can cease with calling my wife names. I know all about her involvement with both you and my mother. So does my father. And, Valerie Rollins, Rome Nyland and the LAPD also know. You don't have any leverage here. I'm holding all the trump cards. Leave my wife alone. My mother's necklace will keep hanging right around my wife's neck."

Rome couldn't believe the audacity of this spoiled little rich boy. "You don't know who you're fucking with."

"No," Vance snarled, "You don't know who you're fucking with. I may only be five-two and weigh one hundred twenty pounds, but I have guns and goons just like you do. The difference is mine are professionals, not street trash like those idiots that answer to your every beck and call. What happened to you? How did you go from being a world-class athlete headed to the Baseball Hall of Fame, to a two-bit street hustler and pimp? Now, for the last time, leave my wife alone. I don't want to see your name in her phone ever again!"

Vance hung up. Never in a million years, would Royale have

imagined that Vance had that kind of gangster in him. He had really underestimated him. But, he was Andrea's son. He had to take after her in some ways. Well, everyone would see how loud the little horse-riding fool would be talking later today when he discovered that he no longer had a horse to ride in the Cash Call Futurity. And, just to fuck with him, he was going to release Andrea and Roshonda's sex tape right now. Vance was about to find out who was holding all the trump cards.

Valerie

There was a soft knock on the door of the bedroom that Valerie was sleeping in. Glancing at the clock on the nightstand, Val saw that it was almost noon. *How in God's name had she slept that late?*

"Who is it?"

"Victor."

She jumped out of bed. "Just a minute."

She made a mad dash into the bathroom and washed her face, brushed her teeth and ran a brush through her hair.

She then opened the door for him as he entered with a breakfast tray that had a little bit of everything on it.

Looking at the waffles, eggs, bacon and sausage, along with butter, syrup, tea and cranberry juice that he was bearing, she commented, "Your house beats a five-star hotel any day."

Victor set the tray down on the table in the suite's small living room.

"That's why I don't understand why you want to move to a hotel."

Val smiled at him.

"Do you want me to pour you some tea or juice?"

"No thanks."

"I just spoke to Rome. When I told him that I thought you were still sleeping, he told me he'd never known you to sleep this late, and that I had better come up here and check on you."

"I can't remember when the last time was that I slept this late. To tell you the truth, I don't feel like getting out of bed today. My body feels like lead."

"Then stay in bed and let me take care of you. There's no need for you to move into a hotel. You are very welcome to stay here."

Lucky jumped up on the couch, landing on Val's lap.

Victor patted the cat on her head.

"See, Lucky has made herself right at home."

"She sure has. I'll just stay put."

Valerie picked up her notebook off the table. "I did a little research last night. I was able to find an obituary on Valerie Anderson. She died in 2005 in Chicago, which is where she was born. At the time of her death she was a retired pharmacist who had worked at Duane Reade. The obituary mentioned that she was a graduate of the University of Louisville. She had one survivor, a son, Valerian Davidson, who resides in Las Vegas. Here's the kicker. She left $2 million to Howard University to establish the Vanteague Davidson Scholarship Fund for African-American pharmacy students."

"I'm aware of that scholarship fund. In fact, I've been donating $1 million a year to it since it began. I just thought the person who gave the endowment was a fan of my father's work. Looking back, when he died, he did leave $5 million to Valerie Anderson, but he left money to all of his employees. I didn't think anything of it. I have really been living my life in a bubble. I am the true definition of a geek. If it's not about science or electronics, I am totally out of the loop."

Val touched Victor's cheek.

"Well, you are a very handsome and nice geek."

Victor couldn't control his urges anymore. He leaned in and deeply kissed Val. This time, she didn't pull back. They were soon entwined in each other's arms, kissing passionately.

"I hope I'm not interrupting anything."

They jumped out of each other's arms to see Vance standing in the doorway with a sly smile on his face.

"Don't mind me, Dad. I don't think I've ever seen you this happy. I say whatever you two are up to, go for it!"

Sitting up straight, Victor asked him, "Do you need anything, son?"

"I wanted to let you know the flight with the horses on it is getting in later than we expected. Turquoise called and asked if Roshonda and I could meet her at her office to look at some houses. I need to stay pretty close to Roshonda with all that's going on, so I'm going to let the staff pick up the horses and take them to Hollywood Park. Then, I'll go over there and make sure they're all right as soon as we finish. Wildin' Out and Full Spectrum will be looking for me."

"That's fine. Since this is Violet's first trip to L.A., do you want to take her out to dinner tonight, or for me to arrange a dinner here?"

"Let's take her out. She loves *The Real Housewives of Beverly Hills.* I'll make a reservation at Villa Blanca, Lisa Vanderpump's restaurant. How about eight?"

"Who is Violet?" Val asked.

Vance told her, "She's my protégé. I intend for her to become the first African-American female jockey to ride in the Kentucky Derby. Her journey to making that history starts next week when she competes in the Cash Futurity. She's fantastic."

Victor asked Valerie, "Do you feel up to joining us?"

"Sure, why not?"

"Okay, son, make it for seven people. I'll invite Rome and Turquoise. You and Roshonda can also inform her about dinner when you go to her office."

"Cool. I'll see you two later."

Vance winked at them, then left.

Valerie told Victor, "I have never been so embarrassed in my life."

"You don't have anything to be embarrassed about."

Valerie decided to change the subject.

"Seriously, what are you going to do about Valerian? All of the signs point toward the fact that he is your brother, who most likely killed your wife."

"For now, the lieutenant has an APB out for his arrest. I'll deal with the consequences when that happens and I meet him face-to-face."

"I guess that's all you can do. The fact that his mom lived in Chicago is also very interesting. I would assume that means that he probably grew up there. I believe that Royale also grew up in Chicago, even though he went to school in Michigan. And, the guys in the group Sweet4U were from Schaumburg, Illinois, right outside of Chicago. I have a feeling that all of these guys have known each other for a very long time."

Victor stood up. "Your clothes arrived last night, but we didn't want to wake you. Relax and get back in bed. The staff will bring everything up and put it all on hangers and in the dresser for you."

He kissed Val again.

"I've never met anyone like you. I see why Rome barely lets you out of his sight. With all the knowledge you have, you could rule the world by yourself. Thank you. I'll see you later."

Chapter Thirty-Four

Thursday Afternoon
Turquoise

Sitting at her desk looking over listings to present to Vance and Roshonda, Turquoise couldn't believe how her luck had improved since meeting Rome. She had gone from a near drought of having almost no sales to finding $50 million properties to show the two of them. This situation with Royale had to stop. Rome was a great guy. Her conscience kept telling her she shouldn't be cheating on him. Since Rome hadn't asked for his Black card back, she had purchased a new outfit to meet with Vance and Roshonda in. Stepping out of her normal corporate-look zone, she was wearing a blue-and-white floral Prabal Gurung tunic with leggings in the same print. She had picked up a pair of navy blue Christian Louboutin pumps to complete the outfit and a navy blue Chanel purse. Since she would be spending the afternoon with someone like Vance, she needed to look like a billion dollars. She hoped there wouldn't be any residual effects on her doing what Royale had asked and changing the time of Vance and Roshonda's appointment. She had also seen Royale copying Vance's number from her phone. Since he knew Roshonda, she wondered why Royale didn't ask her for the number. Sylvia's voice on the intercom interrupted her thoughts.

"Mr. and Mrs. Dumas are here for their three o'clock appointment."

"Show them to the conference room, ask them what they want to drink, and, I'll be right there." She picked up her notes.

"Showtime!"

Stepping in to her conference room, Turquoise couldn't help but to stare at Roshonda. It was obvious why Vance was so in love with the young woman. Her beauty was ethereal. Today, she was wearing a red silk-crepe jacket and a tulle skirt of the same color. Turquoise had seen the suit in the window of Dior. Vance was wearing a warm-up suit and sneakers. The couple looked totally mismatched.

"How are you two doing today?" Turquoise asked.

"We're hanging in there. It's been a tough few days, but we're making it," Vance responded.

Sylvia walked in with a tray.

"Here are your drinks."

She handed Roshonda a glass of champagne and Vance a bottle of water. Turquoise turned down the lights and put the projector on.

"Let's get to it. I would like to get started with these three exquisite homes. This is the first property. Fifty-eight million dollars, it is on Crescent Drive in Beverly Hills. It is called Le Palais. The Crescent Palace. This home is a new, French chateau-styled estate that is steps away from the Beverly Hills Hotel. It boasts seven bedrooms and eleven bathrooms."

Turquoise continued, "Now the next estate you see here is listed at $44 million. It is on Redford Drive in Beverly Hills. It has eleven bedrooms and twelve bathrooms."

Roshonda loved them.

"They're both lovely."

"If you want something smaller, there is a house available on Mountain Drive for $15,995,000," Turquoise explained to Vance and Roshonda. "It has seven bedrooms and seven bathrooms. The nice thing about this house is its stunning spiral staircase accentuated by a two-story window. The grounds are truly majestic."

Turquoise turned the lights back on.

"Would you like to see one or all three of these houses?"

Vance thought about it for a minute.

"Let's start with the first one."

The huge prices of the mansions were overwhelming to Roshonda.

"Are you sure your father wants to spend that much? Fifty-eight million dollars is a lot of money to spend on a wedding gift."

"It's actually already my money. My father established a trust fund for me to purchase a home with whenever I got married when I was a teenager. There's more than enough money in it to pay for that house and to furnish it."

Turquoise grinned. "It sounds good to me. Let's go see it in person."

As she followed Vance and Roshonda out of the door, Turquoise fought back the urge to start laughing at how crazy they looked together. Roshonda was wearing a pair of black-and-white striped flats, but Vance didn't even come up to her shoulder. Turquoise thought to herself, *I guess that long money he has makes him look like he's seven feet tall to her! More power to them.*

Royale

To make sure he had an airtight alibi following his conversation with Vance this morning, Royale and two of his singers were having lunch on the front porch of The Ivy. It was now one o'clock. Operation Steal Horses was beginning to unfold. He would sit right here where he knew some camera had to be recording his every move for the next two hours. That way, no one would ever connect him with the horse kidnappings. It was going to be a nice and slow lunch. He had decided not to tell the boss that Vance had called him this morning about Roshonda, and that he had released the sex tape. He didn't feel like hearing his mouth about that one.

"Are you ready to order?" the waiter asked.

"Yes, first you can bring us a bottle of Cristal, and, I'll have a Ciroc straight up. Ladies, would you like appetizers?"

Lily, an up-and-coming pop star, stated, "I'll have a Caesar salad and a cheeseburger." Olivia, who was more of an R&B diva, told the waiter: "The creamed corn soup sounds good to me, and the chicken tandoori for lunch."

Royale told him, "I'll have the Cajun prime rib as a main course."

He settled back in his seat, wishing he could be a fly on the wall when that pompous-ass Vance found out his horses had been kidnapped and saw his wife's and mother's bare asses splashed all over television and the Internet.

Chapter Thirty-Five

Los Angeles International Airport

The FedEx hangar and office were a couple of miles from the main airport. A crew of Bugatti Blades pulled up in back of the hangar with two men in each of the two horse trailers. Six more crew members followed in a black Denali. Another Denali with no passengers completed the convoy. The guys in the horse trailers went into the hangar. There were only two workers in there.

"What's up?" one Blade asked. "We're here to pick up the horses."

"Okay," the FedEx worker told him. "That flight isn't far from here. It should be here momentarily."

Before he could finish his sentence, the Blade took out his gun, and fired two shots to each of the guys' foreheads using a silencer. He and his partner quickly took the uniforms off of both of the workers, and switched their clothing for theirs. The Denali with no passengers was driven right into the hangar. The guys placed the dead men into body bags, then threw them into the back, covering them over with a black blanket.

Two of the other guys then entered the office out front. There were only two workers in there also. The poor guys didn't even see them coming before they were immediately shot dead. Their uniforms were also quickly removed. Instead of putting their bodies in the truck, the guys found a storage room in the back, then tossed them inside. They quickly took their positions behind the front desk. A Blade ran into the office.

"A FedEx plane is landing. Let's do this."

One guy stayed in the office, while the other one went with his man. All the guys out back had their ski masks on. They crouched down low in the hangar and in the driver's seats of the two trailers. The plane came to a slow stop in front of the hangar. The first person off the plane looked like he may have been a veterinarian. He was wearing a white doctor's coat. He was followed by a procession of five men leading five horses. The Bugatti Blades all had pictures of Wildin' Out. They knew he was a gray Camargue, a rare breed of horse that was raised in London, England. They had been instructed not to make a move until he was led off of the plane.

Wildin' Out was the next horse that the Blades laid eyes on. He trotted off of the plane in all of his championship breed glory. As the horse and his handler came down the jetway, two of the Blades jumped up and held guns on the men leading the other horses. Another Blade then shot the guy leading Wildin' Out with a silencer so the horses wouldn't get spooked, grabbed Wildin' Out, then led him into a trailer. The Blade jumped in the horse trailer next to the driver, then pulled off as fast as possible.

Instinctively knowing that something was wrong, one of the other horses reared back on his hind legs, kicking one of the Blades to the ground. Furious, the Blade shot the horse. One of the stable workers screamed, "Rusty!" and kneeled down to see about the horse. The last one to lead her horse off the plane, Violet McClean, saw everything that was happening out on the jetway. She made a fast decision and jumped on her horse, Très Jolie. Although there was no saddle on the filly, Violet crouched down, grabbed Très Jolie's reins, gave her a stiff kick, and rode her off the plane. She grabbed Full Spectrum's halter as they rode past him. He kicked into full gear. Before the Blades had a chance to even think, Violet, Très Jolie and Full Spectrum were already out on the street, running for their lives.

She rode straight through a traffic light, causing a car to crash. She saw that the street sign read La Cienega Boulevard. A horse rider for most of her twenty-three years on this earth, Violet knew that Hollywood Park was off La Cienega Boulevard, not far from Los Angeles International Airport. She raced the horses as fast as she could along the side of the road. At that moment a police cruiser saw her and put its sirens on. The officers inside of the car motioned for her to stop. Violet brought the horses to a halt.

She yelled down to them, "Officers, I'm Violet McClean from Dumas Farms in Versailles, Kentucky. There has been a horse kidnapping back there at FedEx. Another horse and one of our guys were shot, and there are guys wearing all black with ski masks holding other horses and my friends hostage with guns."

One policeman got out of the car with his radio while the other one did a U-turn and headed toward FedEx. He spoke into the radio, "We need backup at the FedEx Hangar off La Cienega at LAX. A horse kidnapping is in progress. I also need cars at the corner of La Cienega and Slauson."

Violet jumped down off of Très Jolie.

"May I please use your phone, officer? I left my purse on the airplane."

"Of course. Here it is."

She quickly dialed Vance's number. Vance was in the middle of touring the mansion with Turquoise and Roshonda. Not recognizing the number on the caller ID, Vance answered with, "This is Vance Dumas. How may I help you?"

Violet was screaming.

"Vance, it's Violet. Wildin' Out has been kidnapped. Rusty and

Jack were both shot. Très Jolie, Full Spectrum and I are on La Cienega Boulevard. We're on the side of the road with a police officer."

"Whoa…whoa…slow down, sweetheart. What did you just say?"

She repeated herself.

"Wildin' Out has been kidnapped! Everyone else has been held at gunpoint and Rusty and Jack were shot."

Nothing she was saying was making any sense to Vance.

"Are you guys still in Kentucky?"

"No, we're here in Los Angeles. Please come fast. Talk to the policeman."

Violet handed the police officer his phone.

"This is Officer Andrew Cousins. My partner and I saw your friend and her horses riding down La Cienega Boulevard. There are two radio cars pulling up here now and my partner went to the FedEx hangar to investigate her story. We're right at the intersection of La Cienega and Slauson, right by LAX… Okay, sir."

He told Violet, "Your friend will be right here. Do you want to sit inside one of the patrol cars?"

"No, thank you. I'll stand here with my horses."

Roshonda saw the look of shock on her husband's face.

"What's wrong, Vance? Who was that on the phone?"

"Violet. She told me that Wildin' Out has been kidnapped from LAX. I don't understand. I received a call that the plane wouldn't be landing until five. Turquoise, can you drive us to the corner of La Cienega and Slauson where Violet says she is?"

"No problem. Let's go."

The three of them jumped into Turquoise's Chevrolet Traverse.

Roshonda still didn't understand what was going on.

"Who is Violet?" She couldn't help overhearing Vance calling whomever was on the other end of the phone "Sweetheart."

"She's my protégé. She's never come up in any of our conversations. I met her when she was a senior in high school. She used to clean our stables in exchange for riding lessons. I saw her talent back then, so I put her through college and paid for her to attend Jockey School every summer. She lives at the farm in Versailles. She's supposed to make her riding debut in the Cash Futurity next week. I have to call my dad."

Vance punched up his dad's number on speed dial.

"Yes, son? Did you and Roshonda like the houses?"

"Dad, I just spoke with Violet. She's in the middle of La Cienega Boulevard and Slauson with some cop and two of the horses. She says that Wildin' Out has been kidnapped. Can you meet me there?"

"Of course I can. Dwayne and I will be right there."

"Dwayne," he called out. "Call the rest of the security force and tell them to get out to the FedEx Hangar at the airport ASAP. Let's go."

Val was heading down the stairs when she heard Victor shouting.

"What's wrong?"

"Vance says his horse has been kidnapped. I'm on my way to meet him now."

Val followed him.

"I'm coming with you."

As soon as they got in the car, Victor got a call from Rome.

"Hey, this is Rome. I just got a text message from a number I've never seen before. It says to tell you that Wildin' Out is safe and you can have him back for $100 million. I've already called the FBI. Where are you now?"

"On the way to meet Vance on the corner of La Cienega and Slauson."

Rome didn't hesitate.

"I'll meet you there."

Chapter Thirty-Six

The City of Angels

I t wasn't hard to spot Violet as Turquoise's car approached the intersection. A car passing by the girl and the horses had called a television station to tell them about the strange sighting of a girl and two horses along with police cars on the side of the road. Before Turquoise could come to a full stop, Vance jumped out of the car and ran to Violet. She jumped into his arms with tears streaming down her face.

Turquoise immediately saw why Vance had never told Roshonda about his so-called protégé. Guessing that she was half Asian/half African-American, Turquoise thought that Violet looked like a beautiful little china doll. She was around the same height as Vance with wild, curly red hair that hung down to her behind.

"What happened, honey, and why are you, Très Jolie and Full Spectrum out here? Where is everyone else?" Vance asked Violet.

"I rode Très Jolie out here, and brought Full Spectrum with us. Some guys wearing all black took Wildin' Out. They shot Rusty and Jack. I left my purse on the plane so I haven't been able to call anyone to see how they are."

One of the police officers spoke up.

"There were several casualties out at the airport. However, other than the horse that was shot, the other horses are in great shape. When you took off, so did the suspects who were still at the hangar."

Roshonda had been observing the way Vance and Violet interacted. She took note of their body language as well as the tender manner in which he treated her. Vance might call this woman his protégé. However, watching these two, she was positive if they weren't still intimate, at one time they had been. She approached them.

"Hi, Violet. I'm Roshonda, Vance's wife. It's nice to meet you."

"It's nice to meet you, too. Vance just told me that he had gotten married the other day. Congratulations."

Rome's and Victor's cars pulled up on the scene at the same time. Rome immediately told Vance, "I received a ransom note for your horse. The kidnappers want $100 million for his safe return. I suggest we all go back to the house and wait for them to get in touch with me again."

Victor remembered that Vance had told him the flight's arrival time had changed. "Son, I thought you told me earlier that the flight was going to be late."

"That's right. I got a call from FedEx telling me that. We need to get these horses off the street and get the other ones over to Hollywood Park so they can be checked out. I also want to see how bad off Rusty and Jack are."

"Two of the trailers we originally hired should be here momentarily to pick up these two, and, the other four are headed to FedEx."

Looking at Rome, Turquoise felt very ashamed of herself. She now realized that Royale might be behind this kidnapping plot. He had used her to get Vance's number and to throw them off of the real time that the planes were arriving by scheduling the house viewing.

Rome touched her.

"Hey, baby. What are you doing here?"

Turquoise gave him a quick kiss. "I was showing Vance and Roshonda a house when Violet called Vance to tell him what happened. Their car is at my office, so, I drove them here."

Val was right behind Rome.

"Hi, Turquoise."

"Hey."

The horse trailers pulled up behind them. The handlers quickly loaded Très Jolie and Full Spectrum in.

Violet told Vance, "I left my luggage and purse on the plane. I need to go back and get everything."

"Okay. Turquoise, can you take Roshonda back to your office to pick up our car? Violet and I can ride with Dad and Val over to FedEx. We'll all meet at the house. I have to find my horse."

Roshonda didn't like the way she was being dismissed while Violet was staying with her husband.

She asked Vance, "Are you sure that you don't want me to come with you?"

"No, you go on back to the house."

He grabbed Violet's hand and led her to his dad's Bentley SUV. Rome opened the door to his vehicle.

"I'll follow you guys to the hangar. I want to check out the situation there."

Val got into Rome's car.

"I'm going to ride with Rome so we can start comparing notes on everything that's transpired here this afternoon."

As soon as she got in the truck, Val asked Rome, "How did Violet and the horses get way over here by themselves?"

"I'm assuming she rode one of them and led the other one by his halter."

"Did you notice the way Vance looks at her? He may be professing all this eternal 'love at first sight' poetic rhetoric about Roshonda, but his heart is with that beautiful little girl."

"Yeah, I noticed all right. I understand why Vance is so taken with her. Victor told me she was fine and it was too bad that I already had a girlfriend."

Val looked at Rome as if he had lost his mind.

"There is nothing that your old ass can do with that child."

She changed the subject. "Do you think Sincere has the horse?"

"First of all, Missy, there's nothing about me, including my ass, that is old. To answer your question, yes, I am positive that Sincere or whatever alias that he happens to be using as we speak, kidnapped Wildin' Out. I already have Alan and his guys on the Internet locating horse farms within a one-hundred-mile radius of here. We'll find him soon. Horses are too big to just disappear into thin air. It's not like they can hide him in a hotel room. They had to take Wildin' Out to a stable not far from L.A."

"Victor may not know that this guy is his brother, but Sincere, or whatever his name is, definitely knows Victor and him have the same father. He obviously wants part of that family fortune, which he probably thinks he is entitled to."

The hangar was the site of a wild scene as the two trucks pulled up to it. There were police everywhere. The horses and their handlers all looked frightened to death. The horse that had been shot was actually trying to stand up.

Rome, Val, Victor, Vance and Violet all jumped out of the vehicles. Violet ran to a man that looked like he must be their veterinarian and hugged him. Rome walked up to the detective who looked like he was running the show.

"I'm Rome Nyland. I am Victor Dumas's private investigator. What do we have here?"

"There are two dead bodies in the back room. They were both shot and apparently worked here. The supervisor says there should have been two other men here. I'm assuming the kidnappers took them. We've notified the FBI that the horse has been kidnapped. And, your staff member that was shot has been taken to Cedars-Sinai Medical Center. His condition is not life-threatening."

"I called the FBI as well," Rome informed him.

The four other horse trailers pulled up.

Rome took charge.

"Let's get these other horses loaded up and over to Hollywood Park."

Speaking to the man he assumed was Victor's vet, Rome asked, "How is the horse that was shot?"

Victor introduced the two men.

"This is Dr. Gavin Henry. Gavin, this is my private investigator, Rome Nyland."

The two men shook hands.

"Pleased to meet you. Rusty's going to be okay. Fortunately, the bullet wasn't in too deep and I have already removed it. As you can see, he's trying to get up. I'll be able to treat him more thoroughly once we get to the stables."

"All right. The rest of us need to get back to Victor's house right away. The local police and FBI should be headed that way now."

Dwayne told Rome, "I have two of my guys over at the Embassy Suites here at the airport to get everyone checked in after they get the horses taken care of."

Vance told his father, "I want Violet to come back to the house and stay there with us instead of at the hotel. She can ride with me to Hollywood Park every morning to work out the horses. I have faith in Rome. I know he will find Wildin' Out right away."

One of the other horse trainers handed Violet her purse and Louis Vuitton suitcase, which was on wheels.

Vance asked her, "Is that everything, sweetheart?"

"Yes."

"All right then, let's go," Rome told them.

They made it back to Bel Air in record time. James Pace and a few of his officers, along with two members of the FBI, were already sitting in Victor's living room. They all sat down with them.

Victor had already made a decision. "Rome, when they text you back, tell them I will pay the ransom. I don't want any harm to come to my son's horse. He's more than worth it."

"I want to try to find the horse before you do that. Val and I are positive that this is the work of your guy, Claude. We can't let him get away with all that has happened these past few days. He has to be stopped."

"I understand that, but, Wildin' Out can make me back that $100 million in no time. He wins all of his races, which bring in huge purses. And, when we have to retire him, I can get more millions for him in stud fees. Let's pay the ransom. I'll get my accountants to start putting the funds together right away. I don't want the horse injured. He's part of our family."

Val spoke up. "Listen, I know this man is responsible for Rome and me being shot at, and Dedra pulling a gun on me. Let's pay him the ransom, but at the same time, we need to trap him and get him off of the streets." Her phone rang. "Hello. Are you sure? Okay, I'll let the authorities know right now."

"What is it Val?" asked Vance.

"That was one of my sources who lives down in the San Diego area. He just saw two young Black guys driving a horse trailer on Interstate 15 down near Corona. They were headed toward San Diego. The tail of the horse hanging out of the trailer is gray. That's definitely Wildin' Out they have in there."

Lieutenant Pace took out his phone. "I'll alert the local police down there."

One of the FBI agents stated, "I'll get some helicopters immediately up over the interstate."

Victor was in agreement with Val. He wanted to get this guy, Claude.

"Rome, send a text back to the number that originally texted you. Tell whomever I want to meet him face-to-face. I'll have the money."

Rome's phone rang and he engaged in a brief conversation. "All right, thanks."

"That was Alan," he told them. "He's located four horse farms less than one hundred miles from here that are expecting new horses tonight. He's going to dispatch guys to each one of them. I'll send the text now for you, Victor."

All of this time Violet had been sitting on the arm of the chair that Vance was sitting in. Roshonda walked in as he told Violet, "We had this great dinner planned for your first night in L.A. at Villa Blanca, Lisa Vanderpump's restaurant. I know how much you enjoy watching *The Real Housewives of Beverly Hills*. As soon as we get Wildin' Out back, we'll go there to eat."

Roshonda eased into the living room just as Violet smiled at Vance and kissed him on the cheek. Rushing over to the chair that they were sitting on, Roshonda pushed Violet off of the arm of the chair onto the floor, then snarled, "Get the fuck away from my husband, bitch!"

Shocking everyone in the room, Violet jumped up and slapped Roshonda.

"I got your bitch, you washed-up, beauty queen whore! Oh yeah, I know all about you. I just pray I didn't catch any diseases from Vance fucking your nasty ass."

Val jumped in, pulling the girls apart, while all the men in the room stood there in awe watching the two beautiful women in action.

Vance yelled at Roshonda, "Are you crazy? How dare you come in here and attack Violet! My horse has been kidnapped. Another one of my horses and one of my best friends were shot tonight!

And, let's not forget, my mother was killed less than a week ago! How dare you!"

Roshonda shot him a venomous look.

"How dare me? First, you make me keep our marriage a secret for an entire year. And, all that time you had this bitch living with you in Kentucky."

"Yeah, well, maybe that's what you get for fucking my mother behind my back." Shocked by Vance's word, Roshonda fled the room. Lieutenant Pace and Rome exchanged glances. At this point, they didn't know what to say or do.

Violet looked at Vance.

"I'm sorry, Vance. I shouldn't have hit her. I should have gone to the hotel."

"No, you are where you're supposed to be, right here with me." This was all too much for Victor.

"Can everyone excuse my son and me for a minute? Val, do me a favor and take Violet into the kitchen. I'm sure she could use a snack after her long trip and the ordeal that followed it."

The four of them left the room. Victor and Vance went into the office. Victor shut the door.

"Son, what are you thinking? How the hell are you going to have your mistress and your wife under the same roof? I taught you better than this. I'm going to have Dwayne take Violet back out to the Embassy Suites with the rest of the staff."

"I'm not going to leave her alone after all she went through today. I'll handle Roshonda, but I want Violet here with us."

"All right. I'll go along with this absurd arrangement because she did save those horses today, and I love Violet as if she was my own daughter. But, I want you to stay in your bedroom with your wife tonight. You are a grown man, but I have always taught you to be respectful of women. There will be no slipping in and out of

Violet's bed under this roof tonight. Do you understand me? You are in an extremely vulnerable situation. You married Roshonda with no prenuptial agreement. Now, you're flaunting another woman right in front of her. She can take you to the cleaners."

"I didn't exactly marry her, Dad."

"What is that supposed to mean?"

"I fabricated the whole thing. The marriage license was fake and I hired actors to pose as the minister and witness over at the wedding chapel. I told you, I was trying to mess with her and Mom. I confessed everything to Violet as soon as I got back to Kentucky, after taking Roshonda away for a few days after the alleged wedding."

There were times like this that Victor realized Vance was more like Andrea than he would have liked him to be.

"Okay, so now she can get you for fraud. I've been wanting to offer her a payoff ever since I found out she was a prostitute. Then, even more when I saw her and your mother in that photo. And, I am going to do exactly that tomorrow. She is history!"

Vance knew he had made a huge mistake.

"I understand."

Valerie came rushing through the door. "The helicopters spotted the trailer. They have lights shining down on it. The police cars should be surrounding it soon."

Victor told Vance, "Get everyone into the movie theater and turn on the televisions so we can see what's going on."

"Yes, sir."

When Vance left, Val asked Victor, "Are you all right? Your son seems to be a regular Casanova. I hope he didn't get those playboy moves from you."

"No, I'm as square as they come. By the way, thank you for locating the horse trailer. I think all that womanizing is the result of

Andrea's blood running through his veins. If you want me to, I'll prove how square I am to you right now."

He kissed her deeply.

"Victor..."

Rome stopped short as he entered the room and saw them kissing. Between the girls fighting and now seeing Victor and Valerie kissing, Rome could not believe how tonight was playing out. You couldn't make this stuff up if you tried to.

"I see you two have become good friends." They broke their embrace and looked at him. "Listen, I came in here to tell you that Alan located a horse farm in Temecula, right off Interstate 15 that's expecting to board two new horses tonight. The police and FBI are on their way there now. I don't think there will be any need to agree to paying these clowns any ransom. Thanks to Val's source, their jig is about to be up."

Chapter Thirty-Five

Royale

Sitting in the back of the lounge area at the Four Seasons Hotel where he had told Turquoise earlier to meet him, Royale was also watching the saga of the stolen horse play out on television. This situation was suddenly resembling the final scene of *Set It Off,* with the helicopters and dozens of police cars chasing Queen Latifah through the streets of downtown L.A. *Where had his foolproof plan gone wrong?*

His phone rang. It was one of his guys.

"Damn, man, what are we supposed to do now?" asked a young Blade named Darryl. "We got nowhere to go. I don't want to start shooting at no cops. I ain't trying to die out here."

Royale hung up on him.

Back in the cab of the trailer, Darryl told Shakim, who was sitting next to him, "That SOB just hung up on me. According to the GPS, we are five minutes from the farm. I say, let's pull over, jump out of this truck, and run into those bushes over there. The lights will be on the top of the trailer. They don't want us, they want the horse. We can lay low over there for a few and then call somebody to come get us. I can't go to jail. I've already got two strikes. If they get me, I'm locked up for life."

"I'm with you, man. My girl just had a baby. I ain't trying to go to jail over no horse."

Darryl brought the trailer to a slow halt. "Let's make a run for it."

The two Blades jumped out and started running as fast as they could. Unfortunately for them, a roadblock had already been set up on the other side of the shrubbery. Shakim and Darryl ran right into the path of the police.

The cops drew their guns, shouting, "Halt! Lay down on the ground and put your hands on your heads!"

The entire scenario was captured on cameras in the helicopters circling above. The police cars that were following the trailer pulled up behind it. All of the officers got out their cars as fast as possible and ran to the trailer. Looking inside, they saw Wildin' Out was just fine. A news crew pulled right up behind them. The cameras were now on the police and Wildin' Out's tail.

Royale's phone rang again. The boss's number flashed on the caller ID. He pushed "Ignore." For now, the safest place for him was here at the bar. The boss wouldn't think to look for him at the Four Seasons Hotel. It was now nine at night. Turquoise was supposed to have been here at seven. It was obvious that she wasn't coming. He wasn't worried about her, though. She knew what would happen to her if she so much as uttered one word to Rome that he may have had something to do with the kidnapping of that horse. He couldn't figure out for the life of him how the cops had discovered what highway that trailer was traveling on. He had to think what his next move was going to be fast.

"Would you like another shot of Ciroc, sir?" the waiter asked.

"Yeah. In fact, send over a bottle. I'm going to head to the men's room. I will be right back."

When he got to the bathroom, Royale did something that he hadn't done in a very long time. He ducked into a stall, then took out a glassine baggie, and snorted a long hit of heroin. Then, he sat down on the toilet, and took two more hits. Listening to make sure no one else was in the bathroom, he went to the sink and washed his face. Damn...that felt good. He went back into the lounge to continue drinking alone and wallow in the misery of defeat.

Chapter Thirty-Seven

Roshonda

Packing her clothes, Roshonda heard a lot of loud cheering coming from downstairs. That must've meant Vance's horse had been found. She couldn't believe that all of this time, Vance had known about her dates with his mother. Between realizing that the real reason she had never been to his home in Kentucky was because he had another woman living there, coupled with how humiliated she was when he took up for his girlfriend instead of her, Roshonda had decided to leave Vance. She was going to hit up the little bastard for every dime that he had and ever hoped to have. She was sitting on a gold mine. She was a woman whose husband had flaunted his mistress right in front of her with no prenuptial agreement. It looked like she was about to get her *Pretty Woman* happy ending after all. Praise the Lord!

Vance entered the suite.

"Going somewhere?"

"Isn't that pretty obvious? This is a suitcase. You see me putting my belongings in it. I'm not sleeping in the same house with you and your girlfriend. What did you expect, for all of us to sleep together tonight?"

"It wouldn't be anything you haven't done before."

"You have lost your mind. What happened to the loving husband that you were this morning?"

"Look, I'm sorry, Roshonda. When I saw you and Violet together, I realized that I love you, but I am in love with her."

"Well, guess what, you little smurf? I was never in love with you. Why do you think I didn't care whether you told anyone that we were married, and never once complained that we didn't live together? I never wanted to be seen with you. Your ass was nothing but a ticket out of Sin City for me."

"As I said, I'm sorry. I never should have played with your emotions the way I have."

"Sorry doesn't cut it, dear husband. Your ass is going to have to pay big time for what you've done to me or I won't give you a divorce."

"You don't have to give me a divorce. Our marriage was never legal. I had the whole charade arranged. From the very beginning, I just wanted to use you to get at my mother."

As hard as she was, Roshonda couldn't help but to start crying. Hysterically, she opened up her Hermès Birkin bag and pulled a long switchblade out of it. She lunged at Vance.

"You think you can do all that to me and just walk away? I will slice you up to ribbons."

Vance was extremely quick. He jumped out of Roshonda's way just as Violet came into the room carrying a gun. She shot the knife out of Roshonda's hand.

Grabbing the knife off the ground, Vance pushed Violet behind him.

Everybody downstairs heard the gunshot at once.

Rome yelled, "Victor and Val, you stay down here!" as he, James and what police officers still remained at the house, ran up the stairs. Bursting in the room with their guns drawn, they saw Violet and Vance huddled in a corner, holding a gun and a knife. As James took the weapons from them, Roshonda closed up her suitcase.

Walking out the door, she told Vance, "It doesn't matter if we are legally married or not. You will still be hearing from my lawyers. Have a nice life."

James took the weapons out of Vance's hand.

"I have to ask who these two weapons belong to, and if the gun is registered."

Violet told him, "The gun is mine. I am licensed to carry it in all fifty states to protect my horses. The knife was what's-her-name's."

Rome told James, "Since Roshonda has left the premises without the knife, you can take it with you, James. I don't believe that after all everyone in this house has been through today that there will be any charges filed."

"That's fine. If we're all finished here, I am going to tell everyone goodnight. Let's move on out, men."

As the police officers left, Victor and Val came through the door.

Victor looked at his son and Violet.

"Now that Roshonda has made her exit, and I see that you two are not bleeding and still breathing, I take it the gun did not connect with whichever one of you three was its intended target."

"I would never have shot her, Victor. I just wanted to stop her from stabbing Vance."

Val almost forgot she had her phone in her hand until it rang.

"You have got to be kidding. All right. I'll let the Dumases know. Just email it to me. Thanks for keeping this under wraps."

Everyone was looking at her with anticipation.

"This is way too much drama for me, but, that was one of the kids over at *TMZ*. They just received a sex tape with Roshonda and Andrea on it. But, they're not going to post it. It's time for a glass of chardonnay."

Rome agreed.

"I can even use a drink after all of this drama."

Victor was of the same accord.

"It's just ten on a Thursday night. Let's all go over to the bar at the Four Seasons. We can also grab a bite to eat and listen to some music. I have a lot to celebrate. I have my championship horse back and I got rid of my whorish daughter-in-law. What more could a man ask for in one day?"

Val's phone rang again.

"Thanks, I owe you one."

"Vance, Wildin' Out is on the way to Hollywood Park with police escorts."

"That's great. You guys go ahead to the Four Seasons and have a good time. Come on, Violet. Let's head out to Hollywood Park to check on the other horses and wait for Wildin' Out. Val, if I didn't think my dad was falling in love with you, I would marry you myself. I'll never be able to thank you for finding my horse so quickly."

She pretended like she hadn't heard the "my dad falling in love with you" part. Val was wearing a striped black/gray flannel Joan Vass tunic with her usual leggings, but she wanted to put on some heels and grab her mink poncho.

"I'm just going to change my shoes and I'll meet you guys by the front door."

Rome's phone rang. It was Turquoise.

"Hey, baby. Did you see everything on television? Yeah, it's great. Val got a tip that the horse trailer was on Interstate 15 down by Corona. The police were able to catch the kidnappers right after that. We're on our way to the Four Seasons. You want to join us? Okay. See you there."

Rome went downstairs with Victor to wait for Val. This had been one hell of a day. Unfortunately, Victor's long-lost brother was still on the loose. None of them were out of danger until they had that bastard behind bars.

Turquoise was still in her office, so she was right near the Four Seasons. She was supposed to have met Royale there hours ago. She was sure he was long gone by now.

Chapter Thirty-Eight

The Four Seasons Hotel

An exhausted, yet exhilarated threesome, Valerie, Rome and Victor, hit the hotel bar at the same time that Turquoise did. Taking a table in the front of the room near the entrance, they had no idea that Royale was in the back of the room, getting more wasted by the minute.

Val couldn't believe the past two days.

"Thank God we were able to get the horse back so fast. But, I can't believe everything that went down between Roshonda and Vance. Talk about wildin' out!"

"What happened with Roshonda and Vance?" asked Turquoise.

Val told her, "They broke up, but only after Roshonda and Violet got into a fight. Then, Roshonda tried to stab Vance, and Violet shot the knife out of Roshonda's hand."

The waiter came to their table.

"Can I help you?"

Rome was the first to order a drink.

"I'll have a Hennessy and Coke."

"You can bring me a Cosmo," Turquoise piped in.

Victor told him, "I'll also have a Hennessy and Coke. Bring a bottle of your best chardonnay for this lady," he said, pointing to Val, "as well as a bottle of Cristal."

Val looked at her watch. "It's too late to eat anything heavy. Do you guys want to order a couple of pizzas?"

They all nodded in agreement.

Val told the waiter, "We'll have two vegetable pizzas as well as two pepperonis. Thank you."

Turquoise couldn't believe she had missed all of the action.

"The minute I laid eyes on Violet and saw how beautiful she was, and how attentive Vance was to her, I realized there was going to be a problem for the three of them. I guess I can kiss my commission on the house goodbye."

"Not yet. I'm going to offer the house to Roshonda tomorrow as part of a settlement. I don't think she'll turn moving into a $58 million mansion down."

"That sounds good to me. Also, Val, I have the five apartments for your adopted families ready for you."

"Good. I need to run some errands tomorrow anyway. Can I come by your office in the morning around eleven?"

"It sounds like a plan."

Turquoise was very pleased that she was still going to make a $10 million commission. All of a sudden they heard a loud commotion coming from the back of the room. Then, two security guards followed by four police officers rushed past them. The shouting got louder.

Val listened.

"That voice sounds familiar."

As soon as those words came out of her mouth, two of the police officers were dragging a drunken Royale past their table. When he saw the four of them sitting there, he halted, zeroing in on Turquoise.

"Where have you been all night, bitch? I've been waiting here for you and blowing up your phone all night."

Val took note of the frightened look that flashed across Turquoise's face.

Rome stood up. "Man, it looks like you may have had a little too much to drink. My lady is looking for a property for you, but that doesn't give you the right to call her out of her name."

"You lame motherfucker. She wasn't your lady when my dick was inside of her the other night."

Before he could say anything else, the cops hauled him off. Turquoise spoke up immediately. "I can't believe he would make up a lie like that. What is wrong with that man?"

Rome told her, "Don't worry about it, baby. Some assholes like him have to have something to say."

Val wasn't too sure about that. She had seen how Turquoise shivered while Royale was yelling. There was something going on between those two and she was going to get to the bottom of it. She couldn't wait for this night to end. All she wanted to do was get in bed and pull the covers up over her head. Her phone rang.

"What's up? You have got to be kidding. Yeah, I'm here with Rome and Victor now. That guy was hauled out of the Four Seasons by the cops for causing a disturbance right in front of us. Okay, let me tell Rome so that he can call his contact down at police head-quarters here. Thanks. That was real good looking out."

"What now?" Rome asked.

"That was my source at a radio station down by Corona. He told me that the guys the State Police picked up driving the trailer want a plea deal. They confessed that they were working for Royale Jones and it was his plan to snatch the horses."

Rome was already out the door, yelling, "Something kept telling me he was involved in everything that's been going on. Let me see where they took him. I'm sure he's somewhere still in this building."

He dashed out of the lounge to the hotel lobby. Looking out the front door and down the ramp that led to the hotel's driveway, he saw that the police had Royale with his hands on their car. They were searching his pockets. Rushing to them, Rome told the officers, "My partner got a call from her associate claiming this man was the mastermind behind today's kidnapping of the race horse Wildin' Out."

The officer told Rome, "We just got that report over the radio. That's why we're searching him now."

As he gave Rome that information, the policeman pulled the bag of heroin out of Royale's suit pocket. He then reached inside his jacket and pulled out a gun. Discovering all of that contraband, he pushed Royale into the back of the patrol car.

Royale looked at Rome and sneered, "Tell your bitch I'll be back soon to get some more of her good pussy."

The patrol car pulled off with sirens blaring. Rome went back inside where the others were. He motioned to the waiter.

"Another shot of Hennessy and Coke, please."

In all of the years that Valerie had known Rome, she had never seen him down two drinks. "What happened out there?"

"Nothing. They took the bastard to jail. He had drugs and a gun on him."

When his drink arrived, he downed it in one gulp, then turned to Turquoise. "Are you ready? I need to get home. I want to get over to the Beverly Hills Police Station first thing in the morning to try to talk to Royale." He turned toward Val and continued, "Val, I know you want to run errands tomorrow and have a meeting scheduled with Turquoise. I have a feeling that Royale and this Sincere are very connected. Tyler told me that Sincere was D.O.D.'s main man, and Sweet Lyrics and Royale are tight. I don't want you going anywhere without Dwayne accompanying you. With Royale locked up, this guy Sincere is going to be on the warpath. I have security traveling with Romey and Davida, too."

"No problem. I'll see you tomorrow."

Victor stood up and gave Rome a manly hug.

"No amount of money could ever be enough compensation for all you and Valerie have done for me. The situation with Wildin' Out could have gone in a much different direction. Thank you. I'll have a bonus for you in the morning."

"We won't be out of the woods until we get this guy, Sincere. I'm also very pleased with all that we've been able to accomplish in such a short time. We'll meet tomorrow after I leave the police station."

Rome leaned down and kissed Val on the cheek.

"Now, you two be good kids tonight."

He and Turquoise left.

Val didn't know when she had felt this drained.

"I guess we should get going, too. Although I do wish I was going home to my own bed."

"What's wrong with mine?"

"Nothing. I'm sure it's very comfortable. That's not why I want to go home. I have to admit, I do want to take this a little slowly. I don't just want to be another notch on your belt, but, I also miss my home. I never even got a chance to put up my Christmas decorations. I realize your wife was just murdered, but don't you want to make your house a little more cheerful? You don't even have a wreath on your door or any lights on the outside of the house."

"Given the fact that I haven't had sex in at least fifteen years, I am not trying to make you another notch on my belt. And, having no Christmas decorations has nothing to do with Andrea's death. I told you when we met last Saturday, my wife and I have been estranged since Vance was a teenager. This is the first time I've been in this house in Los Angeles in years. When I come to town, I normally stay at the Hotel Bel-Air. There aren't any Christmas decorations because we don't have any. Andrea stopped putting up Christmas decorations when Vance was very small. She was never even around for Christmas or any other holiday for that matter."

Val was still focusing on him not having sex for fifteen years.

"Why haven't you had sex in such a long time? Is there something physically wrong with you?"

"I hope not. I guess it still works. It seems to react whenever I get close to you. Believe it or not, Andrea is the only woman that I have ever been with."

"You can't be serious."

"I wish I wasn't. I told you I'm a geek. Do women throw themselves at me? Yes, they do. But, after all that Andrea put me through, I just didn't want to deal that way. And, I was still legally married to her until Saturday. Besides, I work all the time. Working with you and Rome these past few days has made me realize what I've been missing. I have never done this much socializing in my life. I've never even spent this much time with my son. I don't go to restaurants or sit in lounges like this. I'm sorry that it took Andrea's death to make all of this happen, but, I'm having more fun than I've ever had in my life."

Thinking about what he just said, Valerie had never seen a photo of Victor leaving a restaurant or attending a gala.

"Look, Val," Victor continued. "I agree with you about taking it slowly. I want whatever we have going on to last. So, I won't pressure you. When it's time for us to be intimate, it will just happen. Now, Rome has an entire crew working over at your house. In the morning, we'll ask him how they're coming along."

"Thanks, Victor. I have a lot to get done tomorrow. Let's blow this joint."

"I need to meet with you before you head out in the morning to give you everything you need for your meeting with Turquoise. Is she your first appointment?"

"Unfortunately, yes."

"Why is it so unfortunate?"

"I know Royale was drunk, and I suspect he was also high on something, but I think he was telling the truth about having an affair with Turquoise. She looked pretty shaken up after he made that statement. I don't want to see Rome hurt. He seems to really like her."

"See, that's what I'm beginning to love so much about you. You are so concerned about everyone. Meet me down in the solarium for breakfast at nine so we can go over everything."

"It's a date."

This time, she leaned over and kissed him.

Chapter Thirty-Nine

Friday Morning
Roshonda

U p early to head to the gym, Roshonda was still in shock how her life had gone from sugar to shit in less than a day. How had she been so stupid to not have that marriage license checked out? She had always thought it was strange that the press never got a whiff of that marriage license. Now she knew why. It never really existed. On the bright side of things, she hadn't had to take care of herself for an entire year. She now had that $1 million Andrea had left her, and if Vance didn't give her the kind of money she wanted, she would threaten to have him put in jail for having fraudulent documents drawn up. She was going to make an appointment with an attorney today. Her intercom rang. Not knowing that Royale had been arrested last night, she was praying it wasn't him still harassing her about Andrea's necklace.

"Yes?"

"Attorney Patricia Wise from the Cochran Firm to see you."

Knowing the Cochran Firm represented all of Victor's businesses, Roshonda told him, "Please send her up."

"This should be interesting."

She answered the door as soon as the bell rang.

"Good morning, Miss Rhodes. I'm Patricia Wise. I've come to see you on behalf of Victor and Vance Dumas."

"Come in and have a seat. Can I get you something to drink?"

"No thank you. I'll be pretty quick."

Attorney Wise sat down, opened her briefcase, and pulled out several envelopes. Handing the large manila one to Roshonda, she told her, "Please read the contents of this envelope first."

Roshonda opened it and pulled out a letter followed by a signature page.

Dear Roshonda:

Let me start out by apologizing for the way that my son, Vance Dumas, handled your year-long relationship. Fabricating a marriage to you was a terrible and dishonest act. However, since he did provide financially for you throughout the entire year, as well as pay a significant sum to release you from your previous employer, I will forgive him. I hope that someday you will too. In lieu of his actions, I am willing to provide you with the home that the two of you looked at yesterday.

The deed will be in the name of Dumas Electronics for five years. After that, if you adhere to all of the conditions that are stated in this letter, the deed will be transferred into your name. You will also be provided with funds to purchase the furniture of your choice for the entire house. In addition, you will be presented with a $2,250,000 check upon execution of this agreement today. Beginning January 1, 2014, $250,000 a month will be deposited into your account and, you will receive $2 million annually for the next five years. My attorney also has in her possession a Black American Express card in your name. Please charge all of your purchases to it for the next five years.

If all of this is agreeable, please sign all three copies of the documents. I wish you well as you get on with your life.

Yours Truly,

Victor Dumas

"Do you have a pen so that I can sign?"

Ms. Wise handed her one. As soon as Roshonda signed the documents, she gave her an envelope.

"Here is your check and credit card. I will give Ms. Hobson instructions to make an offer on the house today. Merry Christmas."

Roshonda opened the door for her. "Merry Christmas to you, too."

Closing the door, she stared at the check and the Black card. The hell with the gym. She was heading to the bank. Grabbing her purse, Roshonda yelled, "Rodeo Drive, here I come!"

Victor and Valerie

Dressed for the day's activities in a gold/black stitched long-sleeved jacket over a black tank and matching boot-cut pants, Val entered the solarium of Victor's house. He was already seated at the table reading the *New York Times*. Looking over a buffet that was set up with around six silver chafing dishes that held bacon, sausage, eggs, grits, waffles, pancakes and toast, as well as fruit, Val couldn't help herself.

"Good morning, this looks like a scene out of *Dynasty*."

She was referring to the breakfast buffet that was always set up on the '80s television series about the wealthy Colorado oil baron, Blake Carrington, and his family.

"Well, we've certainly endured as much around here in the past few days to rival the show."

He stood up and kissed Val. "Good morning to you, too. I actually had the staff put out the buffet because Vance and Violet ate earlier before they headed out to Hollywood Park. I also didn't know if Rome or his policeman friend might be dropping by. This house has seen more activity this week than it has in years. Normally, there's no one here but the staff."

Val put a little bit of sausage and eggs on her plate, then sat down next to Victor.

"Well, I think everything is lovely."

Victor reached over to the pile of items he had on the table. He first handed her a checkbook along with a signature card.

"This is the checkbook for the Andrea Dumas Foundation. As we discussed, the account has $5 million in it. You and I are the only signatories on the account, but you will not need my signature to write a check. Just sign this card right here. You can pay Turquoise in full for the families' rent for two years on the apartments that she has. To be on the safe side, you should go with each of them when they select furniture. I don't want them using those funds for anything else. This is the check card for the account, an American Express card with the Andrea Dumas Foundation on it for purchases you need to make, and an American Express card with your name on it."

Once again speechless, Val signed the card. When she opened the checkbook, the first check was made out to her for $50,000, signed by Victor. "Before you start protesting, the check that I gave you last Saturday was payment for public relations work. This one is for heading up the charity until we find a permanent person."

"Thank you. You are so kind and generous. You know, years ago I saw a movie called *Rich and Famous*. It starred Candace Bergen and Jacqueline Bisset as two best friends who were both authors. The one that Candace Bergen played was commercially successful and very rich. However, Jacqueline Bisset's work was critically acclaimed, but she never made the big money. That's been the story of my life. My work is critically acclaimed. I'm famous, but not rich. You can't begin to understand the difference in my life that your hiring me has made."

"You can't begin to understand the difference you've made in my life just being around you."

Unable to stop themselves, they started kissing again.

For the second time, Rome walked in on them.

"Oh come on now. You two are acting like horny teenagers. There are a lot of rooms in this house. Why don't you try getting one?"

Val stuck her tongue out at him.

"Victor thought you might be stopping by. Good morning."

"Help yourself to some breakfast, Rome."

"Thanks."

Rome filled a bowl with fruit.

"I was over this way after dropping Romey at school. I thought I would drop by to let you know that James summoned me downtown to his office. He says he has something urgent to tell me about Royale that he didn't feel comfortable discussing over the phone. I'll let you know what it is as soon as I hear what he has to say. Royale is in a lot of trouble. His little gang buddies turned on him, and that didn't look like a small amount of drugs he had on him last night either. I don't know if the gun he was carrying was registered or not."

"I told Victor I thought he was on something. Is Dwayne ready to leave, Victor? I need to stop by the Rite-Aid on the way to Turquoise's office."

"Yes, he's out front in the car."

"Rome, how is the work coming at my house? When do you think I will be able to go home?"

"As cozy and you and Victor look, I kind of thought you might want to take up residence here."

"I'm serious."

"Since we are already working in there, I told them to paint the entire house, so it's going to take a little longer than I originally anticipated. Then, they'll lay the carpet in the living room. You'll be happy to know though that some of the MacKenzie-Childs furniture for the living room arrived yesterday from New York.

You should be back in before Christmas. I know how much that means to you. What else do you have to do today?"

"I'm having lunch at one in the Polo Lounge with the event planner to see her final plans for the Santa Sleigh Ball. Then, I'm getting my nails, feet and lashes done. From there, I'm going to the Beverly Center to do some Christmas shopping and pick up a few things for myself. I should be finished with everything around seven at the latest."

"Okay, so why don't we all meet at Villa Blanca at seven?" Victor asked. "Vance wants to have the dinner that he originally planned last night for Violet."

Rome was already up on his feet. "Sounds like a plan. That way I can finish with Jim and make Romey's basketball game."

"It won't give me any time to get back here to change clothes for dinner, but that's fine."

Victor told her, "You don't need to change. You look beautiful."

"Well, thank you, kind sir. I'll see you two this evening."

After running into Rite-Aid to pick up some much needed personal supplies and food and cat litter for Lucky, Val hit Turquoise's office at eleven on the nose. Turquoise was in her outer office, talking to her assistant.

"Good morning, Valerie. This is my right-hand girl, Sylvia."

"Hi, Sylvia. It's nice to meet you."

"It's nice to meet you, too."

"Come on back to my office."

"This is very nice," Val complimented Turquoise as she sat down.

"Thanks."

"So, Turquoise, are you going to tell Rome that you've been sleeping with Royale?"

"I can't believe even you would come into my office and insult me this way. That man was drunk and lying."

"Drunk or not, I think he was telling the truth. I saw the way you looked at him when he first appeared at our table. You don't have to worry. Your little dirty secret is safe with me. It's obvious that you have Rome pussy whipped out of his mind. I'm not going to say anything to him because I don't want to see him hurt. He was almost destroyed by Romey's mother and her constant cheating on him. I just don't see how you could cheat on a man like Rome with that slimy Royale."

"Once again, I did not cheat on Rome. Can we get down to the business that you came for? Here are the leases for the five apartments. They are out in North Hollywood and really nice. They are all two-bedrooms as you requested and are $1,500 a month. That includes electricity."

"Okay, so what does that come to with your commission with the rent paid in full for two years?"

Turquoise took out her calculator.

"Okay, the rent and security comes to $216,000. My commission is $72,000. That comes to $288,000."

Val took out her new checkbook. "Let's just make it an even $300,000. Consider the extra money as a bonus for finding the apartments fast. Maybe you can get Rome a nice Christmas gift with it."

She handed Turquoise the check.

"When can I pick up the keys? I want to have everyone in their new homes by Christmas Eve."

"I'll have the keys for you on Monday."

"Good. There are at least three families that are staying in horrible shelters downtown that I will move in on Monday. I'll get them beds that same day and then the rest of the furniture during the week. Thank you. Don't forget our conversation. You hurt Rome and your ass is mine."

"Goodbye, Valerie."

Rome

Leaving police headquarters, Rome was dumbfounded by the information that James had laid on him about Royale. He punched up Victor.

"Yeah, Victor. Listen, the information that I have for you about Royale is a little too heavy to discuss in a public place. Can we meet at your house at seven?"

"I was going to call you and suggest that we meet here anyway. Vance and Violet are pretty worn out from their work-outs with the horses and their trainers today. They also spent time at the hospital with Jack, so they weren't up to going out either. I'll have Dwayne bring Val here when she finishes up."

"Fine, I'll see you then."

Hanging up, Rome looked at the clock on his dashboard. It was already four. He had enough time to drop the money he promised Tyler off to her, catch Romey's basketball game, then make it to Victor's by seven. He was planning to take tomorrow off. This had been one rough week. As he drove downtown, Rome couldn't help but to think about Royale's claims that he was having an affair with Turquoise. He really wanted to believe her story; that it wasn't true. But, why would Royale even go there if it weren't? The judge had denied Royale bail and he had refused to speak to Rome. So, he wasn't going to find out anything about the two of them from him. Sooner or later, the truth would come out. It always did.

Valerie

After lunch with her event planner, then spending two hours at the nail salon, and another two hours at the Beverly Center, Val was wishing that she could sink into a nice soft bed instead of having dinner at a restaurant. Dwayne got out of the car to help her with all her bags. In addition to buying Christmas gifts, she had also done quite a bit of shopping for herself. She had picked up five new tunics and several pairs of leggings since she didn't want to wear the same clothes around Victor's house every day. She also bought several dresses and three nice pairs of Louis Vuitton shoes. She had noticed that despite all of his wealth, Victor's briefcase was old and worn. So, she bought him a new one at Louis Vuitton for Christmas with a matching wallet.

"There's a change of plans, Valerie," Dwayne informed her. "Whatever information Rome has for all of you, Victor says it is very private. So, he arranged dinner for everyone back at the house."

"Thank God. I am exhausted."

She couldn't believe how fast this day had flown. It was already five minutes to seven. Pulling up to Victor's house, Val wondered if they were in the right place. There were Christmas lights in every window and there was a big huge wreath on the door.

Dwayne told her, "Go on inside. I'll see that all of your bags get up to your room."

Stepping inside, Val couldn't believe her eyes. This place had been transformed into the North Pole. There was evergreen and holly crawling up the staircase and a huge tree in the foyer.

Victor called out, "We're back in the dining room!"

The dining room was even more shocking. There was another huge tree in there. A beautiful MacKenzie-Childs Christmas runner was on the table and it was all set in Tiffany Christmas china. Val knew that pattern anywhere. A delicious-smelling buffet was set out on a banquette that was also decorated for Christmas.

"Rome told me how much you love Christmas after you left this morning. He also told me that you have some salt and pepper shakers that your friend Kenneth gave you, but your dream has always been to have an entire set of Tiffany Christmas china. Given that Rome instructed my decorator to order your new furniture from MacKenzie-Childs, I assumed you must love everything from there, too."

"How did you do all of this today?"

"That's what I have a staff for. Come on, let's eat. I loved that food so much the other night that I had my other driver pick up takeout from Mr. Chow."

Once they all sat down, Rome began his story about Royale Jones.

"Royale's fingerprints came back as Rolondo Jemison. He's a career criminal who everyone has assumed was dead since 2010. He is Royale's cousin."

"I knew he was a lot lighter than I remembered Royale being."

"I told Tyler the same thing."

"But, there's more. The Bugatti that he was driving was registered to Andrea. And, there was a secret compartment in it that had around $10,000 worth of cocaine in it. So, they charged him with impersonating Royale, kidnapping Wildin' Out, felony drug possession, and Andrea's murder. I know Roshonda told us he was still in L.A. at the time she was killed, but the District Attorney feels that he could have hopped on a plane, killed her, then flown right back here. As soon as they release the Bugatti, I'll have it towed over here."

"If he's Rolondo, what happened to Royale?" Vance asked.

"The police don't know and Rolondo isn't cooperating with them. The bad thing here is we still don't know where Sincere is. I still feel that he murdered Andrea and is the mastermind behind everything that has transpired in the last week. Since we've been able to stay two steps ahead of him and Royale is in jail, if I were him, I would leave the country. But, until the race is over, I'm keeping the extra security on all of you and the horses."

All this information had exhausted Vance.

"I need to lay down after hearing all of this. I'm grateful to God that we're all still in one piece. I'll see everyone tomorrow. Maybe we can all finally get Violet to Villa Blanca. Goodnight."

Rome was feeling exactly like Vance.

"I'm going to make an early night of it, too. I am beat. I'll talk to all of you tomorrow. Turquoise is coming over tomorrow to decorate, so I'm going to stay home all day."

Only Val and Victor were left sitting in the dining room.

"I can't believe you had all of these decorations put up for me. Seeing all of this has really brightened my day. I love Christmas so much that I must have been one of Santa's elves in a past life. Thank you."

"No, thank you for bringing Christmas back into my son's and my life. For the first time since I bought this place, it's not just a house. It's a home."

The two of them headed up the staircase. Standing in front of Val's room, she asked Victor, "Would you like to come in?"

"I thought you would never ask."

Not even switching on the lights to see where they were going, Victor and Val fell across her bed kissing passionately. Always conscious of her weight, Val undressed very fast and ducked under the covers. Taking off his clothes, Victor told her, "Don't be so shy. Your body is as beautiful as the rest of you."

For someone that hadn't had sex in fifteen years, Victor found his way around Val's body as if he had a road map. He made tender love to her. He was so passionate that when they both climaxed at the same time, it took every restraint in Val's body to stop her from screaming.

Victor licked her nipple.

"See, I told you that it still works."

Chapter Forty

Eight Days Later
Betfair Hollywood Park

"Welcome to the thirty-third running of the Cash Call Futurity," said the announcer over the sound system at the racetrack. "This is the One Million-Dollar Road to the Derby Showdown!"

Electricity was in the air at Betfair Hollywood Park. Standing between Victor and Rome in line at the buffet in the back of Victor's private suite, Val was very excited. Since she was still staying with Victor, she wasn't able to wear the St. John suit she had told Rome about the previous Saturday. She hadn't been able to go back in her house. So, she had purchased an Albert Nipon suit. Winter white, the jacket and skirt glimmered with metallic thread running through it. She was wearing a white hat with gold flecks in it that matched the suit perfectly. Beige Christian Louboutin Mary Jane pumps and a new beige and white check-ered Louis Vuitton bag rounded out her outfit.

Although things had gotten a little frosty between Rome and Turquoise after Royale's comments the previous week at the Four Seasons, the two of them were still a couple. Stunning as ever, Turquoise was wearing a David Meister blue gold sequined dress. She wore a royal blue Fascinator on her head and gold sandals.

"Let's take our seats," Victor told them. "Vance is riding Full Spectrum in the next race. The horses are coming out on the track now."

While all the other jockeys wore a combination of bright colors, Vance and Violet wore all black. It was Dumas Farms' quiet statement that they were a Black-owned farm and all of their horses were ridden by Black jockeys.

"All we want to do today is beat the Todd Squad."

"Who is the Todd Squad?" asked Turquoise.

"Any horse trained by Todd Fletcher and ridden by Julian Castellano from Winstar Farms. They are our biggest competition."

"And, they're off!

"Number seven Full Spectrum ridden by Vance Dumas has jumped way out in front of the other horses. It's number two, Snitch, trying to come behind him. Number four, Dark Skies, is a distant third. Number four, Dark Skies, is passing number two, Snitch. But, number seven, Full Spectrum, is at the finish line. It's Number seven, Full Spectrum! The Winner!"

Val, Victor, Turquoise and Rome were on their feet cheering.

Val hugged Victor.

"Wow, that was some race!"

"I'm going to go down and congratulate Vance. You three stay here. I'll take you all down with me after the final race."

"Are you sure you don't need me to come with you?" asked Rome.

"No, I'm fine. We haven't had one incident in the last week since Royale, or I guess I should say Rolondo, has been in jail. Maybe the D.A. is right and he did kill Andrea. You stay here and keep the ladies company. I'll be right back."

He kissed Val on the lips and left.

Rome asked Val, "So, when's the wedding?"

"Shut up, smarty pants. Whenever yours is. We can have a double ceremony. I'm sure that Turquoise would love that. Wouldn't you, Turquoise?"

Turquoise shot Val a murderous look.

Victor decided to make a stop in the restroom that was right outside of the suite before getting on the elevator that went down to the tracks. He needed to wash his hands after eating barbecue ribs. He turned on the water at the sink.

"Hello, big brother. It's nice to finally meet you in person."

Victor looked in the mirror to see Claude Hoskins standing behind him holding a gun to his back.

"Good afternoon, Valerian. How are you? It is a pleasure to meet you, too. Although it would be even more of a pleasure for me if you would put the gun away."

"I bet it would."

"What do you want from me? You've already killed my wife."

"Andrea was never really your wife, brother. I met her in Chicago when we were kids. You know, our mutual daddy never wanted my mother and me, brother. He gave her a few measly dollars to live off of when she told him she was pregnant with me, told her to leave Louisville and sent her to Chicago. From the moment I was born, my mother taught me to hate you. I have followed your every move throughout your entire life. I still have some relatives on my mother's side living in Louisville. Remember your old girl-friend, Louise? Well, she's my cousin. She told me that you were a little nerd who didn't even have the nerve to get her in the sack. But, I knew you wouldn't be able to resist Andrea. So, out of her love and devotion to me, she seduced you and got you to marry her. Every penny you ever gave her, she in turn, gave it to me. But, she was never really your woman. In fact, Vance isn't even your son. He's mine."

"I am going to ask you again. What do you want from me?"

"I want you to pay me the $500 million that Andrea swore she was leaving me."

"Since you say you knew my wife so well, don't you know she

was a pathological liar? She didn't even have $500 million to leave you. You have money. When I discovered your existence last week, I went through my dad's old records. He always took care of you and left you and your mother $5 million when he died. I am not going to give you one single dime!"

"Well, I guess I will have to kill you right here."

Valerie had gotten up to go to the bathroom. She heard voices inside of it as she tried to open the door. Listening more carefully, she quickly realized it was Victor talking. She then heard Victor say to someone, "Killing me is not going to get you any money."

Then, the person he was talking to told him, "Yes, but I hate you. So, putting an end to your charmed life will give me a whole lot of satisfaction."

Val started banging on the door. "Victor, it's Val. What's going on in there? Let me in!"

Her sudden yelling caused Valerian to turn around. He may have been shadowing Victor his entire life, but he somehow did not have a clue that Victor had spent years taking martial arts classes. As a result, he was a black belt in karate.

Victor whirled around, kicking the gun out of Valerian's hand. As agile as Vance was, Victor grabbed the gun and pointed it at Valerian. He then opened the door for Valerie. Rome had heard her yelling from inside the suite. He dashed into the room and immediately put Valerian in a chokehold. By then, two security guards and three policemen also ran into the bathroom.

Rome handed one of them Valerian's gun.

"Arrest this man. I believe he just tried to kill Mr. Dumas and if you dig further, you will also probably be able to charge him with the murders of Andrea Dumas and Ashton Oaks as well as the attempted murder of Platinum Pizzazz, whose real name is Jo Ella Conrad."

As they took Valerian out of the room, he sneered at Victor. "As long as I'm still breathing, it's not over, brother. But, until then, take care of my son."

"What did he mean by that?" Valerie inquired.

"He says Vance is his son, not mine. What he doesn't know is that because my wife slept with anything that moved, I had a DNA test done on him years ago. Vance is my son without a doubt. Come on, let's get back to the races. We don't want to miss Violet's debut."

Valerie gave Rome a high-five. "It's finally over. You did it again, partner."

"No, partner. We did it again!"

When the three of them got back to their seats, the eighth race was getting ready to start. The gun fired and the horses were off!

"Number six, Très Jolie, is off to a fast start. She's right in front. Number five, Eleven Flowers, is coming fast up on number six's right. Number six is in the lead again!"

Val jumped up. "Come on, Violet!"

"Number two, Native Dancer, has moved into second place. Number six, Très Jolie, is keeping a narrow lead. Number five, Eleven Flowers, is back in second place. She's neck in neck with Très Jolie!"

"Run, Très Jolie, run!" Victor yelled.

"Number six, Très Jolie, is keeping the lead. It's Très Jolie, over the finish line. Violet McClean from Dumas Farms has won her first race!"

The four of them cheered loudly, jumping up and down.

Val was so happy!

"What a historical moment in Black History. Val, I'm so proud of Violet. Let me go collect my winnings and get ready for the final race of the day. I know Vance and Wildin' Out are going to take it."

Rome turned to Turquoise, who had been very quiet all day. "Are you all right, baby?"

"I'm fine. I was thinking about that wisecrack Val made about us getting married. Why haven't you ever been married, Rome?"

"I really don't have an answer for that question. I've never been that guy who juggled a whole lot of different women around. Davida always insisted that she didn't need a piece of paper to solidify our relationship. But, my son told me yesterday she's getting ready to marry some doctor she's been dating. Up until I met you, I hadn't been serious with any woman since Davida. Why are you asking me this now? Do you want to get married?"

As Victor was returning from getting a drink at the bar, he asked, "Did I just hear you propose to Turquoise? Congratulations, you two."

Sitting down next to him, Val asked, "What are you congratulating them for?"

"Rome just asked Turquoise if she wants to get married."

She looked at Rome. "You just did what?"

Rome didn't know what to say. He was just asking Turquoise a question. He had not meant for the question to be an actual wedding proposal. *What was he going to do now?*

Turquoise threw her arms around his neck.

"Yes...yes...yes."

The announcer's voice broke into all of the confusion..

"Please rise for the singing of the National Anthem, which will be performed today by the one-and-only Mariah Carey."

As soon as Mariah finished, the starting gun was fired and the horses were out of the gate.

"Number nine, Wildin' Out, takes an early lead. Dirty Swagg, number six, is in second, with number ten, Black Caviar, close on his tail. Number two, Selena's Song, moves past Dirty Swagg.

She's trying to catch number nine, Wildin' Out. Number two, Selena's Song, passes number nine, Wildin' Out. They're almost at the finish line. Number nine, Wildin' Out, sprints ahead of number two, Selena's Song. Number nine, Wildin' Out, from Dumas Farms wins the $750,000 Cash Call Futurity race."

Valerie gave Victor a big hug, as did Turquoise and even Rome. Everyone in the suite came up to hug him. Val started to cry. She couldn't believe it had been two weeks since she'd met this wonderful man in Las Vegas. In that time period he had lost a wife and she had lost her best friend of more than thirty years. But, more importantly, through all the danger and pain of the past fourteen days, she and Victor had found each other. You never knew what God had in store for you.

Chapter Forty-One

Later That Night
The Santa Sleigh Ball

With its Art Deco styling, the Crystal Ballroom was the first ballroom at The Beverly Hills Hotel. Through the years, it had graciously maintained its art deco style, capturing the expansive history and grace of this magnificent hotel. With its private foyer, built-in storage and dance floor, and French doors looking out on the Crystal Garden, the room was gorgeous. Crowned by spectacular chandeliers, the Crystal Ballroom opened to floral gardens. For tonight's Santa Sleigh Ball, Valerie's event planner had placed four huge gold-colored Christmas trees with white lights and gold and silver balls adorning them in the gardens.

There was also one huge Santa's sleigh outside with what appeared to be real reindeer attached to it. Inside of the ballroom, there were more Christmas trees than one could count. Oversized Christmas stockings with handles on them, the gift bags placed at every red-and-green-decorated table throughout the room were stuffed with beautifully and brightly wrapped packages.

All of Val's favorite celebrities such as La Toya Jackson and Jeffré Phillips, LisaRaye McCoy, Vivica A. Fox, Omarosa Manigault, Tyler Perry, Freda Payne, Leon Isaac Kennedy, Jocelyn Allen, Russell Simmons, Florence LaRue, Kim Coles, Tangi Miller, Jamie Foxx and Blair and Desiree Underwood were all out in full force tonight.

Loretta Devine and her husband were also present, and Eddie Murphy had just entered the room, making a rare fundraiser appearance.

The mothers of the five families that Victor had adopted were also in attendance. They were all single parents. Victor had given them all allowances to buy new ensembles for the evening.

There were also many representatives from different sickle cell organizations, who the funds derived from tonight's event would be benefitting, in the ballroom.

Holding tightly onto Victor's hand wearing a bright red Adrianna Papell ballgown, Val watched Vance and Violet making smooth moves out on the dance floor. With Solange Knowles spinning old school sounds from the deejay booth, practically all five hundred guests were grooving like it was 1999. No longer wearing the riding silks Val had seen her in for the past week and a half, Violet was dressed to the nines in a Don O'Neil, purple, curve-hugging sequined gown with velvet insets.

"They make such a cute couple," Val told Victor. "But for the life of me, I don't get how she handled the whole Roshonda situation. I mean, Violet knew about Vance's marriage charade from the start, but she quietly stayed down there in Kentucky while he was also playing house with Roshonda here in Los Angeles. That is too much for me!"

"I guess my son had Violet under the same kind of spell that you have me under. I think they will work it all out. Roshonda actually gained a lot more than she lost over the past year. She never has to worry about working again in her life if she manages her money correctly over the next five years."

"From the looks of things, Roshonda certainly got over Vance quickly."

Approaching them on the arm of Joshua Louis, who played

basketball for the Los Angeles Clippers, was none other than Ro-shonda. Instead of wearing a long gown, she had on a Naeem Khan beaded black nylon tulle dress with a nude silk georgette lining. It gave off the illusion that she was naked underneath. She looked risqué, yet beautiful.

Roshonda kissed both Val and Victor. "This is Joshua Louis. Joshua, this is the fabulous Valerie Rollins and Victor Dumas."

Val smiled at the tall young man.

"It's nice to meet you, Joshua. I am a big fan of yours."

Shaking Joshua's hand, Victor told him, "So am I."

"It's good to meet you both, too. I listen to you every morning on the radio, *Gossip On The Go With Valerie Ro.*"

"The room looks beautiful, Val. This is a lovely party."

"Thanks. You two have a good time and thanks for coming."

As they walked away, Victor said to Val, "Thank God they're heading in the opposite direction of Vance and Violet. Let's hope there won't be any more catfights between those two women tonight."

Val started to laugh, then did a double-take. Jermonna was stand-ing right in front of her.

Hugging her, she screamed, "Oh my God! J Body. What are you doing here?"

While she was glad to see her little buddy, Val wished that she had stayed in rehab longer. Just as she was about to utter those thoughts to Jermonna, Dr. Drew Pinsky stepped up behind her. Pointing to him, Jermonna told Val, "I received a call from Dr. Drew at Hazelden the other day. He asked me if I felt up to return-ing to Los Angeles to finish my rehabilitation on *Celebrity Rehab.* I'm finally going to be on a reality show."

"That's wonderful. I've actually been on his CNN show many times. How are you, Dr. Drew?"

"I'm fine, Val. How are you,? When are we going to get you back on my talk show?"

"You know that I'll be happy to come on the show whenever Emily calls me. Dr. Drew and Jermonna, this is Victor Dumas."

Jermonna looked slyly at Victor.

"Oh, so the rumors are true. You two really are an item. I saw that picture of you two kissing. Get it, Val!"

Val hugged Jermonna again. She was so cute. A few weeks in rehab had done wonders for her. She looked like a new person. Tonight Jermonna was wearing an Art Deco-inspired gold, black and white sequined dress with fringe by Gucci.

"I just came by to show my support and give you this check to help buy Christmas gifts for your adopted families. I have to get back to the clinic. I'll see you on Christmas Day. Are we still having dinner at your house as usual?"

"Yes. I've been staying at Victor's house ever since Dee Dee committed suicide in my living room. Rome and Victor are having everything redecorated over there for me. Hopefully, I should be able to get back in there on Monday so that I can get things ready by Christmas Eve."

Every time Valerie mentioned going back to her own house, Victor cringed. Although she had only been there for two weeks, he couldn't imagine his house without her. He had to somehow stop her from leaving.

"Fantastic. This Christmas I'll be sober and won't do anything to embarrass you. Goodnight. I love you, Val. Thanks for always sticking by me. It hasn't been an easy thing for you to do. I promise you, though, this time I'm going to do the right thing and stay clean."

"I love you, too, J Body. Take care of her, Dr. Drew."

Vance and Violet joined Victor and Val on the side of the dance floor as Rome and Turquoise arrived.

"I was wondering where you two were. Let's sit down at our table. Stevie Wonder is about to perform."

Like Roshonda, Turquoise had also opted to wear a short dress. She had on a pale silver beaded sheath that had huge silver sequins on it. She wore a gray mink shrug over her dress.

As they took their seats at the table, Val leaned over to Rome and asked in a low voice, "Are you really getting married?"

"We'll talk about it later."

Vance suddenly stood up. "Violet and I have an announcement to make. During her physical for today's race, we found out that we are having a baby. So, we are getting married on New Year's Eve. You don't have to worry, Dad. This marriage will be legal! Everyone at this table is invited."

Val started to cry. "A baby! After all of the horrible endings for far too many lives we have witnessed over the past two weeks, God is bringing a new life, a new beginning to Vance and Violet."

Raising her glass of champagne in the air, Val continued, "A toast to Vance and Violet. Congratulations on both of your victories today. To the future of the brand-new life that will soon enter this world!"

Vance kissed Violet and raised his champagne glass.

"To a new life!"

As if on cue, the sound of Stevie Wonder's voice, singing "Isn't She Lovely," filled the Crystal Ballroom.

Victor took this moment to tell Valerie, "When I see you I want to run to you as fast as I can. I can't wait to start our future together. Will you marry me?"

Valerie hadn't heard those four words directed at her from a man's mouth since she was nineteen years old. Thirty-one years. Not only was she not getting any younger, but being so close to losing her life twice in the weeks leading up to this evening made her realize life was no dress rehearsal.

She whispered softly in Victor's ear, "Yes."

All of the deadly stuff players had been eliminated from their lives. This was gearing up to be a Christmas of Miracles.

Epilogue

Christmas Day
Valerie

It was only seven a.m. Everyone at Victor's house was still sleeping except for Valerie. From the time when she was a child, she loved to rise early on Christmas morning and stare at the tree. Sitting in Victor's kitchen savoring a cup of Constant Comment tea, Val was having a hard time fathoming all of the wonderful changes that had occurred in her life in such a short time.

After she accepted Victor's marriage proposal, Valerie never moved back into her cozy little house. She could no longer imagine waking up without Victor lying right beside her. He had a moving company transport all of her clothes over. The two of them donated most of Andrea's clothes and shoes to the families they were taking care of. They gave her massive fur collection to several charities to auction off. Now, Valerie's wardrobe was hanging in Andrea's vast closet. Valerie split up her furniture and other belongings between the five families. Although all of them were coming over for today's Christmas dinner, they were happily ensconced in their new apartments.

Victor had given Val his guest house to convert into her office. The three levels were now filled with all of the beautiful MacKenzie-Childs furniture that he and Rome had purchased for her. She had turned a room into a library with her hundreds of books and framed photographs. Victor also had a room transformed into an actual radio studio for Val. Her ISDN line now set proudly on a MacKenzie-Childs armoire next to a matching floor lamp. They had decided to wait until Vance and Violet's wedding was over to start planning their own. But they were looking to tie the knot some time in 2014.

Val wanted a simple ceremony at First A.M.E. Church followed with a small reception at home. Happy to be back at work, Val had broken another huge story. When the police took Platinum Pizzazz's fingerprints while the rapper was in the hospital, it was discovered that her birth name was Hope Richards, not Jo Ella Conrad. The poor girl had been kidnapped from her family in Wichita, Kansas, at the age of three. They had been looking for her all of these years. Thanks to God her parents had the fore-sight to fingerprint her when she was a baby.

Since she was a first-time offender and had been totally oblivious of D.O.D.'s true identity as a drug dealer and gang member, the District Attorney had dropped all of the charges against Platinum Pizzazz. She recently signed a new deal with record executive Sylvia Rhone's label, Vested In Culture, and was expected to burn up the charts when her new single was released in a few months.

"Good morning, my love. Why are you sitting down here all by yourself?" asked Victor.

"I didn't want to wake you. I was thinking and wondering what I did to deserve all of this happiness."

"I hope this will make you even happier. I thought I would give you this before this house gets filled with the masses for all these Christmas activities you have planned for all of us today."

Val opened up the small box he set before her to see the biggest diamond ring that she had ever laid eyes upon. Victor took it out of the box and put it on her finger. It was a perfect fit.

"Merry Christmas. I love you."

"I love you, too. This is too much. Thank you. It's beautiful."

They started kissing.

"This is getting old." Rome walked into the kitchen. "Christina let me in."

Val told Victor, "I forgot to tell you that Rome and I have a tradition of having breakfast on Christmas morning together. Then, we deliver gifts to the homeless shelters around the city. This year, we're just giving everything to our little families. I can't wait to watch all the kids open their gifts when they get here this afternoon. Where is Romey?"

"I dropped him off at his girlfriend's house. She's leaving town for the rest of the holidays this afternoon with her family. He wanted to take her a gift before she left."

"When did he get a girlfriend? Boy, am I getting old."

"He's had her for a few months now. She's a very sweet girl."

Rome couldn't help but to notice Val's new ring. "That's quite an impressive rock. I bought Turquoise an engagement ring also for Christmas."

Other than telling Victor, Val had kept her suspicions about Turquoise and Royale/Rolondo to herself.

"I'm happy for you. See, you thought I was joking about us having a double wedding. Well, partner, it just might happen. Congratulations! We both finally got it right. Merry Christmas!"

Rome kissed Val on the forehead and gave Victor a hug. "Merry Christmas to you, too!"

About the Author

Busy is the only way to describe Flo Anthony. Under the umbrella of her own company, Dottie Media Group LLC, partnered with Superadio, Flo hosts the daily syndicated radio shows "Gossip On The Go With Flo" and "Flo Anthony's Big Apple Buzz," taking the scoop of the entertainment industry nationwide to top markets including New York City, Pittsburgh, Oklahoma City, Charlotte, North Carolina, Rochester, New York and Reno, Nevada. The show is heard by 3 million listeners daily. A triple media threat, Flo also writes a weekly syndicated column, "Go With The Flo." A stringer for the *New York Daily News'* "Confidential" column, she is also the publisher/editor-in-chief of *Black Noir Magazine*. Not to be left out of cyberville, Flo has joined the blogosphere, with Glitterai Gold at floanthonyblogspot.com. Flo is seen almost daily on TV One's *Life After*, and, after twenty years as an entertainment journalist, she continues to be a familiar face on entertainment shows such as *The Insider* and *Entertainment Tonight*. In the past she has been featured on such shows as *Dr. Drew, Showbiz Tonight, Joy Behar, Joan Rivers, Geraldo, Inside Edition, Maury Povich, Montel Williams, Leeza Gibbons,* Fox News Channel, MSNBC, CNBC, WPIX and *Good Day New York*. A former publicist for legends like Muhammad Ali, the late Butch Lewis, Michael Spinks, Larry Holmes, Lynn Whitfield, Leon Isaac Kennedy and Tyra Banks, Flo still reps a very exclusive group of clients. Flo worked at the *New York Post* for almost a decade where she was the first African-American female to work in the Sports Department and first African-American to work in the Entertainment Department and the world-renowned Page Six. She was also the first African-American to write a weekly column in the tabloid, the *National Examiner.* A graduate of Howard University and a member of Delta Sigma Theta Sorority, Flo resides in the East Harlem section of New York City. Visit her at www.florenceanthonysblacknoir.com